With papyrus scrolls being expensive and writing and recopying the Good News Story Collections tedious, the original Storytellers and Editors had to use their words carefully. They wanted the story to be there and feel real. Still they had to keep it brief and trust the readers and hearers to use their imaginations to jump into the stories and have them come alive. Lorne Brandt's book is one example of such a jump. He both pulls you into the story and invites you to engage your own imagination to bring it to life. For those whose commitment to Holy Scripture makes them uneasy with such imaginings, Lorne fills in the spaces without significant changes to the original versions. For those who are comfortable with going further afield, Lorne extends both the invitation and permission to do so. Read and find yourself in Mary's company.

—*Ray Friesen,* retired pastor and author of Jump into the Story and Wandering the Wilderness.

A Sword Shall Pierce Your Soul

~ THE STORY OF JESUS' MOTHER ~

LORNE BRANDT

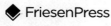 FriesenPress

Suite 300 - 990 Fort St
Victoria, BC, V8V 3K2
Canada

www.friesenpress.com

Copyright © 2020 by Lorne Brandt
First Edition — 2020

All rights reserved.

No part of this publication may be reproduced in any form, or by any means, electronic or mechanical, including photocopying, recording, or any information browsing, storage, or retrieval system, without permission in writing from FriesenPress.

ISBN
978-1-5255-8181-6 (Hardcover)
978-1-5255-8182-3 (Paperback)
978-1-5255-8183-0 (eBook)

1. FICTION, CHRISTIAN, HISTORICAL

Distributed to the trade by The Ingram Book Company

Dedicated to

the memory of

my mother Margaret,

who first taught me

these stories

2020

Richmond, British Columbia
Canada

Cover: photo of author's own wall hanging,
a gift from an Afghani Muslim refugee friend

Table of Contents

Preface — 1

I. Beginnings in Galilee — 3

  Chapter 1. The Engagement — 3
  Chapter 2. Night Intruder — 8
  Chapter 3. Now what? — 14
  Chapter 4. Breaking the News — 18
  Chapter 5. The Honorable Thing — 24
  Chapter 6. More Night Disturbance — 26
  Chapter 7. Spreading the News — 29
  Chapter 8. New Plans — 34
  Chapter 9. It is Decided — 38
  Chapter 10. Marriage After All — 42
  Ch. 11. The Wedding — 44
  Chapter 12. Getting Away — 49
  Chapter 13. Staying with an Aunt — 54
  Chapter 14. Home Again — 60

II. New Beginnings in Bethlehem — 63

  Chapter 15. On the Road Again — 63
  Chapter 16. Unexpected Delivery — 67
  Chapter 17. Good News at Midnight — 71
  Chapter 18. In the Temple — 76
  Chapter 19. Settling in Bethlehem; More Surprise Visitors — 83
  Chapter 20 – Refugees! — 90

III. Jesus Grows Up — 95

  Chapter 21. Nazareth at Last — 95
  Chapter 22. First Passover in Jerusalem — 99
  Chapter 23. Jesus - Lost! — 105
  Chapter 24. The Firstborn Son Grows Up — 110

Part IV. The Mission Begins — 115

    Chapter 25. Jesus is Baptized — 115
    Chapter 26 – At a Wedding with Jesus and his Friends — 119
    Chapter 27 – Rejection! — 123
    Chapter 28. A Mother's Concern — 129
    Chapter 29. Lives Are at Risk — 132
    Chapter 30. The Women in Jesus' Life — 135

V – Mission Accomplished — 143

    Chapter 31. An Unexpected Awakening — 143
    Chapter 32. A Rigged Trial — 148
    Chapter 33. Enemies Get Their Way — 152
    Chapter 34. After the Crucifixion — 158
    Chapter 35. The Darkest Sabbath — 163
    Chapter 36. The Tomb Is Empty! — 167
    Chapter 37. Unbelievable News — 169
    Chapter 38. Through a Locked Door — 174
    Chapter 39. Mary Sees Jesus at Last — 178
    Chapter 40. Reunion in Galilee; The Sword — 181
    Chapter 41. Epilogue - To the Ends of the Earth — 187

End Notes — 193

Biblical References Behind the Story — 195

Preface

Firstly, this book is a sub-genre of fiction called historical fiction. Not everyone who likes to read fiction will enjoy historical fiction. Some claim history is of no interest to them. It might too often have been taught as a dry collection of chronological data. However, the very word should tell us there is a story here. The key is making the story come alive.

Secondly, this book is a sub-category of historical fiction drawn from the Bible. As such, the story needs to be authentic enough. This means incorporating the reality of the times: the customs, the culture, yet without being academic.

Biblical historical fiction poses a special risk because the Bible is regarded, particularly by Jews and Christians, as a sacred text. Some would say that does not allow for adding to the details of what is already written. However, these holy writings are based on historical story, as opposed to a foundation of mythology. I believe supplementing the underlying story, fleshing it out with more detail, helps to deepen our appreciation of the narrative and what the characters experience. That is one of my goals in writing this.

I also want to comment about names. Some writers nowadays choose what might be somewhat more authentic versions of biblical names than what we are familiar with in English. That opens up the question of what version of name to use, Aramaic, Hebrew, or perhaps even, in some instances, Greek or Latin. To avoid that, I have elected simply to use the names we are familiar with from English translations of the Bible.

A special word is in order though about my use of names for the deity we, in English, call God. Here, I have chosen to use Lord, where it might be in the text as such, or where it fits. I have sometimes used the name, The Highest One, as we know the Jews of the time were very careful about using a name for a being they had become increasingly to believe was of utmost holiness and far beyond them. The expression they had come to use in writing were the Hebrew letters JHWH (in English), "I am who I am", for how they believed God had identified himself to their prophet Moses. This has been written Jehovah in the past, but more recently Jahweh, in keeping with the Jewish practice of saying as little as possible of this sacred name. This is the name I will often use.

This not being an academic text, there will be no references to biblical passages within the story, nor any footnotes. However, should the reader be interested, they can compare the fiction to the biblical account by going to the real text, the Bible. To that end, a beginning list of textual references is compiled at the end of the book.

Indeed, part of my reason for writing this particular story would be the hope that it would bring new readers to turn to the text. I invite you to see what the Bible, which has been referred to as a light and a lamp, can reveal. Readers familiar with the original story will, I hope, find that my account enriches their experience.

What then is the story here? It is a story of, without a doubt, the most famous mother in history. Of course, her renown hinges entirely on whom the son she bore is reputed to be. But who was he? Whom did she think he was? What was her experience as his mother? What did she think of what he came to see as his purpose? How did this all impact her? Every mother has dreams for her child's future. The question is, did he fulfil her dreams for him – or not? And where does that sword enter the story?

I. Beginnings in Galilee

Chapter 1. The Engagement

What a beautiful spring morning! The scent of hibiscus and bougainvillea filled the air. The deep blue sky was being infused with a golden glow from beyond the hills to the east. It was the kind of crisp, fresh morning that made you want to stretch your arms to the sky and just sing and dance!

Mary walked into her home and set down the heavy jug of water she had brought from the village well. No one else was in the house, so she assumed her mother Anna had gone to the market to get the best of the morning produce. She knew her father Joachim had gone to work. Quietly, she turned and slipped back out and quickly and lightly skipped up the street toward the eastern rim of the hill on which her hometown, Sepphoris, was built.

Ever since her parents had seated her and told her they thought they had found a husband for her, she had been restless. It wasn't the unease of wanting to find out the unknown, although there was an element of that. It was the growing excitement of what this meant for her future.

Her parents had told her they thought they had found a good match in a young man named Joseph. They had impressed upon her how auspicious they thought this was, as Joseph was from the lineage of the long-ago King David, just as she was. To be able to trace your ancestry back like that was supposed to be a good sign. It meant you cared about your family and heritage, and that was important.

But Joseph, this man who had thus entered Mary's dreams, came from Nazareth. Mary had seen Nazareth before; after all, it was only a couple of miles to the southeast across the valley. However, she had never really paid it any attention. No one much did. It really wasn't known for anything.

Mary knew though, that her father had come to know Joseph as someone having skills as a builder, and that was a trade much in demand in the city of Sepphoris. Following a recent rebellion of Galileans from the area, the Syrian Governor had leveled the city and much of it had been burned. Now, he was determined to build it up as a city he could approve of, and of which his Roman overlords could also be proud. There was a veritable building boom going on. Indeed, this was the reason Mary's family had moved to Sepphoris from Jerusalem, where she had grown up. Mary's father was an experienced builder and developer. That meant his ability to earn a living for his family would be quite secure here. Joseph's having gotten employment here meant the same was true of him. Apparently, Joachim had been impressed enough with the quality of Joseph's work that he had sometimes even put in a good word for him among the citizens of the city.

Mary had seen the young man when he had come looking for her father to inquire about a job prospect or get directions to a waiting employer. He was actually rather handsome in a dark brooding way. Mary had seen him glancing her way on these occasions too. Mary's parents had also told her Joseph was very devout. That was important to Mary, as her parents had instilled in her a strong faith, a great love of their religion and a good knowledge of the history of their people.

With all of that, there had really been no grounds for Mary to object to her parents' plans. After all, this was the way things were done. As an obedient daughter, Mary went along with her parents' proposal. The memories of the recent engagement ceremony were still vivid in her mind. Mary knew from talk she had heard that such rituals were rather more elaborate and even costlier down in Judea, where her family had come from. However, here in Galilee, things were much simpler.

On the appointed day, as arranged by their rabbi, Mary and her family had put on their finest clothes, taken a small dowry and flask of wine and gone across the valley to Nazareth. The closer they had gotten to Joseph's home, the faster Mary had felt her heart beat. This was, after all, the most important thing that had ever happened in her life. They could already see, as they approached, a small group of excited relatives and neighbors gathered around the entry to Joseph's parents' home.

As they approached, Mary and her parents saw that the rabbi had already arrived. The waiting group quietly pulled aside as the rabbi entered. Mary and her parents waited outside. Mary could not help but feel nervous as they stood amongst these politely smiling strangers. Before she had time to think about how all this was making her feel, the rabbi was back at the doorway, beckoning them to enter.

When they had followed the rabbi in and let their eyes adjust to the lower light from within, Mary saw Joseph standing between his parents. Their eyes met and Mary saw Joseph's dark eyes shine as a shy smile pulled at the corners of his mouth. Mary had never really looked that closely at Joseph before and did not want to stare, but she could not help but feel an attraction. She wanted to reach out and touch Joseph's arm, to feel him, to reassure herself that this was real. This was the man who was going to be her husband.

Mary's train of thought was suddenly broken by the rabbi taking Joseph's father, Jacob, by the arm and leading him over to her father. Joachim quickly turned and passed the wine they had brought to Joseph's mother, Naomi. Joseph's father bowed as he thanked Mary's parents for their daughter. Joachim offered Jacob the dowry, then also bowed and thanked them for their son. Joseph's father bowed again, accepted the gift and passed it to his wife. Both men in turn offered prayers of thanks to Jahweh for this engagement. After offering a similar prayer, the rabbi lifted his eyes heavenward and uttered a solemn prayer of blessing on the occasion and the couple.

Then the rabbi turned and gestured for Mary and her mother to join them. The parents were now standing on either side of their children with the couple in the middle. The rabbi took Joseph's right hand in his and reached out with his left for Mary's right hand and placed it in Joseph's palm. Mary trembled with excitement as she felt, for the first time, Joseph's strong hand close around hers. She looked shyly into his face and saw that he was struggling to hold back a wide grin. She almost laughed, partly at how he looked, partly with nervous joy, but caught herself as the rabbi announced their betrothal. On completion of that part of the ritual, Rabbi ben Levi then turned his eyes heavenward and prayed another blessing on the couple, asking Jahweh to make them fruitful in bearing many sons.

When the rabbi was finished, he turned to Naomi, Joseph's mother and said, "Let's celebrate." She passed him a goblet and the wine which he poured into the cup. Lifting it in thanks, he then gave it to Joseph and Mary's parents who all took a drink. Then the rabbi passed it to Joseph and

Mary. They both took a sip after which the rabbi emptied the goblet with a satisfied flourish. Then, after congratulating them all, the rabbi excused himself with a deep bow and left.

Joseph's parents offered Mary and her parents to stay for the evening meal. They politely demurred, according to custom, but graciously did accept the offer. Not to do so would have been equally unacceptable. That was the first time Mary and Joseph had actually spent that much time together and actually begun to get acquainted. Now that they had finally really met and completed the engagement arrangements, Mary knew they would soon be living together. She could hardly wait.

As Mary's mind played over the thoughts she had been entertaining ever since their engagement, she reached the top of the hill and slowly walked down the eastern slope to the edge of the city where the hill dropped away into the valley. She stood and gazed across the valley. Actually, one really could not see the buildings of the village of Nazareth, but even knowing they were just over the brow of the hill was enough. Her heart quickened as she thought that beyond the forest across from her lived this intriguing young man she was now engaged to, and where soon she might make her – no, their home.

Even though people often spoke derisively about Nazareth, Mary harbored no ill will towards it. She was a young woman who had learned to accept her lot in life and be satisfied with whatever Jahweh laid out for her. If she were to marry Joseph and move to Nazareth, she knew it would be all right. In fact, she might even like it better.

Sepphoris sometimes seemed like too worldly a place for Mary. There was so much that went on that was really contrary to her faith as she understood it from her parents. Indeed, if it was not for the good jobs her father had gotten here, her parents had said they would never have moved here. They had come from Jerusalem just before she was born. Her father had become well-known in his business as a land developer, and this had landed him the jobs in this growing city.

But Mary had also often heard her parents talk about how the citizens of Sepphoris were becoming too much like the pagan Greeks and those unwelcome Romans. Furthermore, she sometimes caught snatches of hushed talk suggesting there was still unrest amongst some of the Jews about this.

Mary's parents sometimes worried that some of the hot-headed Galileans who talked like this were going to cause them all trouble again. Every day they prayed to Jahweh for his protection and provision and trusted that he would look after them. Mary sighed and turned back towards home. When she entered, her mother turned from where she was preparing lunch and asked, "Where have you been child?"

"I went for a little walk," Mary replied. Never being one able to hide the truth, she added shyly, "I went to the top of the hill to look at Nazareth."

"Ah, child," her mother responded, "If our prayers are answered, that will be your home soon enough. And to tell the truth, I will be glad for you to be away from this city. It's not really a place I want to see my grandchildren grow up in. Of course, your father and I will miss you, but you won't be far away. Come, help me prepare lunch and then we have to work on dinner. Your father will be home soon."

The afternoon flew by as Mary helped her mother, then joined her parents for dinner. Mary often felt she was more blessed than others of her age. Since she was the only child, she got to eat with her father and mother both. In larger families, the males got served first, then the women got to eat. But Mary enjoyed the opportunity to talk with both of her parents. It was one way she got to learn things because, as a girl, she could not go to the synagogue school.

After the meal was done and everything cleaned up, Anna said, "Come Mary, let's start to take a look at what we have that you will have to take with you when you move into the home of this young man you are engaged to." Mary felt her pulse quicken again. She pinched herself mentally. Was this really happening to her?

That evening, as she said her prayers before lying down for the night, Mary thought her heart would burst. She had so much to be thankful for. She just felt so blessed.

Chapter 2. Night Intruder

Not many days later, Mary's mother, Anna, announced, "Mary, you know your father and I have been talking with Joseph's parents. You know that when a young woman is engaged, the custom is for her to move into the home of her husband-to-be."

Mary nodded. She knew this was coming. As one would expect, part of her was excited at the prospect. But there were also the unknowns; she hardly knew this family. However, she trusted in two things: Jahweh's guidance and that her parents had her best interests at heart. She knew that both they and she had been praying about this. So far, everything seemed to be going along as smoothly as could be expected under the circumstances. This too gave her hope that this was all in the will of Jahweh.

Anna was speaking further, "I will help you prepare what you need to take along with you. Naomi is making a place for you in their home. You will be to Naomi what you now are to me. However," she wagged her finger at her daughter sternly, "You will not be sleeping with Joseph until you are married."

Mary had inhaled sharply as her hand had flown to her chest, "Of course not, mother, how could you-?"

"I know, I know," Anna's face had broken into a big grin. "I was just teasing you. Anyway, let's get to work."

That evening, when Joachim arrived home from work and the three of them had finished dinner, he straightened up from his reclining eating position and said, "Well, Joseph brought news when he met me at work this morning. He says they have a place all ready for you now. So," he smiled across at his daughter with warm affection, "The time has come for you to leave our home. Of course, you are not that far away and we will always be here for you. You will always be our child."

Anna, now sitting up next to Mary, laid her hand on Mary's arm, and looking lovingly into her eyes, added her own heartfelt encouragement. "Yes, you will always be our daughter. May Jahweh bless your union with Joseph and make you a blessing in that family." She squeezed Mary's arm, "And may he bless you with children, as he wills."

Mary hardly knew what to say. She had hardly expected this day to arrive so soon. "You know I will do my best to be a good daughter, wife and mother, with Jahweh's help," she added.

Over the next couple of days, the move was completed. Mary found that Naomi was a pleasant and helpful woman, not unlike her own mother. Mary was relieved at that. She had heard stories of harsh mothers-in-law and had sometimes feared that possibility. Jacob was quieter than her father, but Mary found herself beginning to love him in his ways too. She learned to call Naomi her mother and Jacob her father.

Then, there was Joseph. Not unexpectedly, things were somewhat awkward between them. Neither knew exactly what was expected of them. As Mary had been discussing this with her mother prior to the move, Anna had declared, "To begin with, just treat Joseph like a brother," then abruptly laughed. "Well, no, that's poor advice! You've never had a brother!"

Nevertheless, Mary consoled herself with the thought that this was the whole point of living together in the engagement period. It gave a person time to adjust, to get to know the other. Mary's good nature also helped smooth the way.

Some nights later, Mary found herself having a wonderful dream. She was surrounded by so much warmth. But then there was light too, growing ever brighter. Mary opened her eyes and shot up from her mat! The room was filled with so much light she could scarcely see. What was happening? She found herself shaking in fear, and then she noticed it. Barely visible in the blinding light was a strange figure standing at the foot of her mat! She was overcome with terror!

Then the figure suddenly raised its right arm, causing Mary to shrink back and twist away on her mat, pulling her covers up under her chin, as if to ward off a blow. She couldn't take her eyes off the apparition. Just when she was becoming accustomed enough to the light to focus on the being in front of her, it spoke:

"I have come to bring you greetings," it said, and now she could see what seemed to resemble a most handsome young man, "I am Jahweh's servant Gabriel. I have come to tell you that you have found great favor in the eyes of the Most High. The Lord is with you."

Mary was still trembling as she tried to concentrate on the figure in the dazzling radiance that continued to fill the room. She could still scarcely organize her thoughts to make sense of this overwhelming scene: 'the Lord is with me? What does that mean? And this figure says he is Yahweh's servant Gabriel? And what did I hear? I have won favor with the Most High? How can that be? What have I done?'

Then the figure, which by now she understood to be an angel, spoke again, as if he had read her mind but was also aware of the dread that gripped her, "Don't be afraid, you really have found favor with Jahweh. What is more, you will become pregnant and give birth to a son, whom you will name Jesus...'

'What? Pregnant? Wait! Wait! Impossible, I've only just been engaged!' she wanted to shout but no sound came, and the angel was still speaking firmly: "Your son will be a great person, called the son of the Most High..."

'The son of the Most High?' This was beyond comprehension, but she had no time to grasp what she was hearing; the figure wasn't finished: "...and the Lord Jahweh will give him the throne of his ancestor David. He will reign over the house of Jacob forever, and there will be no end to his kingdom."

Finally, as if sensing his admonition not to be afraid was having no effect, the angel held his breath. The unexpected lull was just long enough for Mary to take a breath of her own and begin to collect her thoughts. The continued presence of this stranger and his confident manner of speaking was still entirely unnerving though. She could not stop shaking, but she managed to calm herself enough to know that she still could scarcely make sense of this.

Burying her face in her hands, Mary thought, the Most High sending angels with messages to humans I have heard of. She wasn't sure though that she had ever heard of a young woman, a girl, receiving such a visitation. And telling her, a virgin, she was going to be pregnant? What was this, this - messenger from Jahweh - telling her? The very idea of her being pregnant was too much. To be sure, she was engaged, but still...

Mary opened her eyes again and looked up. Was it just her imagination or did the light seem less intense, and was this apparition less foreboding looking than she had thought? She felt brave enough to ask the obvious question:

"How can this be, since I am a virgin?"

The angel replied, "The Spirit of Jahweh will come to you, and the power of the Most High will rest on you..." By now Mary found she could listen and the angel's words, as incredible as they were, began to sink in as he went on, "Therefore, the child to be born will be holy; he will be called the Son of Jahweh...." What? Was the angel still saying the same thing? Hold on! The Son of Yahweh? Since when did their one god, Yahweh, have children? And by a human? Was this heavenly being talking about Yahweh or some pagan god? Who really was this talking to her?

No, this was too much. This made no sense at all. How could she be expected to believe this? Was it still all a bad dream after all? If only, but the angel was not finished, "Look, I know this is obviously very heard for you to believe. Would it help if I told you your Aunt Elizabeth has also become pregnant with a son..." Now, what did this have to do with her, Mary thought, and in Elizabeth's old age? But that's what the angel was saying, adding, "although she was called barren, she is now in her sixth month! Nothing is impossible with Jahweh."

The angel fell silent, clasping his hands reverently in front of his chest as he continued to stand at the foot of her mat, as if waiting for a response. Had he just told her this about her aunt to give her an opportunity to test whether what he was saying was true? Mary now remembered that indeed, her Uncle Zechariah, Elizabeth's husband, had reportedly been visited by an angel. The devout couple had been childless and had really given up having a child, although they had never stopped praying for that. Zechariah was a priest, after all, and Mary knew he had a most sincere faith. The angel had told Zechariah their prayers were going to be answered and they would have a child. Not just any child. Yes, what had that angel said?

Those memories flooded back and Mary realized with a shock that what that angel had told her uncle was very similar to what this being was telling her. Indeed, that angel had also said his name was Gabriel. He had told Zechariah they would have a son who would be great in Jahweh's eyes, who would be filled with the Spirit of Jahweh. What's more, he was going to have the mission of preparing their people for the coming of the Lord, the Anointed One. This was a dream Mary's people had held for centuries. Even now, it was not unusual for someone to announced that this long-awaited one, the Anointed One, Messiah, was coming.

Just a minute, Mary realized abruptly, had this visitor not told her she was going to give birth to the Son of Jahweh? Was that not another name for The Anointed one. Mary inhaled sharply. This was unbelievable. This was unfathomable! She, a nobody from Nazareth, the mother of the Anointed One? Impossible! But, she could always contact her aunt to find out if it what this angel was saying was really true. But if this really was an angel, and everything he had said actually was from Jahweh, who was she to question it? She remembered all too well what had happened to her uncle for doubting the angel. He had been struck speechless and was told by the angel this was a consequence for not believing the message. He would not regain his speech till his son was born. Mary shivered at the thought of what had happened to her frightened uncle. Well, she was no less frightened. What might happen to her if she doubted?

As all these thoughts were racing through her mind, Mary realized with a start that the angel was still standing patiently in front of her and gazing at her. Was he waiting for her to answer? Suddenly she felt she needed to respond. But what could she say? It still all seemed unreal. She didn't know what she should say. She thought of everything she knew about Jahweh, and how she had always tried her best to follow The Law and be obedient and faithful to his will. She still had no real understanding though, of what was happening. Just the same, she pulled herself together with everything she had and looked up at this awesome creature in front of her.

Mary forced herself to speak as calmly and clearly as she could, the only words that in the moment seemed appropriate. Nevertheless, she could hardly believe what she was hearing herself say. It felt as if it wasn't really her speaking, "Yes, I am a servant of the Lord, at least I have always tried to be." She sighed and raised her hands in mute resignation as she looked into the angel's face, "I have nothing to say," she paused for a long moment, then finished, "Let this happen to me according to what you have said." No sooner had she said this than the figure disappeared with a flash, and the light with him.

Mary blinked. It was dark, and suddenly she shivered with the night chill. She shook her head as if to clear her thoughts and the emotions that were flooding over her, and looked around. Even in the dim light coming through the small window above her head, everything seemed as always. Then the frightening reality of what had just happened began to dawn on her and she knew for certain it was an angel she had seen, whether in real or in a vision, that didn't matter.

Now what? She couldn't fall asleep again. That much was certain. There was just too much in her head for her to process enough for that. She needed to talk to her someone. Could she talk to Joseph's parents? They really hardly knew each other. What would they say? Would they believe her?

Chapter 3. Now what?

Mary ran to Jacob and Naomi's bed, "Mother, Father," she whispered loudly, trying not to make too much of a disturbance while waking them from their sleep, "I just saw an angel!"

Suddenly the whole experience overwhelmed her and she found herself sobbing in Naomi's arms. Naomi held her close and stroked her hair, "You must have been dreaming. No angel has come to Israel for centuries. And especially not to a girl."

Mary pulled herself up and looked Naomi in the face through her tears, "But that's not true," she countered. "You can ask my parents. An angel came to my Uncle Zechariah not long ago. The angel said his name was Gabriel just like this one. My Uncle Zechariah and Aunt Elizabeth had not been able to have children. They had prayed diligently for a child, just like Samuel and Samson's mothers in our ancient stories. The angel Gabriel had told our relatives they would have a son who would prepare the way for Jahweh's Anointed One." Mary paused respectfully. "No mother," she finished resolutely, "I was not dreaming. Didn't you see the light? It filled the room!"

"What light?" Naomi asked, "We were sound asleep."

Then Mary realized the awful truth. Of course, only she had experienced this. She had been the only one to see and hear the angel. How then could she convince anyone else of what she now so strongly believed to be true. How could she break the news of what the angel had said about her going to be pregnant? Who would believe that this was to come about through some action of Jahweh? That she would carry in her womb the Anointed One? Desperate to get the whole story out, to get Naomi to believe her, Mary thought, I have to convince my family of this. I need their support. Mary no longer doubted what she had heard.

"Mother," Mary pressed on firmly, and by now Jacob had pulled himself up to rest on his elbow on their sleeping mat and was listening as well, "I saw an angel and he told me his name was Gabriel."

That got Jacob sitting right up cross-legged before her and now both he and Naomi were giving her their full attention. They both knew from their religion's holy writings that there was an angel called Gabriel. And Mary had told them this angel had recently visited her uncle. It still seemed a rather farfetched story. Mary took a quick breath before she carried on, not knowing how the rest of her story would strike her in-laws. To be unmarried and pregnant – she didn't want to think about the possible consequences of that, but she couldn't stop, "He told me I was going to become pregnant, not from a man but by Jahweh's Spirit. He said the baby was to be named Jesus and that he would be great…" Mary couldn't hold back now, but tried to remember it all, "… and will be called the Son of the Most High, and Jahweh, the Lord, will give him the throne of his father David. He said this son would reign over the house of Jacob forever, and his kingdom would never end," Mary was almost out of breath when she finished.

Jacob and Naomi were stunned. Their new daughter-in-law, pregnant, by the action of Jahweh's Spirit! And her son to be a king? They knew from discussions they had with Mary's parents prior to the engagement of their son to Mary, that she was a descendant of their ancestor King David, just like their son. That part was right. Some of this began to make sense but it was still all too much.

"Oh, and…" Mary continued, "We were talking about my Uncle Zechariah, remember? The angel also said that my Aunt Elizabeth has become pregnant, with a son. In her old age! He said she was already in her sixth month!"

Suddenly an idea occurred to her, "We could send a message to my Aunt Elizabeth to see if this is true. If it is, then maybe what the angel told me was true too. Please?" she implored excitedly, "If it is, wouldn't that make you believe me?" Something inside her made Mary wish she could visit her relatives and find this all out for herself, but she knew that was probably too much to hope for. However, Mary was convinced of what she had experienced alone in the night. This was not her imagination, or a terrible dream; she sorely needed her family to believe her.

"Whoa, whoa, hold on," Jacob broke in, spreading his hands out as if to call a halt to things. Everything was happening way too fast.

Naomi just shook her head as if trying to clear up her bewilderment: "Your barren aunt? Pregnant? In her old age?"

"Yes," Mary gushed, "The angel said nothing was impossible with Yahweh."

Naomi couldn't argue with that. Slowly, another thought formed in her mind. Mary's idea was not a bad one. That was something they could check. If Elizabeth was indeed expecting, that would corroborate Mary's story. Besides, if Mary was going to be pregnant, there could be a lot of trouble. People would talk. It could be good for all of them for Mary to be away for a while.

Naomi took a deep breath. "Jacob," she said turning to look at her husband, "What do we do make of this?"

"Right now, I have no answers," he answered, shaking his head vigorously as if to clear his brain.

"Mary, my daughter," Jacob said as he leaned forward, looking into her anxious face, "I don't really want to doubt you, but are you sure about all this?" It did seem too fantastical not to be true. There was much in it that rang true. His new future daughter-in-law had so far proven herself in every way and he did not want to have her question their growing relationship by her thinking he seriously doubted her.

As if reading his thoughts, Mary straightened up and turned to look Jacob in the eye, saying as calmly as she could with the excitement she felt, but with a boldness she felt she needed, "Have I ever lied to you?"

"No, no, Mary, you have not. I think right now though, all we can do is keep this in our minds and try to get some sleep and talk about it further in the morning. We'll pray about it and we'll all be able to think better then."

"So, you believe me then?" Mary added.

"Yes, yes Mary," Jacob said quietly but firmly, "I do." In his own mind though, he wasn't really sure he did, but for her sake he wanted very much to accept what she had told them. He could see that Mary needed that and deep down he knew he would do whatever he could to protect his new daughter.

"You too mother?" Mary said, looking at Naomi.

Jacob was nodding behind Mary, his eyes pleading with his wife to agree. "Of course, child," Naomi joined in, "How could I not?"

But there was still one more thing on Mary's mind. "Can we send a message to my Aunt Elizabeth's to find out if what the angel said is true?"

"Wait, wait, not so fast," Jacob smiled wearily. He had never seen Mary like this. But then, if everything she had just told them was true, who wouldn't be worked up? He smiled and lifted his hands again as he said resignedly, "Right now, we all need to get some sleep. Maybe things will be clearer in the morning. We have a lot to think about, and maybe a lot of planning to do. Most importantly, what will we say to Joseph? What will he think? But let's leave that till morning. We can all think and pray about it tonight and trust that Jahweh will give us guidance as to how to proceed."

Mary gasped! Of course, Joseph! How could she forget? And her parents too! All this time Joseph appeared to have remained asleep in his temporary quarters, which was separate from the main body of the house. What would happen to their engagement if she was found pregnant, but not by him. People would soon find out and tongues would wag. Mary knew that in their law there was a death sentence for someone thought to have gotten pregnant out of wedlock. To be sure, that had not actually happened to anyone she had ever heard about. She sighed, both her heart and her thoughts still troubled. What would they talk about in the morning? How could she sleep with all of this on her mind? Oh, she couldn't bear the thought of what this could do to their future.

Chapter 4. Breaking the News

To begin with, Mary felt she would never sleep. On one hand, she was so exhausted. On the other, the emotional stimulation of the angel's visit and the conversations of the night had still not diminished enough to let her sleep. However, it was not long before the intensity of the past minutes – or was it hours? – ebbed enough to allow her to fall into some semblance of sleep.

Before Mary knew it, she was waking up as the sun was streaming in through the small window of her room. 'Oh,' She thought, 'It's getting late.' She started to stretch and then sat bolt upright! Last night! What had happened last night?

She tried to organize her thoughts as she rose and wrapped her cloak tightly around herself. She went over to the ledge near her bed and poured a little water from the jug there into the basin beside it and splashed some on her face. She ran her fingers through her hair as she hurried out to look for Naomi. Sure enough, Naomi was already warming some breakfast for her when Mary came into the room.

"Mother," she cried, "Do you remember last night?"

"I certainly do," Naomi responded, "How could I forget it?"

'Oh, good, thought Mary, 'I wasn't dreaming after all.'

"Mary, have some breakfast," Naomi said, "Then we need to talk."

Mary nodded and sat on the floor beside her mother-in-law to eat what had been prepared. She couldn't help but feel a bit uneasy with that tone in her Naomi's voice. She still did not know her in-laws that well and wondered what they might have been saying about it all.

Naomi did not wait for her to finish eating. "So," she said, "The angel Gabriel visited you and said you were going to be pregnant and have a son named Jesus. You know Jesus means 'Savior,' right?"

Mary nodded. "And," Naomi went on, "This son is supposed to become the King of Israel. How can that be? And what does it mean?" They were as good as nobodies in their world when it came to that sort of thing. This was something neither of the two women could grasp. Mary was beginning to understand the matter-of-fact side of her mother-in-law.

"Well," Mary gently broke the silence that followed as they struggled to understand this. She continued, "We are descendants of King David, are we not?"

"Yes," Naomi replied. "That is true. And you said the angel did mention that. All I can say is, if this is what The Most High wants, he can bring it to pass. But you will need His protection because you know what the consequences for being pregnant in your circumstances can be."

Mary's face paled and she trembled as she remembered her fears of that. She looked wide-eyed at her mother-in-law. She was so blunt! She had indeed heard what could happen to women who became pregnant out of wedlock. The thought made her shiver with fear.

"And not only that," her mother-in-law was continuing, "As you brought up last night, what will this mean for your engagement? I can only imagine how Joseph is going to react to the news of your being pregnant. Obviously, we will have to tell him, and your parents too."

Naomi had still more to say, "Now, we don't yet know what all of this will mean, for all of us. We have a lot to consider, to deal with. There is one other concern, perhaps not demanding attention as immediately as what I have stated so far. That is this business of this child becoming a king. I know it seems beyond us. But you know what could happen if word of that gets out. Our king does not take kindly to those whom he perceives as a threat to his position. Then there would be the Romans. What would this mean to them? These are subjects quite over our heads right now. However, if what the angel said is true, we have to think of all these things."

Suddenly Mary felt like she was going to be ill. She felt a headache coming on. This was getting to be too much. Were her short-lived dreams to be so quickly shattered? But she knew Naomi was right. Telling both Joseph and her own family was something they had to do.

"Jacob and I talked," Naomi went on. "we will have dinner tonight with Joseph as usual and break the news. We did not tell him anything this morning. He's gone off to work now. There's no sense putting it off more though. Better get it over with sooner than later," she finished, looking at Mary as if expecting an answer.

Mary was trying desperately not to let her thoughts run away with her, and in most unpleasant directions. Oh, what was happening? Yesterday morning she had felt so carefree and happy compared to the heaviness she was experiencing now. Mary wished Naomi wasn't so practical. She needed more time to process all of this.

Mary nodded meekly. What else could she do? Arrangements had been made.

On one hand the day seemed to drag on forever. On the other, dinner couldn't come soon enough. She dreaded what was coming. Keeping busy assisting Naomi prepare for dinner helped keep some of those thoughts at bay and pass the time.

Eventually, Mary heard the voices at the door that told her Joseph and his father had come home. She approached the door and bowed as she greeted the men. She had brought a basin of water for Joseph and his father to wash their feet before they all sat down for dinner.

Mary guessed from the subdued nature of everyone's behavior and the lack of conversation that Jacob had already said something to Joseph but she could only imagine what. She looked tentatively at the dark, curly haired young man across from her, wondering what was on his mind. She just wished she could take his hand and tell him everything was all right, was going to be all right. But could she? Was it going to be all right?

After eating in near silence, Jacob finally leaned back, wiped his mouth and said, "Mary, I told Joseph you had some very important news for him, but I have not said anything more. I thought it best it came from you."

Mary was taken aback. What? Jacob wanted her to break the news to Joseph? What could she say?

Sensing her fear, her father-in-law tried to reassure her. "Mary, just tell him exactly what you told us last night. It will be all right," he said encouragingly.

Mary knew Jacob was trying to support her but she was still panicking inside. She looked at her mother-in-law, whose only response was a subtle nod of agreement with her husband.

Mary gulped; this was all happening much too fast, but it seemed there was no alternative. She breathed a quick prayer to Jahweh for the right words to say, took a deep breath, and began.

Joseph's eyes grew wider and wider as he listened. Sweat began to break out on his forehead and upper lip. Were his ears deceiving him? All he heard was that his beautiful, lovely Mary was pregnant? How could she have let this happen? What would happen to them? To her? He didn't want to think about it. Was their marriage over before it had even begun? Were his dreams not going to come true? This was too upsetting for Joseph. He could no longer concentrate on everything Mary was saying. He could not bear to hear it all. His mind was already running away with him.

Besides thinking about what his seemed to say about Mary and what it meant for their relationship, the possible price they might have to pay dawned on him, especially for Mary. Being engaged and then found pregnant by someone else was, according to their law, adultery, and so punishable by death! He couldn't imagine his fiancée being stoned by those who adhered strictly to their law if they found out. And how could they not obey the Law? Stoning was the penalty for being pregnant outside of marriage.

It was simply unfathomable. His sweet Mary really had gotten pregnant by someone else? How could that have happened?

"Joseph," Jacob broke in before Joseph's thoughts could get too carried away. "I know this is a lot to take in. I am not sure you have heard it all. Look at me, son."

Joseph straightened his shoulders and faced his father.

"I don't know everything that is going on in your mind, but I can imagine. I need you to hear me clearly," Jacob said in a take-charge tone of voice, "This is something that your mother and I only found out about last night," he continued slowly. "Mary appears to have been visited by an angel that appeared to her Uncle Zechariah a few months back and told him he and his wife were going to have a son. From the sounds of what Zechariah has said, the son he and Mary's aunt are expecting seems destined to be the forerunner of this Anointed One that Mary is to bring into this world."

Joseph's eyes widened. How much more was there to this? It was becoming even more unbelievable. The Anointed One coming in their lifetime? After centuries of waiting? As if from a distance, he heard his father continue while he struggled doggedly to keep his focus on what he was hearing.

"Let us reassure you Joseph, Mary has not been unfaithful to you."

"Oh, no," cried Mary, "I could never do that!"

"But then, how-" Joseph blurted out.

Jacob was not finished. "No, Mary has reassured us of that and I trust her," he continued firmly. "Furthermore, I have never seen any evidence of anyone being around her, or of anything untoward happening – until last night. I can well imagine you didn't hear everything Mary said. It is a lot to take in.

"But please, know this," Jacob went on, "Remember, it appears to have been an angel who told Mary all this. She did not make this up. Nothing else has happened. The angel said Mary would become pregnant through the power of Jahweh, and bear a son who will be The Anointed One. Don't ask me to really understand that either. But I think we have to take Mary at her word. I don't know what else we can do and we have to start somewhere." Jacob paused, "And remember, both of you come from the line of King David, and if, even now, Jawheh is preparing Mary's cousin to run before him, in the power of Elijah, which is how Zechariah heard it – it could make sense."

Jacob wished he could believe what he was saying as much as he was asking Joseph and Mary to do. However, someone had to try and keep things under control and who else but him, as the father figure they depended on. Joseph and Mary would need all the support they could get and the baby would certainly need a father.

"It is all too much," Joseph jumped up and blurted out angrily, "Do you really expect me to believe all this? It's just too strange. I've never heard of anything like this."

Mary could see the sweat on his brow and the confusion in his eyes as Joseph glared at them, clenching and unclenching his fists, as if to challenge them to argue back. Just as suddenly, his arms dropped to his side and Mary noticed how helpless he looked, standing before them all. Jacob saw how Joseph was struggling to save face, to keep control. He fought for words but nothing seemed to come to mind that could ease Joseph's anger and fears at the moment.

It was Joseph who broke the silence. He held up his arms defensively, "I don't know what to do? I have to go. I have to think about this." He headed for the door, fighting to keep control, and before anyone could respond, he was gone.

That brought Jacob to his feet. He rushed after him while Mary, rendered speechless by this, buried her face in her hands and began to weep. Was this the end of her dreams? Naomi took her in her arms and whispered in Mary's hair. "Oh, my daughter, what will become of this? What is going on?"

Both were still sobbing when Jacob came back in. Seeing what was happening, he got down beside them and wrapped his strong arms around them both. It was all he could do to choke back his own sobs, but he was able to say hoarsely, "I was able to get Joseph to stop and listen to me before he went on. I asked him not to be hasty, to think about this, to pray about it. I urged him to come and talk with us about it again. What else could I say? He agreed he would."

Naomi nodded and released her hold on Mary, who then straightened up and began to dry her eyes. How her heart ached.

Chapter 5. The Honorable Thing

Joseph, after leaving his parents and Mary, had gone back to his new quarters with his heart torn by mixed feelings. Part of him was still angry. Just when life was beginning to look like it was working out – this! The more he thought about it, the more confused he became. Gradually, the thoughts racing through his mind slowed in the growing dusk. His mood calmed and he became aware of how his heart ached. Suddenly he found himself sobbing. At the same time, he sensed the anger inside him was still there. How could this happen? What had he and Mary done to deserve this? He wiped his eyes in the gathering darkness. His head hurt; he just did not know what to think.

Then again, if this really was from The Highest One, as Mary had said, a message brought by an angel - wow! Joseph shook his head. Was there anything more that could be done now? His mind was in turmoil.

But if Mary was pregnant, did that not mean she had broken their Law?

Joseph did not know what to believe. 'I really hardly know Mary,' he thought, 'but just the same, I don't want anything to happen to her. She is supposed to become my wife.' Indeed, Joseph could hardly bring himself to think of what he knew was the consequence of such behavior. According to their Law, she could be stoned to death. Then, what about me, he wondered? People will think I am the obvious culprit. Could I suffer the same punishment? He could not help but think of what this might mean for himself. He really could not see a way out of this dilemma. In the end, the only thing that was left was to pray to Jahweh for wisdom. If this was his doing, would he not give us the answers we need?

Then, Joseph had an idea. Maybe he could talk to Rabbi ben Levi and see what he would advise.

Joseph didn't know if he could wait till tomorrow to see what kind of answers might come with time. At the same time, he felt a certain dread about what they were all facing. Eventually, he just knew he had enough for this day. He lay back on his mat, pulled up his cover and tried to sleep.

Sleep did not come quickly though. As Joseph tried to sleep he kept thinking about it all. As was his habit when he was in such distress, Joseph tried to recall comforting words of scripture. Then, in his desperate straits, he poured his heart out in prayer to Jahweh.

As he thought about it further, lying there and not able to sleep, it came to Joseph, that perhaps the only thing he could do now was break off the engagement. How could he marry someone who was pregnant with – someone else's child? But he did not want any harm to come to Mary. He did not want to get into trouble either. If this was the path to be taken, he would have to do this very quietly, just between his family and Mary and her family. That was the only honorable thing he could see doing – for now. People might still talk. After all, the engagement had not been a secret. Oh, there was just too much to consider. But at least he felt that he had come to one possible decision with that. He really could see no other way, nor could he think clearly anymore. It was not long before sleep finally came.

Chapter 6. More Night Disturbance

Joseph was exhausted, but in his troubled state, he slept fitfully. He was in that tiring state of being half awake and half asleep when all at once he felt a strange and comforting warmth about him. When he became aware of it he also noticed it was becoming increasingly brighter. Was he dreaming? But no, it was as if he felt something, a presence in the room. He was overcome with terror. What was happening? He opened his eyes to a sudden blinding light filling the room! Then he saw it – the radiant figure of a young man at the foot of his mat. Joseph was speechless but then the figure spoke in a clear, calm voice:

"You are Joseph, a son of David," the figure began. "I have come to tell you not to be afraid to take Mary as your wife. The child she is carrying is from Jahweh's Spirit. Mary will give birth to a son and you are to name him Jesus, which means Savior, as you know, because he will save his people from their sins."

Joseph gasped. This stranger was telling him the same things he had heard from Mary! The same things Mary had said such a night visitor had told her. Had she not referred to the figure as an angel? Named Gabriel? This angel, if that's what it was, was addressing everything that had occupied Joseph's mind these last dreadful hours. Who was this and how did this figure know what had been on his mind? He scarcely had time to gather his thoughts, realizing he had all kinds of questions for this person. However, before he could summon the courage to open his mouth, the visitor was gone and all was dark as before.

Joseph bolted up from his sleep. There was nothing abnormal around him; the room felt cold and dark as usual at night. Then he realized, it had all been a vision. Or was it real? He sat briefly in stunned silence. Then, as the force of what had just happened began to dissipate, he started to go over what he had just heard. 'Joseph, son of David.' Yes, he was a descendant of Israel's great king. But he had never been greeted that way before. What did this mean? Mary had said the angel had told her she was going to be pregnant – by the Spirit of The Highest One? But this angel said Joseph was still to marry her? And this child was going to become the Savior of his people? This was still all a lot to take in. It was beyond his comprehension.

This person - and it must have been an angel like Mary had seen, with that heat and light, and those words – knew all about his dilemma, his fears. He had told him not to be afraid, but to take Mary as his wife. This, this angel, had also told him that Mary's child was from the Holy Spirit. That meant Mary had not gotten pregnant from any other man. That should have been a relief, and it was, but it was still all a bit much to really sink. What was this all about? Who would believe such a story? Mary had said her night visitor had also said she would have a son that should be named Jesus. But it seemed her visitor had talked about him being a king. This messenger, however, had talked about this child saving his people from their sins. What did that mean? Only Jahweh could do that.

Now what? Should he awaken his parents and tell them what had happened or wait till morning? He certainly had a lot to talk about with them and with Mary and her family. Anyway, he had no idea what time of night it was. Because everything was very dark, he guessed it was not yet anywhere near morning. But could he sleep till then?

Joseph lay back on his mat and breathed a prayer, asking The Highest One for guidance. As he prayed further and thought about all that had happened in the last twenty-four hours, he felt the strange beginnings of hope return. Both he and Mary had received the same kind of visit. They had received essentially the same message. And it came just after their engagement. There must be a connection there. Yes, if Mary is to have a child, better it have two parents.

Again, the thoughts of what people would think when they found out crept into his mind. There would be some shaming, especially for Mary. That's just the way it was. Then he remembered that, before falling asleep, he had reasoned that possibly breaking off the engagement was the path to take. When he reviewed that now, especially in light of this further message, he began to have second thoughts. Why did he think that would have been the right thing to do? That would perhaps make people think he was not the guilty party for getting Mary pregnant, so he would not suffer the same shame and blame. Oh, some would still wonder, still talk, but what could one do about that? There would always be people like that.

If he thought about Mary though, for he did care about her, that would still put her in a bad light. She would still be in trouble. In fact, as he debated further within himself, he realized that would leave Mary in a worse predicament than if they remained engaged. How honorable is that? Since they were already engaged, maybe they could arrange their marriage sooner rather than later. At least that way, people would think it was his son. Sure, there would be some judgment, but not as harsh as if Mary were left on her own. They would not come under the same censure together as either of them would alone.

Indeed, had that not been the messenger's initial statement? 'Don't be afraid to take Mary as your wife.' Again, this unsettling guest had said this was all from Jahweh. He still could not understand that. Why would The Highest One make a young virgin pregnant? That seemed to go against their Law, which had come from Jahweh to begin with. However, it was as if the guest, the angel, was telling him to go ahead with the engagement because it really was acceptable to The Highest One. Or was he actually being told what to do? Was this really all some strange plan of Jahweh's?

Impossible as it all seemed, when he mulled it over like this, he could see some sense in it. He didn't understand it, but the messages to Mary and him were plain enough. He could not explain it, but his earlier anger and confusion, the hurt, was beginning to be replaced by a strange sense of comfort and strength. This brought some relief. He thought he ought to thank Jahweh for giving him some direction by sending this messenger to reinforce what Mary had said. However, he knew he still needed to ask The Highest One for help.

Joseph still did not think things were settled though. There was still a lot on his plate, Joseph felt. It remained rather overwhelming. He needed to talk about this again with his parents, maybe the rabbi as he had thought in the evening. They then needed to talk with Mary and her parents. Now he was too tired to dwell on how those conversations could go. In fact, this had all left him rather drained. He lay back on his mat again and made himself comfortable. He remembered the prayer of thanks he had thought he should make. As he struggled with what to say, sleep overcame him. This time he was more tired but also beginning to feel a little more at ease. With that, it was a much better sleep than that with which the night had begun.

Chapter 7. Spreading the News

Before long, Joseph was awakened by the crow of a rooster. He knew that meant it was time to get up and go to work. For a moment though, he had to collect himself as to where he was. All the events of yesterday and especially last night were flooding back. He dashed out to where his mother was ready with some breakfast for him.

"Mama, mama," he cried, "Is Papa still here?"

"Yes, Naomi said, "He's around somewhere." Turning towards Joseph, she quickly inquired, "Did you sleep well? How are you this morning?"

"I don't know yet," Joseph answered as he hurried on outside into the fresh air of the morning and saw his father puttering in the garden.

"Papa, Papa," he said anxiously, "Remember what Mary told us? About the angel?"

Jacob straitened up and turned towards his son, "How could I forget something like that?" he said wryly before Joseph could finish, "You were quite upset, even confused, when we told you. For which I can't blame you. You heard quite a strange story and you had lot on your mind."

"Yes, yes," Joseph raced on, "But last night the angel came to me."

"What," his father exclaimed, "Two angels two days apart? After so many years of silence from Jahweh? That's a bit much to take in, believe me. Are you sure you weren't dreaming about Mary's experience with all that on your mind?"

"No, father, no," replied Joseph with some impatience, then rushed on, "In fact, the angel told me much the same as was told to Mary. He said I was to have no fear and we were to marry anyway. But he said more. Besides the same things Mary told us, about her getting pregnant by the Spirit of Jahweh and giving birth to a son, the angel said we are to name him Jesus, because he will save his people from their sins!"

Jacob rested his chin on his hands as he listened to his son, "Wow," he exclaimed as he tried to absorb Joseph's words, "This is still beyond anything I have ever heard. Jahweh making someone pregnant. A virgin at that! And both you and Mary get this message!" He paused. "But there is some reassurance in what you say. If the angel told you it is all right for you and Mary to get married, I believe this tells us Jahweh knows that some of the fears we had about all of this are not going to be as bad as we thought. That's good news too, don't you think?" he looked up at Joseph standing there.

Joseph nodded.

But, Jacob reflected, "This child is to grow up to be our Savior?" He shook his head. "What in the world does all this mean? Who has ever heard anything like this? I wish I knew more of what it meant. However," Jacob finished thoughtfully as he rested his chin on his hoe, "If this is true, if it is from The Highest One, we will find out in time." Then he added, straightening up, "Have you told your mother yet? And of course, Mary?"

'No," Joseph replied, "I thought I should tell you first."

"Very well," Jacob answered, "You know how your mother can sometimes worry and this news could certainly add to that. Let's go in and have something to eat while we talk about this together."

The two of them re-entered their home and reclined around the food Naomi had set out for them. Mary had been helping Naomi and she too settled down to eat with them. Jacob lifted his eyes heavenward and asked for a blessing on the meal and then they ate in silence for some time before anyone spoke.

Joseph could hardly contain himself but he thought he should wait for his father's leading. He could not help but steal a glance at Mary from time to time, wondering how she would take the news he now also had to share. Eventually, Jacob pushed back and crossed his legs to sit upright, "Naomi," he began, "and Mary," he nodded in Mary's direction. "Our son appears to have had the same kind of night visitor that Mary reported."

Naomi and Mary gasped and straitened up as one, eyes wide, "What? Joseph, what did the visitor, the angel, tell you? Tell us!" Naomi gasped.

"The same as to Mary," Joseph began, repeating the whole story he had told his father.

Naomi looked at Jacob, then Mary, "Jacob, what does this mean? What are we to do?"

Jacob considered things for a minute and then replied, "I think we just have to wait and see what The Highest One is doing. I guess it won't hurt to go ahead with the engagement and even the marriage. That was apparently the angel's word. I think that's good news. However, I am still concerned for Mary – and you too Joseph.

"There are several reasons why I think it's still wise for us to keep quiet about this. First of all, you know what some might look for in terms of punishment for being pregnant under these circumstances. We don't want anything to happen to you." He looked at Josepha and Mary, then went on.

"We know what the old Law says but we also know many of our leaders in these times do not believe Jahweh is that punitive, as to want people killed. He would rather be gracious and forgive they say. It sounds like the angel was reassuring in this regard, but we can still do our part not to invite more trouble than we need to."

Jacob hesitated briefly before going on, "There is still another very important reason why we have to keep quiet. You know how King Herod feels about any challenge to his rule, and the angels are telling us this boy is to be a king? And then there are the Romans. What will they think?"

Then he leaned forward and intoned ominously, "I hear some of our Galilean hotheads are again planning a revolt. Ah," Jacob leaned forward and lowered his voice, "they are crazy – just between you and me I say that." He straightened up again, "We just don't need trouble."

Joseph had heard some of his young friends talking of this too but he had kept quiet. Violence was not his way.

"Mary," Naomi spoke, "you have not had a chance to say anything. What does all this sound like to you?"

All eyes were on Mary. She was quiet for a moment before answering. "Father," she said," looking at Jacob, "I think your words are wise. You have already been thinking about this. Of course, I am glad the angel said it's all right for us to marry." She smiled. "That means Jahweh is all right with all of this. It is, after all, his doing. It is good to hear the reassurance too.

"Otherwise, I really have nothing to add. I do feel better with keeping quiet about things. I am also glad we all agree that since this has all been begun by Jahweh, we continue to follow his leading."

"Good," Jacob said, rising from his place at the meal, "We will proceed as we have all discussed." Then he added, "Joseph, you had wondered about getting advice from our rabbi. At some point, it might be good for us to consult with Rabbi ben Levi. First though, we need to go and talk to Joachim and Anna about this too. We still have not shared any of this with them. It has all been happening so fast." He sighed. "What do you all say?"

Joseph turned respectfully towards his mother. She was briefly silent before she answered, "Absolutely. We are two families caught up in this. We will probably come up with a better way forward if we seek it out together."

Joseph looked back at his father and shrugged, "I have nothing to add. I think you are both right."

Mary looked at them all and nodded. "Yes, of course we have to tell them. Thanks father," she said to Jacob.

"All right then," Jacob said, rising to his feet, "Come, my son. You need to get to work. I'll come with you as far as Mary's parents. It's on your way. Hopefully Joachim will still be home."

Joseph got up, leaning over to kiss his mother on his way out, then shyly reached over to grasp Mary's hand. "Please both pray for us," he said, before the two men turned and walked out into the new day. They pulled their cloaks tighter around them as they stepped out into the still cool morning air.

They walked in silence around the side of the hill on which Nazareth was built, and then downhill on the path that lead across the valley to Sepphoris and Joachim and Anna's home. In the distance, they could see its imposing buildings and walls, bright in the morning sun. Joseph could not help but wonder how what the things he and his father had to tell them were going to be received. He knew he would find out soon enough.

Chapter 8. New Plans

Joseph could not help feeling apprehensive as they approached the home where Mary had lived until just a few days earlier. As if reading his mind, his father eased his anxiety somewhat by stopping Joseph with his hand on his shoulder and turning to face him before they got to the door, "I am your father, I will talk first. You might have something to add in its turn." They turned to enter the home.

"Greetings and peace to your household," Jacob called as he stepped into Joachim and Anna's doorway.

"Peace to you," Joachim replied, as he stepped from the shadows and welcomed the two of them in, "What brings you two here so early in the morning? I hope you bring good news. Come in, rest your feet."

Jacob was relieved to see that Joachim was still home. He was anxious to share what had happened in their home over the last couple of days. He and Joseph sat down across from Joachim and Anna. "I believe we do bring good news," Jacob answered, trying to sound positive. "I believe we do. You see, Mary had a visit from what we can only understand was an angel a couple of nights ago."

"What? Our daughter? An angel?" Joachim was incredulous. "And since when do angels speak to young women?"

Seeing the shock in Joachim and Anna's faces, Jacob held up his hand, "I know, our apologies for not telling you sooner. But you see, before we could really come to terms with that and what it meant, Joseph had a visit the next night from the same angel that visited Mary."

Anna gasped and exclaimed, "This is unbelievable!" before clapping her hands over her mouth., waiting for Jacob to go on.

"Yes," Jacob went on, "The angel said the same thing to both of them. The Spirit of the Lord is making Mary pregnant-"

"What? Am I supposed to believe that?" Joachim leaned forward and broke in, "I have never heard anything like that in my life!" Anna's eyes widened even more.

"I know, I know," Jacob replied. "Don't you think we questioned it when it happened first to Mary? But when it happened again to Joseph, there did not seem to be any doubt." Seeing that their hosts were anxiously waiting now, Jacob continued, "What's more, as far as we can understand, this child is to be The Anointed One. The angels said this child was to be the Son of Jahweh."

Joachim leaned back, shaking his head and spreading his arms in disbelief, "This is getting more preposterous all the time. A human being having a child from Jahweh. I'm sorry, but that sounds sacrilegious. Indeed, the scriptures do talk about the Messiah as the Son of The Highest One, but I thought the Messiah would come straight from heaven as our deliverer, not be born of a human.

"Can such a thing happen just out of the blue? I mean, does this sound like what the prophets have said? Don't prophets come and tell us more details about how and when such things are going to happen? Is Elijah not supposed to return before The Messiah comes? Should this child, this king-to-be, not be born out of some royal family, maybe in Jerusalem? This just doesn't sound right."

Joseph could scarcely contain himself. "Father," he said eagerly, looking towards Jacob, "May I?"

"Go ahead," Jacob gestured.

"Joachim, Anna, let me fill you in on the details. You know both Mary and I are descended from David, right?" They both nodded. Joseph went on, "The angel mentioned that as, of course, that is the line of the Messiah. We know that. So that makes sense." Again, the couple nodded. "But you mentioned prophets. You have relatives in Judea. Zechariah and Elizabeth?"

Now Joseph really had their attention.

"How do you know them?" Joachim started.

"Oh," Joseph blurted, "The angel told Mary that your relative Elizabeth is six months pregnant, and that her child is to be the forerunner of the Messiah."

"Wow," Joachim exclaimed, "This is getting more fantastic all the time."

"Yes," it was Anna's turn, "This is just as unbelievable as everything else you have been saying. Elizabeth is – was? – barren! Oh, if this is true, how wonderful for them!" Her face beamed, thinking of how delighted her sister must be.

"Yes," Joachim continued, his eyes narrowed as he tried to digest this all, "If the angel said all that, well, it would fit what we have been taught to expect. Still-" he shook his head. "What does this mean, for us, for you and Mary, and Joseph?"

"Well," Jacob answered, "Believe me, we had questions about that too after Mary received the first message. You know what our Law says about single pregnant women. We too wondered what we should do. However, before we could come up with any answers, before we even got to tell you, as I said, the angel had visited Joseph and added to the story."

"Yes," Joseph broke in again, "The angel - by the way, he said his name was Gabriel, and we know that angel name from our scriptures – told me to go ahead and marry Mary regardless."

Joachim spread his arms and sighed, "Well, that is good news, a relief. At least our families can go ahead with our plans for Joseph," he nodded at the young man, "and our daughter." He shook his head again, "If this is all to be believed."

"Joachim, my friend, and Anna," Jacob spoke up. "I think we have to believe this. What choice do we have? Two visits by angels. Let me tell you, our children were quite shaken by all this, as you can well imagine. Well, we all are. But, as you are recognizing, the details all add up. The messages are consistent with one another and with what we know from our holy writings. There is still more, actually."

"What?" Joachim almost laughed. "All right, tell us everything, please."

"Joseph, you go on," Jacob said.

"I think what father wants me to add is that the angels said our child was to be named Jesus, and they specifically said that was because it means that he will save his people from their sins. Oh, and one more thing, Mary wondered whether we could send a message to your relatives to verify what the angel said. Actually, she kind of wants to go there herself, but I don't know if that's wise."

"Save his people from their sins?" Joachim was incredulous. "What has that got to do with being our king? Isn't Messiah supposed to come and free us from all our oppression and restore the kingdom of Israel, make it even better, to last - forever? What does a king have to do with our sins? That's between us and the priests and Jahweh.

"As for contacting our relatives, sure we can do that." Joachim continued. "But Mary going there? Well, we will see. Come to think of it, there might be some merit in that. We have to think more about this though before we make any such decisions."

"None of us has all the answers to all these questions," Jacob reminded them. "All we can conclude is that if two angels came and gave Mary and Joseph two similar messages, that fit with other facts, as we have described, this must be the will of Jahweh. There is some assurance and guidance in what the angel said, such as that Joseph and Mary should marry, and what to call the baby. However, otherwise, we concluded all we can do is trust Jahweh, pray about this and wait to see if there is any more guidance in all of this."

"You are right," Joachim responded. "What else can we do? All I know is, this has been rather exhausting."

Anna nodded. "Thank you, thank you for sharing everything with us. At least we can go forward together."

"And I have to go to work," Joachim said, realizing time was slipping by. Noting the water container and bag Joseph had brought, he added, "How about you, Joseph? Looks like you were going to work? Shall we go?"

Chapter 9. It is Decided

When Joseph arrived home that evening, he joined Mary and his parents for the evening meal as usual. They ate in relative silence and Joseph assumed they were still all thinking about the recent events and decisions. No doubt Jacob had filled them in on how things had gone in their discussion with Joachim and Anna that morning.

As they were finishing up their meal his father broke the silence, "Joseph, after our visit with Mary's parents this morning, your mother and I talked. Mary has been included too," he added, nodding at Mary. "You did say the angel told you it was all right to get married to Mary. That this is all the work of The Highest One. If this is so, we trust it will all work out. What else can we do? Therefore, we think we should go ahead with the marriage. Better to get married now. Later, when it is obvious Mary is pregnant, you and she are both more likely to come under condemnation by legalistic busybodies. This way, if you have been married for some months by that time, people will think it is your legitimate child. What do you think?"

Joseph's heart jumped at the words. He wanted more than anything to marry the beautiful Mary. However, he did not want to appear too excited at the prospect. He waited briefly before responding as calmly as he could, "I am most thankful for your thoughts father. You know I want to marry Mary. You are my elders and your wisdom means a lot to me. I know you are both trying to do what is best for us. It does indeed appear that this is the will of The Most High. But do you think we should still talk to the Rabbi first?"

Even as he said this, Joseph was aware of how strange it sounded. Not that long ago his and Mary's parents had talked of the two of them marrying. Now, it seemed this was actually the will of the Lord. How many young couples could say that with such certainty? Thinking about it like that, this was a wonderful blessing. If it was the will of The Most High, their fears of what might happen to them because of Mary's condition would surely not materialize.

"As for the rabbi," Jacob smiled. "We have been praying about this too. I think at this point we can go ahead without talking to ben Levi. Will Jahweh speak to him any more than us? We are all Jahweh's children. Besides, who knows what his opinion will be about Mary's becoming pregnant, or whom He might talk to and spread news we want to keep quiet for a while."

Joseph thought about Mary and their recent engagement. He knew the engagement period was generally understood to last a certain length of time. Now it seemed it was going to be cut short!

"May I ask," Joseph said, turning to Mary, "What do you think?"

"Oh, Joseph," Mary replied with a beautiful smile, "I want to get married as much as you do."

This suited Joseph completely. So did his father's comments about not consulting the rabbi at this time. He had really not been keen on sharing all this again, especially outside of their immediate circle. Who knew where the tale would go? "But how do we go about this though?" he asked.

Jacob responded to Joseph's question, "We can speak to Mary's parents. You know about the concerns regarding the unrest developing around us. Under these circumstances, it is better we do these things now while we can. Who knows what the future brings? We might actually have to make plans for our safety if things get ugly."

Joseph did not want to think about these troublesome things going on around them, but he knew his parents were right.

"I will come with you tomorrow morning and ask Joachim if we can arrange a time to talk about this – as soon as possible. There is still the matter of Mary's idea of going to visit her relatives in Judea," Jacob finished.

Joseph had almost forgotten about that and his heart sank a little again. He did not look forward to the thought of her traveling down there and being away from them. There were so many angles to this.

Next morning the sun was barely up when the chill morning saw Jacob and Joseph walking across the valley to Sepphoris together again. Joseph noticed how, even though there were still many questions and a lot to work out, his heart and his footsteps were lighter than when he had walked this way the day before.

When they reached Joachim and Anna's home, Jacob called out, "Blessings and peace on this home!"

Joachim appeared in the doorway and his face broke into a big smile when he saw his friend Jacob, "Welcome, welcome, peace also to you. Come in, come in. What brings you back so soon?"

"Thank you," Jacob said has he crossed the threshold, with Joseph close behind.

Hearing that it was Jacob and Joseph, Anna turned to add her greetings and welcome.

"Yes, sit, sit," said Joachim, "Have you eaten?"

"We have, thank you, "Jacob replied. "But coming back to your question about our appearance this morning – Joseph's mother and I have been thinking, and Mary and Joseph are in on this. We have some ideas we would like to discuss with you. Soon, if possible."

"Why not this evening?" Joachim answered, turning to Anna, and then seeing no disagreement, spread out his arms as if already welcoming them, "Come with Naomi and Mary for dinner with us!"

"That is more than kind," Jacob protested. "Since I brought up the idea, it is our wish you eat with us."

"Oh, no. I insist," Joachim grinned. "Please do not refuse me my friend," Joachim raised his arms in a welcoming gesture. "After all," he leaned forward and laid his hand on Joseph's shoulder and smiled at him, "It is about our children."

"Well, thank you then," Jacob said somewhat formally, "We will be here." He then rose, bowed in thanks, exchanged Jahweh's blessings on the day with his hosts, turned and left.

"How are you then Joseph?" asked Anna, rising to bid the men farewell, as Joachim and Joseph would now continue on to work together. "This must all be very difficult for you. I am sure Mary has all kinds of questions too."

"I am doing all right," Joseph tried to sound more confident than he was.

"It sounds like we all will have more to talk about tonight," interjected Joachim, "but right now, we have to go and earn our living for today, right Joseph?" he commented, pulling himself to his feet and preparing to go to work, "Anna will have a busy day preparing for our meal tonight."

Joseph dutifully picked up his lunch bag and flung his water flask over his shoulder and followed Joachim out the door. Turning back on the threshold, he looked at Anna, smiled, offered a firm "Goodbye" and disappeared down the street.

Chapter 10. Marriage After All

That night at dinner, Joseph and Mary's parents discussed how they would like to proceed. They agreed that it would be good for the two young people to marry, and soon. This wasn't the usual custom – engagements could last a year - but these were unusual circumstances. This would help keep tongues from wagging too much as it became ever more apparent that Mary was pregnant.

However, even more so, the two families believed The Highest One was behind all this. Therefore, it should be all right. Their fervent prayers had helped them feel better about all this too. They had not received any response or information suggesting anything negative to be concerned about, beyond what they had altogether already thought about. If people asked questions they would simply say that they had consulted Jahweh and this seemed the way to go.

Then, there was the matter of going to visit Anna's sister. The sense had developed that this was still a good move. It could further reduce the risk of gossip and unpleasant consequences for the young couple. Besides, it would give Mary a chance to connect with her relatives and share experiences with Elizabeth.

Joachim stated that he had already sent word to Zechariah and Elizabeth to see if Mary's visit would be all right. If and when they received an affirmative response, they would make arrangements for Mary to go there safely.

"Actually," Joachim said, "If we can arrange the marriage for as soon as possible, I think it would be good for you," he looked straight at Joseph, leaned forward and continued intently, "to take Mary. You have both been that way before. We would send a servant along and arrange for a ride for Mary. That way, you could spend some time together and get to know each other better. What do you think?" he asked, looking at Mary and then Joseph in turn.

Joseph could hardly believe his ears. He wanted nothing more than to spend time with Mary. This was such unexpected good fortune. Suddenly, things seemed to be moving rather rapidly. His heart skipped a few beats as he saw Mary's face beaming with one of her radiant smiles.

Mary's face was glowing when she answered her father, "Papa, I would love that very much. Wouldn't you Joseph?" She finished, looking at him.

"I – I – I can't think of anything I'd rather do more," Joseph stammered.

Joachim chuckled jovially, "It's a deal then. We will just wait for the right time to go. Meanwhile, we will have to plan the wedding," he concluded seriously, then broke out in a big smile of his own as he looked towards Joseph's parents. They also smiled as they nodded their assent.

"Of course, there is one more thing," Joachim went on. "Remember, Joseph, you said yourself it might be good to consult with Rabbi ben Levi. We will have to meet with him to plan the wedding – you, your father and I. Right Jacob?"

"You are right, Joachim," Jacob replied.

"It all just seems so much," Naomi sighed, "What is Jahweh requiring of us?" she mused.

"Who knows?" Joachim remonstrated expansively, spreading his arms wide for emphasis, "The ways of the Lord are mysterious and beyond understanding. It is up to us only to obey. And Jacob, we'll talk and arrange to meet the rabbi. Is it all right if I look for him?"

"Oh, yes, Joachim, I'll wait for word from you," Jacob replied, then added, "Joachim, you and Anna both, we owe you a lot. Thank you so much."

"These are the things we have to do for our children," Joachim said with a shrug. "Meanwhile, we all still have our normal routines to follow. Tomorrow is another work day. Thanks be to Jahweh for that."

"Yes," Jacob answered, rising along with Naomi to leave. Joseph and Mary also rose to follow them out. They all exchanged farewells and the four vanished into the night.

Ch. 11. The Wedding

Joseph sometimes found it hard to concentrate on his work in the following days. He wanted to please his employer and do the best he could. He was determined to learn from him and others he saw working around him. With a baby on the way, he knew he would soon need to be independent. The pending change in his status to that of a married man, which was going to happen very soon now, had unexpectedly made this more pressing. He felt good about the skills he was acquiring as he worked with stone, plaster and wood. There was so much to learn. He hoped that someday he could also learn to work with marble.

He also took notice of the detailed work of the mosaic tilers in the finer buildings he had occasion to be involved. Their artistry amazed him. He felt uncomfortable with some of that work though. These artisans often incorporated human figures into their murals and floors. In Joseph's mind, that was against the law of his people. They were not to make any image of anything human, lest it become an object of worship. He felt especially guilty when these mosaics were built on the background of floors and walls he had helped make. He made sure to pray and ask Jahweh for forgiveness if this made him break the Law by preparing the surface for this work. He would also try to remember to include a prayer about this with the sin offerings he would bring to the temple in Jerusalem when he would get there with his family.

As he worked, his thoughts frequently strayed to his personal life. He thought about the angels' visits to Mary and then himself. He thought about how fortunate he was to have become engaged to Mary. She was not only beautiful and had the most pleasing disposition: she was ever polite, courteous, obedient and helpful. She was always so positive. There was nothing about her not to love. Now that they were engaged and living together, he was getting to spend more time with her.

Mary had met both of their parents' approval, so that carried a lot of weight in his estimation of this young woman. There was also something so innocent and trusting about her that it stirred his deepest feelings, emotions he had not known he had. He was aware of how much he wanted to care for and protect her. He sometimes wondered how much of that might be called for in the days ahead. Most importantly, he was challenged by her faith. Girls were not allowed to go to synagogue school as he had been fortunate to do until he was twelve. This meant they did not get to hear the scriptures read other than in the synagogue on Shabbat. That made it all the more amazing that she knew as much about the stories of Israel and about the law as he did. He realized that said something positive about both her parents and herself, as where else would she have learned this if not from her parents? In their moments together, Joseph, impressed by the significance of this pregnancy, had promised Mary that they would not consummate their marriage until after the child's birth. He felt that what was taking place inside Mary was too holy to be disturbed by earthly pleasures, though there was nothing he wanted more than to be totally one with her. Mary had been utterly impressed by this expression of Joseph's commitment and self-discipline; it only deepened her love and respect for this quiet but sometimes moody young man from Nazareth.

Time flew by and one day when he and Mary, already seated with Anna and Jacob, ready for the evening meal, were surprised by Joachim walking in.

"Peace be upon this household!" he boomed. Then he announced with a huge smile, "It's all arranged, in one week you young people will be married!"

Mary gasped and leapt to her feet, threw her arms around her father and kissed him, "Oh, Papa, I am going to be the happiest wife in the world. I just know Joseph is going to be a wonderful husband and father too," she added, turning her warm smile on Joseph.

That week flew by. Preparations were made for a small gathering of their two families and some close relatives and friends. When the day came, Joseph and Mary were given brand new clothes to wear. It was the custom to display their wealth and status this way, such as it might be. In their case, it was not very extravagant. Joseph's family was rather poor and Joachim and Anna were not the type of people to show off whatever their position might be.

Just the same, when the day arrived, Mary wore a beautiful new blue dress with a white shawl about her head and shoulders. It was trimmed with lace which widened at the front to create a veil over her face. Her wavy brown locks were nicely combed down to frame her face along her chin. Above the top of the lace dangled a row of shiny new silver coins. Topping that off was a crown of pink almond blossoms encircling her head. When she turned her head, Joseph caught a flash of silver earrings dangling below her ears. Looking down, Joseph noticed she even had new sandals. She had never looked so beautiful.

Joseph had managed to acquire a new dark brown cloak to cover a new white tunic. His curly, dark hair and beard, such as it was, shone with oil. His yarmulke was neatly fastened at the back. He had not acquired new footwear but had thoroughly cleaned and oiled what he had.

Tradition held that some of Joseph's friends would have come from his home with music makers to fetch Mary and her family from their home to accompany them in a joyful procession to Joseph's place. Truth be told, this was often truer in Judea than in Galilee. Sometimes these young men would sing and make merry in ways that were not altogether honoring to Jahweh. There singing was sometimes suggestive of not outrightly lewd. Many Galileans frowned at that, looking at it as another sign of how much their southern kinsmen were giving in to the pagan ways of Greece and Rome that threatened them at every turn. It was easier to avoid all that with what they had planned. Both Mary and Joseph's families were too devout to stoop to that custom anyway. In addition, under their unusual circumstances, both families did not want to do anything extra to attract more attention and questions.

Instead, they all assembled with the few invited close relatives and friends at Jacob and Naomi's home, having arranged for the rabbi to join them here. Joseph and Mary, especially, felt quite self-conscious. They were sure not many knew what was really going on in their lives. However, they still could not help feeling somewhat vulnerable, particularly when people looked their way. At the same time, as they had talked things over amongst themselves and with their parents, they became more confident and stronger in their conviction that what they were doing was right.

There had been questions about why marry so soon when the engagement had only been a couple of months earlier. Joachim and Jacob had simply affirmed to all who asked that this was revealed to them as the will of The Highest One. That unusual answer usually caught the questioners so off guard they scarcely knew how to press the issue further. In any case, when they did, the two fathers were steadfast in their decree and offered no more.

Carpets and blankets had been spread around the small front courtyard of the home. It was a warm, sunny day with a clear blue sky overhead. An awning had been extended out from the house to provide some shade for the couple and those who would sit near them. The young couple was given seats of honor at the center. The faced the leader of the local synagogue, and Rabbi ben Levi, who stood before the group.

The rituals of a first century Jewish marriage were followed, although the whole affair was somewhat abbreviated at the request of the families. Thus, it was not long before it was time for the young couple to rise together and face the rabbi. When he had intoned a prayer of blessing for this marriage, he spread his arms and, with a wide smile, pronounced them husband and wife.

This was the signal for an act both young people had eagerly anticipated. Joseph moved somewhat nervously towards Mary, then they were both in each other's arms and Joseph leaned down, and having lifted her veil, pressed his quivering lips against Mary's. Their parents and the guests cheered as they held each other tight for a long moment before parting. Mary placed her hand in Joseph's and they once again faced the rabbi. Taking their hands in his, he raised them up as he ended the formal part of the event with a prayer to Jahweh for a blessing on the couple and a wish for many children.

When the brief ceremony was over, Joseph turned and, taking Mary's hand in his, led the happy group to the tables of food that had been set up in the courtyard. In spite of their efforts to keep things low key, some of the villagers had realized what was occurring. They now made their presence heard with a cacophony of pipes, cymbals and tambourines from the street beyond the gate. Joseph and Mary were left with little choice but to invite the well-wishers to join them. They wasted no time pouring through the gate, joyfully dancing around the couple, showering them with grain and their own well-wishes and blessings. All this made the wedding more normal and helped put the couple more at ease as they all celebrated together.

The guests and the religious officials did not overstay their welcome. Having been allowed to share somewhat in the festivities, they soon left, again playing their music as they sang and danced a song of blessing on their way out. This left only Joseph, Mary and their parents to take pleasure in this time together.

When their scaled back but still joyous evening celebration came to an end, the wedding party that remained, still the only ones to know the underlying story, did not include the usual ceremonies of the bride being led to the groom's bed. To be sure, a bed had been prepared for the newlyweds to share. Before Mary's parents left, the four elders accompanied the couple to their bed and formed a circle around them. Together, they lifted their hands to Jahweh, while uttering the traditional prayers of praise and thanksgiving. They ended with blessings being wished upon the couple, before kissing them and leaving them to each other.

Joseph drew shut the curtain placed around their bed while Mary shyly lowered herself to the sleeping mat. Joseph dropped his cloak at the end of the mat as he lowered himself beside her. Taking her up in his arms, he gently lifted off her headgear, twirling her shining hair through his fingers as he pulled her tightly to him. He leaned down and kissed her forehead, moving his lips down over her fluttering eyelids and cheeks to her lips. They kissed one another passionately as their bodies pressed against each other. Joseph gently laid her down with him.

They both knew what they had promised one another, but that did not mean they could not enjoy one another's bodies. Even under their unusual circumstances, the couple realized there were untold new pleasures to enjoy. Passion they had never experienced was aroused as they tenderly undressed each other. Then they fell to hungrily exploring one another's bodies with caresses and kisses. Eventually, they clung together as they pulled a blanket over themselves and drifted off to sleep in the bliss of one another's arms.

Chapter 12. Getting Away

The newlyweds gradually became accustomed to this blessed new experience. Joseph continued to go off to work in Sepphoris and Mary happily helped his mother with the household, all the while also slowly preparing for the arrival of a child. It did not seem long before word came from Judea that Zechariah and Elizabeth would be delighted to have their niece visit.

The messenger that had returned also confirmed that, yes, Elizabeth had told him she was pregnant, as the angel had promised. Furthermore, in her bliss at what was coming for her and Zechariah, she had told the messenger to tell Joachim and Anna again the story of how this had come about. They had heard some of it but perhaps not all the detail the messenger now reported.

An angel had visited Zechariah when he was serving in the temple and told him what was going to happen as an answer to their prayers. Understandably, Zechariah had doubted this, with their being so advanced in years. As a result, Jahweh had struck him speechless until such a time as their son – it was going to be a boy, whom they were to name John – would be born. The angel had also told Zechariah that this boy would be great in the sight of the Lord. He was never to drink wine or strong drink, and he was going to be filled with the Holy Spirit, even before his birth. The angel had said this son would 'turn many of the people of Israel to the Lord, Jahweh. He would go as a forerunner before the Lord in the spirit and power of the prophet Elijah.' The intent of this was to 'turn the hearts of the fathers back to their children and the disobedient to the wisdom of the just, to make ready for the Lord a people prepared for him.'

This story would have seemed unbelievable to Joachim and Anna if it were not for the events that had also been happening in their home and in the home of Jacob and Naomi. This indeed confirmed what the angel had also told Mary. Her story agreed with what they were hearing from Judea. Just the same, it added more to their wonder and amazement at the things they were getting caught up in.

And why their families? The ways of The Highest One were indeed mysterious and beyond comprehending. It was still all somewhat of an unknowable prophecy, beyond anything they had ever experienced or imagined. On one hand, just the way it was all occurring had a foreboding element to it. There were the unknowns and risks they had already discussed. They had questions about what kinds of lives these young men – John and their Jesus – were to live.

However, in their deep faith, they did not want to focus excessively on the negative. For both couples, even related to each other, to be chosen for what sounded like such significant roles in Jahweh's plans was beyond what they could ever have imagined. By all accounts, their sons were to be dedicated to sacred missions. This was a great honor. They could not overlook that. Better to give thanks and praise to Jahweh for blessing them so richly with the choices he had made and the tasks he had entrusted to them than worry about the dangers. If this was all the will of The Highest One, they had trust that he was still working out his plans. It renewed their faith in the Jahweh they had always been taught had made a covenant with their people, a promise that included the coming of a Messiah to be their king. Now, it seemed these prophecies were going to be fulfilled in their lifetime; the covenant was being kept. After centuries of waiting, and wonder of wonders – they were key actors in the story now!

Of course, besides all this, Anna wanted badly to know how her sister was doing. The messenger said she seemed to be well and had told him to reassure Anna of that. Furthermore, she was already into her sixth month.

So, plans were quickly put in place for Mary and Joseph to go to Judea, much to Mary's delight. She had been wanting to go ever since the angel had told her about Elizabeth. Joachim arranged with their trusty servant Eliab to accompany the young people. He had helped them on trips to and from Judea and Jerusalem before.

The morning of the trip dawned bright and sunny. Joseph could barely contain his excitement as he raced over the hill and across the valley to Sepphoris. Mary had gone back there to spend the night with her parents before being away for some time.

When Joseph called out a greeting from the doorway, Joachim bounded to the door and clapped his big hand around his shoulder, "Come in my son, come in. Have something to eat before you leave."

Joseph protested that he had already eaten but even Anna prevailed upon him and he ate more. They did have a lot of walking ahead of them. He had already seen Eliab loading up a donkey in the street with food and bedding for the journey. He had brought some bread, dried figs and raisins of his own.

When they had all finished breakfast and farewells were said, Joachim invoked a blessing from Jahweh for safety and good health for the three of them as they travelled. Besides their own food and bedding, they also carried some gifts for Zechariah and Elizabeth. Then they were off.

Eliab walked in front of the donkey, holding the reins. Mary sat astride and Joseph walked alongside. Mary shyly reached out her hand and Joseph took it in his as they plodded along in silence for a while. It was still early and, in some ways, they barely felt awake. They were both filled with excitement though. Just married, and here they were, making their first trip together. Joseph's heart was almost bursting with pride as he walked proudly alongside his bride. He sensed the increasing responsibilities that were being placed on him as a man now. He was no longer a boy.

It was a beautiful spring day as they began their trek to the southeast. They drank in the fresh scents of the green hills, the bees buzzing about the flowers covering the hillsides, and the singing of the birds. Following the customs of their people, they did not take the most direct route from Nazareth to Judea. The Jews of the time considered the peoples living south of Galilee, the Samaritans, unclean, as they were not pure Jews and did not believe, worship or live according to The Law the way the Jews did. This added a couple of days to their journey to Jerusalem, but they did not want to risk difficulties going through Samaria. The citizens of that area were not always friendly to Jews either, knowing how they were viewed. Thus, it was getting late in the day when they arrived at their first night stop, Beth Shan, the ancient city – town really – the Greeks and Romans called Scythopolis. This was a major crossroads between the east-west route from the eastern cities of the Decapolis to Palestine and the Mediterranean. There were many travelers stopping for the night but their presence was not that unfamiliar to these three. Nazareth and Sepphoris were not that far from this route so many of these traders and pilgrims passed that way too.

They had stopped for lunch on the way and now, after stopping to rest and have a little evening meal, they found a sheltered place to sleep for the night. They wrapped themselves in their blankets against the cool night air. Joseph felt a thrill as Mary turned to him and yielded the curves of her warm body to his protective arms. He could hardly believe his good fortune to be together like this with his beloved Mary. Eliab slept next to them, near their donkey, in order to be something of a guard for them.

In the morning, after eating a bit more of their carried food, they turned south through the Jordan Valley. They walked past fields of corn and grain, groves of olive trees and figs. To the left lay the blue hills of the Transjordan. On their right were the barren and grassy hills of their own land.

Three days later, getting dusty and tired by this time, they reached Jericho. Here Eliab found them a citizen willing to let them share the family's upper room for the night. He took care of the transactions required to make it possible. They rested easier that night, the young lovers once again thrilled to sleep in each other's arms.

Next morning, having eaten the last of their provisions and having refilled their canteens with water, they set out on the last leg of their journey together. The plan was that Joseph and Eliab would accompany Mary to Jerusalem. Here they would stay with Anna's sister and her husband. From there this aunt's family would accompany Mary to the home of Zechariah and Elizabeth in the village in the Judean hills in which they lived. Joseph and Eliab would return to Nazareth. Mary and Joseph did not relish the thought of parting for however long Mary would stay with her aunt, but that was what their parents had arranged so they complied. Joseph knew he needed to get back to work. He was going to have a family to support.

The twenty miles or so from Jericho to Jerusalem were noted for the rough terrain in between. To begin with, it was bleak, hilly and dry. It was a steep climb from the Jordan Valley to the mountains on which Jerusalem was built. The winding road past rocky ledges and caves was also notorious as a hiding place for thieves who sometimes attacked travelers violently. For that reason, Eliab had made arrangements for the three of them to travel with others going up to Jerusalem. If this had been a feast time the road would have been filled with pilgrims making their joyous way westward together, but that was not the case now. Still, there was always the belief that there was some increased measure of safety in numbers. The trio also said an extra prayer for safety before they set out.

Before the day had ended the three travelers arrived safely at Mary's relative's home in Jerusalem. They were welcomed enthusiastically and quickly given refreshments after their long and wearying journey. Mary brought her uncle Benjamin and Aunt Tirzah greetings from her parents and thanked them for the hospitality they were receiving. Naturally, they had a lot to talk about. The evening was getting late when Uncle Benjamin said, "Well, you have come a long way. You must be tired. Come, rest for the night and we'll look after the next stage of your trip tomorrow."

Under the circumstances, as guests, there really was no place for the couple to sleep together that night. They settled for a quick embrace before they kissed each other good night. Mary slept with her relatives while Joseph and Eliab were given a place of their own to rest.

Next morning, their hosts provided a good breakfast and saw to it that the men had adequate provisions with which to start out on their return journey. Joseph and Mary hugged each other tightly as they bade each other a tearful farewell. Then, Joseph and Eliab were off, back to Nazareth. Both needed to return to their work. Mary, sad to be without Joseph, yet excited at the prospect of spending time with her aunt, prepared to travel the last short distance for her time with Elizabeth and Zechariah in Ein Kerem.

Chapter 13. Staying with an Aunt

As was the case with many of the priests who served in the temple, Zechariah and Mary's home was not far from Jerusalem. Mary's uncle Benjamin walked with her the last few miles west to their village.

The Levites who served in the temple in Jerusalem tended to do quite well. They received a share of the offerings brought to the temple and since so many came to worship there and fulfil a variety of sacred obligations according to their Law, that tithe could amount to a good sum. This explained the well-built home Zechariah and Elizabeth had. It was not ostentatious, but certainly better than what Mary and her family had, even in Sepphoris. There were extra touches given to the stone and plaster work around the gate to their courtyard as well as framing the doors and windows. The latter were nicely fitted with wooden latticework. Even the heavy wooden gate and the door of the main entrance were oiled to a shine, hung with shiny brass hinges, and featured an overlay of carved pomegranate leaves and fruit.

Benjamin approached the gate and announced their presence. A few seconds later the gate swung open and there were Mary's uncle and aunt. Elizabeth reached out and took Mary in her arms and kissed her on the cheeks. "We are so glad you have come and thank the Lord you got here safely." Then she stepped back and looked Mary up and down. "You look so beautiful."

Mary protested with a greeting of her own. When Elizabeth heard Mary's greeting, she burst out in a joyous laugh as she clasped her hands tightly to her own swollen belly. Mary had noticed the movement.

"Oh," Elizabeth exclaimed, "this is so exciting, even my own baby has leaped in my womb."

Then Elizabeth broke into an entirely unexpected torrent of words, crying out with a loud voice, "Mary, you are most blessed among women, and blessed is the child in your womb! Who am I that the mother of my Lord should come and visit me? You are even more exalted because you believed that what was spoken to you by the Lord would be fulfilled."

Mary was stunned by his unusual greeting. She had never heard anything quite like it. Where did that come from?

As if reading her mind, Elizabeth exclaimed, "What was that? Where did that come from? I felt as though power just came over me and made me say that! Could it be Jahweh's Spirit?"

After a stunned pause, Elizabeth came to, "Come, my girl, you must be tired. Let's go in and let you get off your feet." Putting her arm around Mary's shoulder she started to direct her into the house.

Mary's mind was racing at all she had heard. She could understand the blessed part. In their society becoming pregnant was usually considered a positive event. But, 'The mother of my Lord!' She had never been addressed like that before. Was Elizabeth telling her something about her baby? What more did this add to the many troubling thoughts she already had about what was happening in her life and that of all around her? Something about that sounded alarming.

On one hand, this just added to Mary's growing uneasiness about her situation. How much did her uncle and aunt know about her situation? It seemed they knew something, judging from what Elizabeth had just said. What had her father passed on to her uncle and aunt when he had sent the messenger to see about her coming? If the messenger knew, who else knew? So many concerning questions. Mary knew she had plenty of time to talk about it all though. She was staying for some time.

In another way though, this filled her with joy! She had been right in wanting to come to see her aunt. They were sharing some unique, as yet not understood, mysterious blessing from The Highest One. Mary felt a bond with Elizabeth she had never experienced before. There was no doubt going to be a lot to talk about.

Elizabeth's spontaneous flood of blessing had almost made Mary forget the niceties generally expressed on safe arrival at one's host's. She looked sadly over at her dear Uncle Zechariah, who was still unable to speak. She greeted him respectfully just the same and he smiled and bowed in return.

Then, before she could go on, Mary suddenly felt as though her tongue was not under her control. She heard herself pouring out a flood of words that seemed to come from beyond herself, just as her aunt Elizabeth had just done. What she was saying was not that different but at the same time obviously applied much more to her. And such beautiful words they were:

"I have indeed been exalted by the Lord, and my spirit has begun to rejoice in Jahweh my Savior, because he has considered my humble state and chosen me as his special servant. From now on, all generations will call me blessed, because our mighty Jahweh has done great things for me. Holy is his name; from generation to generation he is merciful to those who fear him.

"He has demonstrated power with his arm; he scatters the proud and arrogant. He brings down the mighty of the earth from their thrones, and lifts up those of lowly position. In this way, he makes sure he can satisfy the hungry with good things, whereas he sends the rich away empty.

"He has helped his servant Israel, remembering his mercy, as he promised to our ancestors, to Abraham and to his descendants forever."

Just as suddenly, the oration was over. Mary was amazed. Again, she thought, 'Where had that come from?'

Elizabeth, who had been gazing in awe at Mary's enraptured face, hearing what Mary was now crying out, said in awe, "Child, that was nothing less than the Spirit of Jahweh speaking through you too! The Highest One has indeed not forgotten us his people. We are hearing his voice in our midst again. You are indeed most blessed to have The Highest One come upon you like this. This is marvelous beyond words. How can we begin to know what it all means? How can we ever thank our Lord for these favors, these blessings to us, among the least of his people?"

Mary had no answer to that. Understanding the full import of what was happening to them was still far away. Right now, she was just happy to be with family whom she could see shared this divine experience. Hopefully, they could help her understand it further. After all, as a priest, Uncle Zechariah had special training, as it was his duty, besides performing his turn at the rituals in the temple, to teach the people about Jahweh, the Law and what was required of them to live as Jahweh's people. Mary felt sure he could also help her understand the significance of all that was happening.

Remembering his need to return to Jerusalem, Mary turned to thank her uncle Benjamin again and wished him well. Then she turned to thank her uncle and aunt again for their welcome. Zechariah and Elizabeth insisted Benjamin share some refreshments with them before he left. He accepted, so after a short visit over a light meal, they all wished Benjamin well as he took his leave.

Mary stayed with Elizabeth about three months and then returned to her home. But during that period, they shared a lot. Mary was blessed by the wisdom of her aunt and uncle. She learned more of how what the angel had said to Zechariah related to passages in their sacred scriptures, notably the prophetic writings. This child-to-be was going to have a special role of some kind in relation to her own child. Mary was not sure what this meant, how it would all unfold, but in some mysterious way in Jahweh's wisdom, this John was going to prepare the way for her son and whatever it was he was supposed to accomplish. Mary felt divided. She could feel a sense of positive anticipation building in her now with some of what she was encountering. However, she still also wrestled with feelings of apprehension and foreboding.

According to the understanding of scripture Zechariah shared with written notes, which Elizabeth could read to a limited extent, John was to bring a message that would tell their people the coming of the Messiah was at hand.

"You," he told Mary through writing and gestures, "Are to bear the Messiah. You will bring him up in the ways of The Lord, making sure he learns from our scriptures what his role is to be. We know he is to bring our people liberation, which we have long been waiting for. How he will do that remains to be seen."

As the three of them talked these things through, comparing what they had been told, Zechariah one day gave this message to Mary, "Even though your Jesus is coming with this great mission, it must be kept secret until he is ready to reveal it on his own terms. I'll tell you why, but you and your parents have probably already thought about this too. Our King, Herod, will do his best to do away with your son if he learns who he is. He will not believe Jesus is the Messiah, and even if he does – he shook his head, who knows?"

Then, even more ominously, he had added, "To tell the truth, I am not even sure our chief priest and the leader council in Jerusalem are ready for a messiah. They have so much power and are making so much money with all that goes on in the temple, Mary, sometimes - and I don't want to scare you – we have to trust Jahweh – I fear for these promised special sons." He shook his head and tears welled up in his eyes.

Mary and her family, Joseph and his family too, had indeed touched on these things. They always disturbed and alarmed her. These words of her uncle did not ease those fears. 'How could our religious leader not want a Messiah?' she thought. They should be the ones to be most welcoming and supportive. Then a thought struck her, 'Maybe that's why her family was being entrusted with these tasks. Jahweh surely knows the heart of everyone,' she thought, 'Jahweh would know whether the religious leaders were the ones to be part of this or not.'

Mary was coming to see that there was a lot more to this than what she, or Zechariah and Elizabeth for that matter, had been told or could imagine. Until things became clearer though, there was little she could do. It did sometimes make her afraid for her future, and that of the baby within her. She tried to resist these ominous thoughts and simply, trustingly, pour out her heart to Jahweh. If this was his doing, it would all somehow take place. She did not know what else she could do.

At the same time, she was happy, in return for all she learned, to help her aunt with housework. Elizabeth was able to teach her things about being a wife and mother in addition to what her own mother Anna taught her, and Mary eagerly absorbed it all. If she had been chosen by The Highest One for a role that she was beginning to understand and could not imagine being surpassed by any other, she wanted to, indeed needed to, give it her best.

It was still troubling to see her dear uncle struggle to communicate while mute. However, with gestures and writing he too had added significantly to her knowledge and preparedness for what was to come. Mary grew to love him dearly for his efforts and they got along all right. During these months, she too felt her babe move in her womb. This experience only deepened her wonder. Something great and momentous was happening with her life: in fact, within her own body.

Chapter 14. Home Again

Mary had enjoyed and been enriched by the visit with her aunt and uncle in Judea. However, she was glad to be home in Nazareth again with Joseph and his parents. She realized how it had barely begun to sink in to her before she had taken off for Judea that now she was actually a married woman, living with her husband in the home of his parents. She was learning how she fit into the family and how she could work together with her new mother-in-law. Of course, it was wonderful to see Joseph after work every day and to be able to send him off again in the morning with a lovingly prepared lunch for the day.

She wasted no time either in going to visit her parents and tell them all about the trip. Joachim and Anna were pleased for their kinfolk in Judea, although they too felt sorry for what had happened to Zechariah.

However, what really awed them was the story Mary repeated about how Elizabeth's pregnancy had come about and what the angel who had spoken to Zechariah had told him about the future of their own son. They had heard some of this from the messenger they had sent to Judea earlier but to hear it first-hand from their own daughter, with more conviction and detail, added to their increasing concern. It also deepened further their puzzlement at what this all signified.

Sometimes they were even fearful about what was going on with their families. Having someone who seemed destined to be a king in one's circles was not something their rulers would look on favorably. Still, they had to trust Jahweh, because they did believe by now that he had spoken to them. After all, there were three instances of that: first Zechariah, then Mary and finally Joseph, and there was no disagreement between these three reports.

Mary told them in more detail, how the angel had told Zechariah that he was to name his son John. This sounded strange, as it was not the name of anyone in the family, as it would have been the custom to name a son after a family member. Then there was the message about what John's future would be. The angel had told Zechariah that 'joy and gladness' would come to them, and 'many would rejoice at his birth, for he was going to be great in the sight of the Lord.' Zechariah had been told that John 'must never drink wine or strong drink, and that he would be filled with the Holy Spirit, even before his birth!' Evidently, the best way they could understand it, was that he would become something of a prophet. He was going to 'turn many of the people of Israel to their Lord, Jahweh.' And he was to go as 'a forerunner before the Lord in the spirit and power of Elijah, to turn the hearts of the fathers back to their children and the disobedient to the wisdom of the just, to make ready for the Lord a people prepared for him.' Mary's parents had heard some of this before but the full import of it had not struck them as strongly as it did on hearing these things again in more depth.

This was most astounding! All faithful Jews knew that the prophet Elijah was to return and prepare the way for the Messiah. This sounded just like what the prophet Malachi had said years before: 'Look, I will send you Elijah the prophet before the great and terrible day of the Lord arrives. He will encourage fathers and their children to return to me.' Was this saying that John was the resurrected Elijah? Mind you, the words were 'in the spirit of,' not that he was Elijah.

There was particularly the phrase, 'A forerunner before the Lord.' That certainly sounded like the Messianic predictions from the prophet Isaiah they were familiar with. Did it really mean that? Could it really be true? That this child in Mary's womb was the Messiah? The only qualification they could think of was that they were descendants of David. But beyond that, they could not imagine how they could be part of something so magnificent.

As these developments continued to occupy their minds, Joachim and Jacob's conversations frequently turned to what all of this meant for Israel and especially for their families. Naomi and Anna had their thoughts and questions too. This should be something to rejoice about, a story too great to hold back. However, there were also too many reasons to keep quiet. There was the concern about the young couple's wellbeing and image, although they were now married, so that was less of an issue. However, the greater concern was what might come their way from their neighbors, their leaders, if they really learned that these two families believed that from them would come the Messiah. Who would believe it?

And that was not even considering what the court of that murderous Herod, let alone the cruel Romans, would do with those who told such stories. There had been far too many 'Messiahs' trying to liberate Galilee and the rest of Israel from Greece and then Rome over the last few centuries. All had been ruthlessly put down by the empire of the day. Often, the whole population suffered as a result. Foreign powers seemed to relish taking these opportunities to rouse terror in the hearts of the subjects of their vassal states, all the more to keep them in their grip. Mary and Joseph and their families certainly did not want to bring such disastrous misfortunes on their heads, let alone on the neighbors and their people at large. Sometimes, their hearts were simply overwhelmed with the heavy responsibility of all this.

Joseph and Mary mostly just listened, trying to take it all in, wondering what it all meant. They heard their parents' concerns and knew of their validity. Yet, they both increasingly felt, given the dangers, a strange peace. They often shared with each other how they felt this way. This mutual understanding of the story they found themselves in only strengthened their belief that they were becoming an important part of Jahweh's incomprehensible plans for his people. Slowly, in spite of their fears, they found their faith deepening. After all, were their scriptures not full of stories about how their great Jahweh always kept his promises? If there was one thing they could depend on, it was Jahweh's faithfulness.

II. NEW BEGINNINGS IN BETHLEHEM

Chapter 15. On the Road Again

When Joseph stepped out to go to work one morning some months later, he saw some Roman soldiers posting a notice at the market. He wondered what it was about but did not want to approach the site while the soldiers were there. Instead, he turned and continued on to Sepphoris. When he got there, he stopped in at Joachim's home to see if he was still there. He wanted to ask him if he knew what was going on.

Joachim was still home, and after exchanging greetings, Joseph asked about the activity he had seen.

"Oh, that," said Joachim, "Nothing scary. Just a nuisance for us all. It seems the new Roman Governor Quirinius from Damascus wants a census. They made a big to-do about it with an official proclamation at the market yesterday. We men all had to go and listen. No doubt checking to see whether they are getting the taxes they want. Taxes, taxes, taxes, that's all they want. But what do we get? H-m-m-ph!" he snorted, "Usually nothing."

"Will this have much effect on us?" Joseph asked.

"Well, yes, our families are supposed to go and register at the place of our birth, or at least where our ancestors originate. Unfortunately, that means more travel for us. You know our families have roots in Bethlehem, right?" Joseph nodded. "In fact," Joachim continued, "Our families still have rights to some land around Bethlehem. Rights that go back to King David's time. Most of his descendants, like so many of our people, have been wiped out over the years. So, with the small lineage we have left, we are still privileged to have land claims there. Although it's not much of a privilege when you consider we will have to go there at the census time to verify our claims there. We'll have to make some plans to look after that when the time comes. Meanwhile, son," Joachim said laying his hand on Joseph's shoulder, "We've got a day's work ahead of us."

When he got home from Sepphoris that evening, Joseph asked his father about this business of land in Judea and having to go there at the census time. After thinking about it for some time, Jacob said, "Joseph, you are younger than I am. You know I can't walk well for great distances. Nor can you mother. Why don't you go on our family's behalf? And take Mary with you to represent her family. She's a woman, but our Law has precedent that women can attest to their rights too. Remember the story of Zelophehad's daughters from the Torah? Yes, and one of those daughters was Tirzah, whom I believe is your aunt's name, right?" Jacob looked at Mary.

"Yes, yes it is," she answered. Joseph and Mary had to admit though that they didn't remember this story. "Well," Jacob leaned back, and Joseph could tell a story was coming. Mary, having overheard this exchange and, being curious, had come to sit down beside Joseph. She had placed her hand on his with a gentle squeeze and smiled at him before turning her attention to Jacob too.

Jacob began, "When Canaan was being divided among our tribes at the time when they were going to enter this promised land, after that Exodus from Egypt, there was this one family without sons. The daughters of this family had the courage to come to their leader, our prophet Moses - imagine that - and ask for a share in the inheritance of their tribe. Unheard of! Everyone knew land only got passed on to sons. But this," and Jacob leaned forward, shaking his finger at his young listeners, "Just shows the wisdom of our leaders and, I might add, the greatness of our Jahweh who, after all, chose them. Moses asked the Lord for wisdom on this and the answer came back, yes, they deserve a share. Then, when it fell to Joshua, that faithful commander of our people, to actually see to it that the tribes got the land Moses had allotted them, these brave women got a share of their tribe's land too. So," Jacob focused his eyes on Mary, "You can go with Joseph to help represent our interests, and even that of your parents. Save them a trip."

Mary's heart skipped a beat. 'Go on another trip with Joseph. How wonderful to be just the two of them again. What's more, I could get to see my relatives in Jerusalem and maybe even Ein Kerem again.' She looked eagerly into Joseph's face. "Can we?" she asked.

"Father," Joseph looked at Jacob somewhat anxiously, "are you sure? Mary is quite far along in her pregnancy."

Before Jacob could reply, Mary cut in, almost immediately questioning her own confidence, "Joseph, we can do it. I'm still all right. We'll take it easy."

"Let's see," Jacob responded, "We will ask Jahweh for his opinion." Turning more to the matter at hand, he finished, "It could all work out, especially if we give you proper documentation to take with you about that. You should be all right. You know the way. And," he smiled at Mary, "it's about time someone of our families pays a visit to that new relative of yours in Zechariah and Elizabeth's family and brings them a token of our well wishes."

This certainly made Mary brighten up at that prospect. "Oh, father," she said, addressing Jacob respectfully as a daughter-in-law might be expected to do, "do you think it would be all right for me to go and see my Aunt Elizabeth and the new baby? That would be wonderful."

Jacob replied, "Yes, it would be good, but we have to be careful, as Joseph already said. You are coming near to the time of having your own son. We don't want to put you and this holy child you are carrying at risk. I will see again about hiring a donkey for you to ride so we can do our best to ease your travel."

"Oh father," Mary replied, "that would be wonderful."

The following evening at dinner Jacob sighed as he began to speak, "I have tried all day to find a donkey for you to use Mary. It seems with all this traveling to complete the census, there isn't a donkey nearby available. Maybe we'll have to rethink our travel plans for you and Joseph."

Mary straightened up and looked at Jacob, then Naomi, "Father, mother, I want to go, even if I have to walk. The Highest One who has cared for us so far will look after us even if we are walking."

Jacob and Naomi glanced at each other. Both thought of how well things had turned out for the couple so far, despite their many earlier anxieties. Jacob spoke, slowly, "I don't know Mary, you are pretty far along in your pregnancy." He was silent for a moment and then he continued, "However, I believe you are right. We don't want to tempt fate, but you are a servant of one who is higher than any other power." Jacob also recalled a certain prophecy about the Messiah being born in Bethlehem but he did not want to bring that up. Then, they would all be more anxious, thinking about the possibility of Mary giving birth away from family and home. For the time being, he kept that to himself.

"It's only fair too though," Jacob added, "that we consult your parents about this too, Mary."

"Oh, certainly," Mary responded, "thank you. We must do that indeed."

Joachim and Anna had the same questions that had already been raised. Again, with some persuasion from their daughter, and reassurance from Joseph that he would look after their daughter, they too relented. Thus, arrangements were completed and a few days later found Joseph and Mary retracing the steps they had taken only some eight months before. The plan was to complete the business in Bethlehem, then stop off at Mary's relatives in Jerusalem to give their greetings before going on for a brief visit with her Uncle and Aunt, Zechariah and Elizabeth, and their newborn son.

Chapter 16. Unexpected Delivery

The sun was low in the west on the fifth day of their trek as the young couple saw the towers of Jerusalem in the distance as they turned south to Bethlehem. Because of Mary's advanced pregnancy, this trip had not proceeded as rapidly as the previous one. When they had gone to visit Elizabeth and Zechariah they had spent three nights on the road; this time it had taken four. They were very relieved though, to realize they would reach their destination that evening.

They trudged wearily across the low valley and up the eastern slope of the hill on which Bethlehem lay. They were trying to get there as fast as they could because Mary had begun to complain of backache. As they approached the town, the pain was coming in waves. Mary had already been holding on to Joseph's arm for some support; now she began clinging to him more earnestly. She did not want to alarm Joseph, so had not told him of this latest change in her pain. He just believed she was tired from being pregnant and walking that distance, and wanted to get them a place for her to rest.

There had been others on the road with them, also coming to Jerusalem and Bethlehem because of the census. Joseph had his own little worry – that there would be no place for them to stay. They finally did come to a place where they could see some other travelers about the premises so Joseph concluded this could be a place that was making space available for the census pilgrims.

They turned aside and Joseph inquired as to whether they had room for two more. The owner of the house was at first dismissive and said they had no room, but apologized when he saw Mary and said they were already full and really could do no more. In response to Joseph's query as to whether there were other places to stay, he really could not say. Joseph was considering going on to look for himself when a sudden cry came from Mary. He turned in dismay as he saw her crumple to the ground. At Mary's cry, a woman whom Joseph took to be the owner's wife, rushed out. Seeing Mary in her condition, the woman ran to help.

The woman turned and said sternly to the innkeeper, whom the couple now understood to be her husband, "Salmon, they can stay at the side of the stable with the animals. At least they can rest there and it will even be a little warmer. At least it will be shelter." Turing back to Mary she said, "Poor child, having to come all this way in your condition."

The innkeeper's wife turned back for a moment and returned with a lamp. "Follow me, this will be shelter. It will be warm enough. The animals won't bother you."

With the woman's help, Joseph pulled Mary to her feet and placed his arm inside hers to support her more firmly as they were led to the dark area alongside the house where the lady helped Mary up to what turned out to be a low ledge adjacent to the animals kept there. There were clumps of straw scattered about the ledge and at one end a pile of hay. The woman set the lamp on a small outcropping of rock above the ledge. Then she quickly pulled together some heaps of the straw for the weary travelers to lie on.

When Mary gasped again as pain struck her once more, the woman looked at her swollen abdomen, then up to meet Mary's eyes, "Are you in labor?"

"I don't know," Mary panted, "maybe?" She looked beseechingly into the woman's eyes, "What can I do?"

Joseph's mind was in turmoil. What was happening to their trip? What seemed to be unfolding in front of him was not something he had at all anticipated! The only thought that occurred to him was that they probably needed a midwife. Where would he find one at this hour in a strange village?

In spite of his confusion, Joseph still had the presence of mind to throw down his cloak on the straw for Mary to lie down on. The woman stood back and said, "You were fortunate to come here and not somewhere else. I am Rachel, and I am somewhat of a midwife."

"Oh, thank the Lord," Joseph said with palpable relief. "I thought I might have to go looking for one."

"Never mind," Rachel said, "We'll be all right. You just wait right here." With that she was off running back towards their area of the house, yelling orders at her husband and family. Soon a child, whom Joseph judged to be one of their children, appeared with a basin of hot water and a cluster of thick cloths which, following her mother's instructions, she placed on Joseph's cloak near Mary's feet.

Rachel meanwhile had helped Mary settle comfortably onto the straw. Having told them her name, she learned their names and then she asked Joseph to sit at Mary's head. Joseph was glad to do so. It seemed that Rachel knew what she was doing. He sure did not know what to do!

Just then Mary had another of her pains. "Yes, Mary," Rachel said, "I think you are going to have a baby." Joseph's eyes widened and he had to struggle to calm the panic he felt coming over him.

"Joseph," Rachel continued calmly but firmly, "put your legs around Mary and let her rest on your chest. It will give her support and make it easier for her. At some point, she will have to push and you can be what she pushes against."

Joseph meekly followed the woman's instructions. He certainly had no other ideas. Meanwhile, she was helping rearrange Mary's garments to make room for the baby to be born.

Mary continued to have these pains and Rachel continued to support and encourage her. Mary was young, strong and healthy, but this was going to be her firstborn, so it took some time for labor to progress. Joseph could feel a weariness settle over him after the long day but what was going on in front of him was certainly not going to let him fall asleep. It felt like forever before Mary suddenly cried out even louder than she had with some of the contractions, "I think the baby is starting to come! I feel like I need to push." Rachel had told her to let her know when she began to have this feeling.

Rachel yelled at her husband again, "Salmon! A knife and more clean water!"

He appeared with a knife which he placed beside the lamp and then took the basin of water away, returning with it filled with clean hot water again.

"Mary," Rachel said, "I know it is hard, but if you can squat – Joseph can put his arms under yours and help you up, it will be much better."

The young couple struggled to comply with continuing to follow their helper's suggestions. When it was evident Mary was having another contraction, she was instructed to push. Joseph had braced himself against her to keep her upright. A few contractions later a head of black hair appeared and with the next contraction they saw the whole head.

"Try to relax and take some deep breath between the pains," Rachel said gently as she grasped one of the cloths next to the basin and carefully wiped the baby's face, especially around the nose and mouth.

Suddenly the baby cried, just as Mary felt another pain coming on. With a cry and extra strain on her part, the baby emerged in its entirety and into the cluster of the clean torn cloths Rachel was holding at the ready. The baby cried again as Rachel made sure its delicate little nose and mouth were free of mucous before she wrapped it snuggly in the cloths and laid it between her and Mary. Then Rachel nimbly tied a knot in the umbilical cord before she reached for the knife and, passing it through the flame, cut the cord. After that she took the baby again and quickly unwrapped it and began to bathe it with the water in the basin, wiping off all the blood and mucous.

She turned to Mary and said, "As you can see, it's a boy." Once she had finished washing the baby she gave it to Mary, who instinctively pressed it to her breasts.

Mary gazed down into her newborn's face, then began to wrap the child more tightly in the cloths when Rachel told Mary, "You are not done yet, there is still the afterbirth."

A few contractions later Mary rid herself of that and suddenly she felt a whole lot better. Instead of the pain filling her mind she was now filled with wonder at this miracle in front of them. What an amazing thing had just happened!

"Joseph," she whispered turning her face up towards his, squeezing his hands once more, giving him a kiss on the cheek, "It's our Jesus."

Joseph did not know whether to laugh or cry. Nor for that matter did Mary. All she could do was look down at the child in her arms and wonder.

Chapter 17. Good News at Midnight

"Mary," her midwife helper broke in, "You need to learn to feed your baby. Let me help you. I'll show you how it's done." She knelt next to Mary and helped her rearrange her garments so her breasts were accessible, then positioned the baby in Mary's arms with his cheek against Mary's breast. The child immediately began nuzzling for her nipple and in no time latched on and began to suck. Mary had seen babies nursed before and knew that when her son was done with the one breast she should offer the other. Having done so, when it seemed he was satisfied and looked as if he were falling asleep, Mary looked around for a place for him to sleep.

"Here," said Rachel, who was cleaning up the things she had gathered to help with the birth, indicating the manger. She stepped down from the ledge they had been on and pushed the manger up beside it. "It would be too crowded with both you and the baby on that ledge. At least his way the baby won't fall off there." As it turned out, the top of the manger was flush with the ledge so it was almost as if the three of them were on one level. "See," Rachel said as she went to one side and grabbed some of the sweet-smelling hay and placed it in the manger to make it more comfortable, "This will be perfect. We'll make sure the animals are kept away for now."

Mary reached over and tenderly laid the newborn, now wrapped tightly in layers of cloth, in the manger and lay by his side, gazing raptly at the sleeping infant. Joseph came and knelt by her side and also looked wonderingly at the child. He placed his arm around her and held her close.

"So," Rachel asked, "Has this baby been assigned a name?" Traditionally, naming was a significant rite shared by the family. "You two seem to be all alone here. How will you name this baby? Or do you know what its name is to be?"

"Jesus," offered Joseph.

"You already have a name? Yes?" Rachel looked inquiringly at Mary.

"Yes, that is his name," responded Mary.

"Savior –" Rachel said, "unusual, but an honorable name. Well, when he is circumcised you can decide for sure."

Suddenly the tranquility of the moment was broken by a commotion outside the home. Before they had time to see what was going on a swarm of men invaded their space. They were climbing over each other in an effort to get close to the young family. It seemed they had eyes only for the baby. Mary and Joseph looked at one another in fear. What was this? More guests? Did they mean harm to her newborn? Instinctively she lifted Jesus from the manger and cradled him tightly in her arms.

"Salmon," Rachel shrieked, "We need your help!"

These men, some only boys really, seemed all excited about something and kept talking about a blinding light, angels and singing in the night sky. The one who must have been their leader suddenly spoke loudly to the others, "Hush, remember what we were told. Remember who this is and why we came here."

Quietening quickly and dropping to their knees, their faces bowed to the ground in front of the astounded couple, the men began loudly praising The Highest One.

By this time, Salmon had appeared. "What is going on here?" he bellowed as he elbowed his way in, attempting to bring some order to the scene.

The older man whose command had just quieted the horde, stood up and bowed in the direction of the four, "Sirs, ladies, we beg your pardon. We were tending our sheep like our ancestor David here on the hills of Bethlehem. We had settled them for the night and were thinking of getting some sleep ourselves." He spoke faster, "But that was obviously not meant to be, at least not yet. Suddenly the sky was ablaze with light. The hills were as clear as day. Then we saw what could have been nothing other than an angel descend in front of us. We were all paralyzed with fear, naturally. Wouldn't you be? But this angel told us, 'Do not be afraid!' We couldn't stop shaking anyway."

He stopped to catch his breath, "The angel said, 'Listen carefully, for I am here to tell you good news. News that will bring great joy to everyone: Today your Savior has been born in the city of David.' Well, that's Bethlehem," the old man said.

"The angel had more to say, 'He is the Messiah, the Lord.' Here, now, in our town? Impossible. We couldn't believe it. But who were we to question an angel? The angel seemed to know what we were thinking because then he said, 'I'm telling you the truth. This will be your proof. If you go into Bethlehem, you will find a baby wrapped in strips of cloth and lying in a manger.'

"So, we came looking in the town for where a baby had been born and some people knew a very pregnant woman had come here last evening so here we are!

"And here is this baby in a manger, just as the angel said. It's a miracle!"

The old shepherd dropped to his knees again, joining his comrades still pouring out excited praises to Jahweh. Straightening up once more, he raised his arms wide and said, "No sooner had the angel said this then he was lifted off the earth and joined in that fantastic light by a huge army of angels, way beyond counting. They were praising Jahweh and saying, 'Glory to Jahweh in the highest, and on earth peace among people with whom he is pleased!'"

Salmon and Rachel were speechless, not to mention the shock Joseph and Mary felt. Only the baby seemed unperturbed.

What was going on?

The shepherds all began repeating the story to them and others who, hearing the commotion, were gathering outside, peering in at the door. They kept on praising Jahweh and finally, turning with one last bow to the astonished foursome, they said, "We need to go now. We have to get back to our sheep."

No sooner had they said this then they vanished into the night. They could be heard as they disappeared, calling out continual praise as they went, sharing the good news with all they met. To Mary and Joseph's relief, the strangers who had also looked in, followed them out.

Salmon and Rachel turned back to Joseph and Mary, "Whew! This is unbelievable; I don't know what to make of this," Rachel exclaimed, "What do you make of it? This baby, the Messiah, the Savior? Indeed, you did say his name was going to be Jesus."

"Yes, yes, we did," Mary said quietly.

"I – I don't know what to say." Rachel was at a loss for words.

"I know," interjected Salmon, "These poor folks have had quite a day. I'm sure they need a rest. I know this all just doesn't seem to make sense. But hey," he said, gesturing towards Rachel, "We can talk more about it in the morning. Things always make more sense after a good night's sleep. Come to think of it, maybe you need a little something to eat. It's probably been a while."

Mary was too stirred by everything that had taken place to feel hungry. "I'll be fine," she said, looking back at Joseph "How about you?"

"I'm all right too he said. Thanks for the offer. I think you're right though about needing some rest."

"Yes," Mary agreed, "Thanks so much for all your help. Rachel, I don't know what we would have done without you. I think," she paused, "we are here only because Jawheh led us here. He knows what we need."

Waving his arm around the dark chamber as he turned to go, Salmon replied, "Suit yourself. We could have found something to eat if you wanted. We did what we could. Sorry again about the lodgings. We can take care of business in the morning and try to find you some better lodgings. Come Rachel."

"Thank you ever so much again," replied Joseph and Mary, almost in unison, "How can we ever thank you for all you've done. The Highest One will surely bless you for your kindness."

"Oh," protested Salmon, "We really have not done anything much worthy of blessing. We are just showing hospitality like anyone should. Shalom to you!"

"We will bring back more oil for the lamp," said Rachel, "You will need a little light to get your bearings when the baby is hungry again. And I will bring some water to drink too. You must be thirsty after all that."

After Rachel had returned with the oil and some water she called back as she left again, "If you need anything in the night, do call."

With everyone gone and quiet restored, Joseph and Mary suddenly realized they were hungry. Mary had still been holding on to Jesus, but now she placed him gently back in the manger and wrapped him tightly with the remaining remnants of cloth. They then unwrapped the last of their food and ate it, drinking some water to quench their thirst before lying down together, exhausted, on the straw next to the manger. It wasn't long before Mary heard Joseph's even breathing signifying he was asleep. Her mind was too full of all that had happened and how it connected with the visits of the angels to herself and Joseph.

What had the shepherds said the angels had told them? That the angels had good news for the shepherds, which was to bring great joy to all people, and that their Savior was being born in the city of David. Yes, they were descendants of David. That was why they were here. And that this child was the Messiah! That's what the angels had told them months before. Everything was falling into place, just as they had been told. Now they were reminded of the messages they had received, but it was still too overwhelming to grasp the full import of all of this. Mary marveled at the detail of what the shepherds reported. They had even been told that they would find a baby wrapped in strips of cloth and lying in a manger!

She raised herself on her elbow and gazed at the form of the infant, calmly sleeping in the shadows next to them. She reached out to touch his cheek again. He stirred momentarily and then settled. Mary's heart swelled with an unbearable joy and feeling of contentment. She lay back down and snuggled up against Joseph as the chill of the night began to make itself felt. Eventually, her fatigue overtook her thoughts and she too fell asleep.

Chapter 18. In the Temple

With Mary having just delivered, and a baby to look after, the young parents soon realized that completing their business and returning to Nazareth was not going to be so easy.

"Mary," Joseph said with a sigh, when he returned to where they were staying a couple of days later, "I finally got registered for the census. I took our documents indicating we had right to land here and so that's why we were so far from home for the census. It was even more fortunate that, when I explained our situation, the officials were quick to allow me to complete the process for both of us."

"Oh, thank you Joseph," Mary replied.

"Yes, in one way that frees us to return home. But you know, with your condition and little Jesus, I don't think we should travel right away."

"But what will we do?" Mary asked.

"You know we can't afford to stay here any longer," Joseph continued, and seeing the concern on Mary's face, added quickly, "I was talking to Salmon. I told him about our plight. He asked what I could do, so I said I was a carpenter. He said he actually had some work I could help him with that might let us stay her a little longer. That was a stroke of luck. At the same time, he said he could spread the word around and see if there were other jobs to be had."

"Oh, Joseph," Mary answered reassuringly, "I'm so glad you are willing to do this for us. We see again too that The Highest One is looking out for us and," looking at Jesus, she finished, "his special child."

Then she looked up again, "I've been thinking too, Joseph. You know how we wanted to visit my family in Jerusalem and maybe even Ein Kerem, when we were done here. They would love to see Jesus. Why, they don't even know he is already born. Of course, neither do our families. All of this has been so unexpected, we've just been trying to cope with it ourselves. We really haven't had time to think about others. We'll have to send word to our families if we are not able to travel soon. They will be wondering how we are doing. Your mother will be worried.

"The other thing is," Mary continued, "Since we are here, so close to Jerusalem, we should see if we can actually go to the temple when Jesus is eight days old, for my purification and his dedication as our firstborn. You remember that is what our Law asks of us."

"You are right, Mary," Joseph granted. "We'll see what we can do. If we do go to Jerusalem, you should be able to visit your family too."

"Yes, that would be nice," Mary agreed. A dreamy look spread across her face as she continued, "Maybe we could stay there for a while. It would be nicer than what we have here," she said, gesturing around their dark quarters. "Although, I am thankful we at least have shelter, and food, so far. Then we could also see about returning to Nazareth. I'm sure my family will help us if we need assistance of any kind."

In a couple of days, between the efforts of their 'innkeeper' and Joseph's own work, the young family soon found a better place to stay. They were able to get their own room with another family.

With his skill at carpentry, Joseph was able to work and save enough money in a few days to allow them to make plans to go to Jerusalem. He also found someone who would give Mary and the baby a donkey ride to the city for a small fee. So, on the eighth day after Jesus' birth they made their way into Jerusalem to the home of Mary's Uncle Benjamin and Aunt Tirzah.

What a surprise they had for Mary's relatives! They were enthusiastically welcomed. Their hosts were happy to see that all had gone well despite the seemingly untimely birth. The young couple did not tell them though about the strange visitors they had and what these shepherds had told them. They had talked things over and felt there were still many unknowns to reveal too much. They weren't quite sure yet what to make of it all and did not want too much to be known. Aware of the political situation and possible danger they were in, they were cautious about how that might be received if the news reached the wrong ears. That was a special concern here in Jerusalem.

They told Mary's relatives about their idea, that since they were in Jerusalem, why not take Jesus to the temple for his presentation as a first-born male, his circumcision, naming ceremony and Mary's purification. If they had not been here it would have been done with family and elders in Nazareth, but that was far away. At least they had Uncle Benjamin and Aunt Tirzah to go with them here. Mary and Joseph talked it over with them and they agreed that would be a good idea. Their hosts also then sent word out to Ein Kerem and made preparations for Zechariah, Elizabeth and little John to come join them all in Jerusalem.

"That way, you can see them all, and they can see your little one, and you won't have to travel so much," Aunt Tirzah said, "You've had your share of adventure for now."

That evening when they were alone for the night, Mary said to Joseph, "I think it is most wonderful and appropriate for Jesus to be presented at the temple. If he is of Jahweh through his Spirit, he is not ours. We do need to show that we do give him to The Highest One for whatever His purposes are for him. If he is going to be our king and Savior, the Messiah, we should do the best we can for him in these matters. We should do what is right according to The Law." Joseph was always amazed at Mary's knowledge in these matters, and her strong faith. He had to concede that she had some good points there. This trip was indeed turning into something far beyond what they could have ever anticipated.

The next day young John and his parents arrived. What a joyful reunion that was! Mary could not help, as she looked at the little boy before her, wondering what it had meant when the angel had told Zechariah that John was going to prepare the way of the Lord. How would their two sons' paths be connected in the future? Only Jahweh knew at this time. How nice too though, to hear Uncle Zechariah talking again.

When Mary and Joseph had some time with Elizabeth and Zechariah alone, they learned that Mary's aunt and uncle had many of the same the same questions they had. They all knew it was never a good idea to say too much about these matters in the political climate of the day. Just as they had discussed back in Nazareth, confirming their concerns in fact, Joseph and Mary found that Zechariah and Elizabeth had the same fears about King Herod. He was known to be terribly paranoid about any threats to the throne. And the Romans – well, they were even more present here in Jerusalem, and they did not tolerate either any threats of what could be seen as revolt against them.

On the eighth day Joseph, having purchased the required offering as a substitute for their firstborn and for purification, the young family went up to the temple, accompanied by their relatives. They approached the priests at the periphery of the temple and were assured their offering was acceptable. They left it with the priests and received the appropriate blessing for having offered this for their firstborn son. Then they were directed to a side chamber of the temple where Jesus was circumcised. Mary could not bear to look when she saw the priest take his sharp knife and begin to unwrap Jesus' garments. A sharp cry told her it was over and she turned to gather Jesus tightly into her comforting arms as the priest completed wrapping his newly shorn organ in a poultice and dressing.

When the priest asked about the name of the child to be blessed, Mary repeated again, "Jesus." The priest did not seem perturbed by this. In fact, he pronounced it an honorable name and only opined that he hoped the little boy would live up to his name. Little did he know how prescient his words were. After laying his hands on Jesus' head and pronouncing his blessing, he told them they had accomplished all that was required and were free to go.

They were barely out in the temple courts when an elderly man appeared, crying out with a loud voice. He almost raced toward the bewildered family. Before they knew what was happening he had taken Jesus out of Mary's arms and holding him up toward heaven cried, "Jahweh be praised. Thank you Lord, for keeping your promises, as you always do. Thank you for sending your Spirit to show me the one whom I am blessed to hold in my arms, the one you promised I would someday see with my own eyes. Now that you've kept your promise, Sovereign Lord, you can let your servant to die in peace. I have seen the salvation that you have prepared in the presence of the whole world: a light, for revelation to the Gentiles, and for glory to your people Israel."

Everyone was stunned. As a small crowd was gathering, the family was beginning to feel a bit vulnerable. But the old man was not finished. After finishing his praise to Jahweh and blessing him over and over for keeping his promises that he would not die before he had 'seen the Lord's Messiah,' he turned to bless the young couple and child. Then, placing little Jesus firmly back in Mary's arms, he gripped her arms and piercing her soul with his sober gaze, declared, "Listen carefully: This child is destined to be the cause of the falling and rising of many in Israel. He will be a sign that will be rejected. Indeed, because of him the thoughts of many hearts will be revealed – and a sword will pierce your own soul as well!"

Then Simeon turned and strode back through the crowd, raising his arms heavenward and continuing to praise The Highest One as he went. Mary was relieved to see that those who had been attracted by the old man's outburst had not lingered. What did this mean though? Suddenly, she felt even more unsafe where they were. She could not but think how this was so like what had happened with the shepherds a few days earlier.

Who else had Jahweh informed of the birth of His son? To be sure, they had the same fears after the shepherds left. Oddly, those fears had never materialized. A few people, likely having heard what the shepherds had announced as they had left the stable the night of Jesus' birth, had come by with some questions. However, Joseph and Mary had been able to politely deflect their questions without revealing too much. Then, things had settled down. What was in store for them she could not imagine. She just breathed a prayer that nothing untoward would come of this. She held Jesus even more tightly and leaned towards her relatives and asked, "Who was that?"

"Ah," said Uncle Benjamin, "that is Simeon. He has been hanging around the temple for as long as anyone can remember. He is forever talking about 'the restoration of Israel.'"

"Indeed," chimed in Uncle Zechariah, perhaps a little more graciously, "He is known to be a righteous and devout man. The Spirit of the Lord has obviously been speaking to him – especially about the coming of this child," nodding towards Jesus.

"Well," replied Uncle Benjamin, "You have all been telling me about these strange and special visitations around the birth of these boys. It seems to grow stranger all the time. Who can tell us what this all really means? Should we ask the priests? Who should know better than they?"

Mary was not sure that was a good idea. She just wanted to keep things as quiet as possible. She believed The Highest One would tell them when it was time to begin sharing more of who Jesus identity, and with whom. What Simeon had said was not at all reassuring. The first part of his outburst had agreed with what she, Joseph and Zechariah had been told by the angels that had visited them. The second part of what he had said really troubled her though. What did that mean, that Jesus was going to be responsible for 'the rising and falling' of many in Israel? Was he talking about a messianic rebellion? A battle of liberation from the oppression her people suffered under? The prophets seemed to have spoken of this. Somehow that did not fit what the three had been told so far. There had been no mention of anything suggesting violence. But that last sentence was the most ominous of all: A sword will pierce my soul? Did that mean a real sword or was it referring to emotions? Indeed, sometimes she felt like her heart had already been wounded by all that she was being called on to bear. All these thoughts raced through Mary's mind as the group stood indecisively in the courtyard.

"Uncles," Mary spoke softly, "Doesn't this make you concerned for us all? What if word gets out to the wrong ears. Who knows how far the word of the shepherds went, and if people know this is what this Simeon was waiting for, and hear that he believes his prayers have been answered…" Mary felt like she was going to cry. It was so overpowering. She just wanted to take her baby and leave for somewhere she would feel safer. But how long would anywhere be safe?

Uncle Zechariah noticed her eyes welling up with tears and her lips tremble. Turning to the others he said, "I think Mary is right to be concerned. Elizabeth and I have had the same fears for our John. We've done what we came here to do. I suggest we go back to your home," he nodded at Tirzah and Benjamin, "for a rest and then we can talk about what to do."

The words were barely out of his mouth when a wizened elderly woman, whom they had not even noticed, joined them. She leaned forward to gaze into Jesus' face and then, turning her eyes to heaven, raised her arms, her face simply glowing, and began to give thanks to Jahweh. She kept on blessing the child and family and praising Jahweh before them all. With a final gesture of grasping Jesus' face in her hands and planting a kiss on his forehead she turned back into the crowd. As she walked off, they heard her speak to those she passed about the child, saying that the prayers of all who were waiting for the redemption of Jerusalem were about to be answered.

By this time, the family was really seeing that there might be good reason to be concerned. Who else was going to come forward? Not wanting to attract any more attention, never knowing where that could lead, they quickly made their way to the outer courtyard. As they went, Mary asked her uncles, "And who was that lady?"

"That," began Uncle Benjamin, "is Anna. She is known as a prophetess, and is a childless widow."

"Yes," added Uncle Zechariah, "She practically never leaves the temple, but spends all her days here in worship with fasting and prayer, even at night."

The family hurried the rest of the way back to Uncle Benjamin's in silence. They were all feeling more than a little overcome by what had just transpired and needed time to collect their thoughts.

Chapter 19. Settling in Bethlehem; More Surprise Visitors

The family talked things over further during dinner and into the evening, recounting the unusual events of the past ten months or so. They had their questions and concerns, worries even. However, considering what had already been fulfilled in the recent past, as foretold by the angel visitors, coupled with what the shepherds and the two in the temple knew, this close group concluded that Jahweh was suddenly, very quickly, accomplishing things they had only heard about for centuries. Ultimately, they praised and thanked The Highest One for what he was doing and agreed they just had to leave things in the hands of Jahweh. They then all retired for the night at Benjamin and Tirzah's home.

Next morning, Zechariah and Elizabeth bade the rest of them farewell and left with John for their home. Joseph and Mary then began to talk over their own plans for returning to their home in Nazareth. They had not gone far with that before a guest called at the door for their uncle.

When Benjamin went to the door, an anxious-looking man bowed low before straightening up and saying that he had an important but sad message. No one had been out of the home since they had returned from the temple, so they had not heard or seen anything in the community.

The man related that a group of Galileans had revolted and attacked Sepphoris. As a result, Governor Quirinius of Syria had sent in his troops and thoroughly demolished much of the residential area of the city as punishment. Needless to say, this was extremely distressing news for the family, especially Joseph and Mary.

Both of them anxiously demanded of the messenger whether he knew anything of the state of affairs with their parents. He went on to report that this was part of the reason for his appearance; he had been sent to reassure them that Joseph's parents were all right in Nazareth. Not knowing where Joseph and Mary were, their parents had thought they could at least get word to Mary's uncle and aunt, with the hope that they would know by now where Joseph and Mary were and pass the message on.

Mary's parents, fearing the worst, had left the city as soon as the Galilean rebels head appeared. They were temporarily staying with Jacob and Naomi but were planning to come back to Jerusalem. That was a tremendous relief to the young couple. Joseph was still concerned about his parents but the man indicated that things were quiet in Nazareth. It did not seem that there were any problems there. Benjamin thanked the man for his news and invited him in for some refreshments, considering the hurried trip he had undertaken.

This alarming news certainly changed thoughts about plans to return to Nazareth. After the man left, Uncle Benjamin and Aunt Tirzah talked things over with Joseph and Mary. Their opinion was that the young couple might as well stay in Bethlehem for now, where they already had a place to live and from where Joseph was finding some work. Uncle Benjamin and Aunt Tirzah offered that they could stay with them in Jerusalem if they wished, to wait for the arrival of Mary's parents. However, the young couple decided they would like to return to their own home and see about visiting Mary's parents later.

So it was, that Mary and Joseph settled into life in Bethlehem. They began to set up a home in which to raise their precious son. Mary's parents did relocate once again to Jerusalem, finding a place to live near the north side of the city wall and Pool of Bethesda, where they had lived before. After settling in, Mary's parents came to Bethlehem to visit the young family. How glad Mary and Joseph were to see them safe and sound and hear again that Joseph's parents were all right. How excited Mary's parents were to meet this very special grandchild! They all had a lot to talk about. It was good for the young couple to be able to share some of their experiences and the trepidations that accompanied them. Anna volunteered to stay with the couple and help look after Jesus. Mary and Joseph certainly appreciated her offer, but after talking it over between themselves, they decided they could manage on their own.

Time passed, and things seem to be settling into a reasonably comfortable routine. A year passed, and then some. Mary and Joseph were beginning to feel more at ease, that life was starting to feel normal. Despite the number of unusual events that Joseph and Mary had by this time been privy to, what happened next was still jarring.

The young family was settling in for the night one evening when there was a big commotion outside their door. Suddenly, there was a firm knock on the door and a voice, speaking their language but with an unfamiliar accent, called out, asking if this was the home of the child who was to be king! Joseph and Mary shot upright from their mat, looked at each other, panic rising in their hearts. Joseph hesitated, but then quickly motioned for Mary and the baby to stay back out of sight and got up and went to the door.

There to his amazed eyes he saw a retinue of ornately decorated camels with richly dressed riders perched atop them. There were several other men milling about, holding the reins of the camels. These Joseph judged to be the servants of the riders. The man at the door bowed when Joseph stepped out. "Forgive me sir, for our late and unexpected arrival" he said in his strange sounding Aramaic. "Our apologies. I am sure we have caught you off guard." Then he asked again, more gently, "Is there a new baby boy here?" Pointing up at the sky, he went on, "See that star?"

Joseph followed the man's finger straight overhead. Well, yes, he had noticed that star on previous evenings, and that it was unusually bright and seemed to move over time, but had not paid it much attention. The man went on, "We," pointing to himself and gesturing towards the camel riders, "are a group of men who study the significance of heavenly bodies. We believe this star indicates the birth of a great king. Therefore, we have set out from our homeland in the east to come and find this king. We followed the star to your country. Naturally, we then went to the palace of your king, as where else would you expect a future king to be born?"

Joseph was already hearing more than he thought he wanted to know. The belief in the birth of a king had spread so far to the east? The east to a Jew meant only Babylon, under whom their ancestors had suffered terribly for decades. Babylon had destroyed Jerusalem and Solomon's Temple. Babylon had almost wiped out his ancestor King David's line, which was supposed to continue forever. But what could he do? Joseph felt powerless.

By this time some of the men were dismounting the camels and beginning to remove packages from the camels' saddlebags. The spokesperson continued, "We got an audience with your King Herod..." Joseph inhaled sharply. King Herod knew about this? Their worst fears were becoming real. Who knew what Herod would really do if he thought a future king had been born. Joseph moved back into the doorway, instinctively placing his outstretched hands on the door posts on either side as if to block it.

The stranger was still talking, "Herod had to call in your seers to find out what this was all about. They told him that in your religion's holy writing a prophet once wrote that someday a child will be born in Bethlehem who will become king of the Jews. With that information, your king permitted us to continue on our journey under one condition. We were to report back to him so he too could come and worship this child. With that, we left Jerusalem and continued to follow the star and it did indeed lead us here. So," bowing again, he asked once more, "Please, where is this baby? We mean no harm. We have only to come to determine if the star means what we believe it does. If so, we are here to pay our respects and bring gifts worthy of a king so great," he said, pointing to the star again, "that the heavens would announce his arrival. It has been nearly two years since we first saw the star until today, but we have not abandoned our quest."

Having noticed Joseph's alarm, one of the other men stepped forward to join his traveling companion. He began speaking in a language which Joseph did now know, but the first speaker translated. "Ah, young man, have no fear. Everything is all right. We know about your king," he assured Joseph. "After we left the palace we spent the night in Jerusalem before following the star here. There, a couple of us had the same dream, which certainly convinced us it was a real vision. The message was clear: We were not to go back to Herod, but to bypass Jerusalem on our way home. Therefore, you need have no fear. The king will not hear any more about this from us. You and your baby should be safe."

Joseph was still alarmed but another of the strangers moved forward in their attempts to reassure Joseph and accomplish their mission. He too spoke in this unfamiliar language and again had it translated. "Indeed, it is as our friend has told you. See," he said gesturing to the other men now standing near them with the large bundles in their hands, "We have gifts for you, and for the child. We want to worship with you, worship the child who is born to be king, and then we will leave."

Joseph really did not know what else to do at that point. The report of the dream telling the men not to return to Jerusalem was somewhat calming, but there still lurked the idea that Herod now knew something was afoot.

Even though these strangers had attempted to sooth his fears by telling him of their new plan of returning home by a different route, he once again could not help feeling his family was not safe. Then again, it was an angel that had told these travelers what to do, just like angels had given him and Mary, and Elizabeth before that, so many instructions. He forced himself to believe that meant Jahweh was still determining the direction of events according to his plans.

Anyway, it was the middle of the night. Joseph did not want to arouse the neighbors with what was going on and raise more questions. Until now he and Mary and their family had managed to keep the identity of their precious child from becoming too widely known. Considering this, and the seemingly harmless message of this large company, he felt as if he had little choice but to welcome these guests and show them in. After all their troubles, these men did not look as if they were going to leave without their wishes being fulfilled. Joseph did not want to be inhospitable either. After all, he was the host here.

"Please," Joseph made one last attempt to assert some control, "Allow me to tell my wife to prepare for your visit. One moment," and he quickly turned and went inside, leaving the door open in his haste.

Mary, holding their little toddler in her arms stepped forward and looked at him, "It is all right. I have heard what these men have said. This must be another of The Highest One's strange plans."

Seeing and hearing this, the eager entourage at the door began to move in. Joseph stepped aside, apologizing for the humbleness of their abode, conscious of their own low place in society, but the guests were interested only in seeing the child.

The distinguished-looking guests with their packages had assembled about Joseph, Mary and Jesus. "Please, please, sit and be at peace," the leader spoke through their interpreter. The family retreated into the darkness and made themselves as comfortable as possible with what was unfolding before them.

When their eyes grew accustomed to the darkness, illuminated only by the flickering light of an olive oil lamp, the visitors saw where Mary had settled in the back with the baby Jesus in her arms. They called for their men to bring in some torches and soon the room was filled with light.

The whole assembly dropped to their knees, placing their bags beside them and fell forward, faces to the ground in obeisance to the one they believed would become a great king. Some of them also raised their hands to heaven and broke out in praise to the 'Lord of heaven, maker of all things, master of all', thanking him that they had been able to see this baby, this future king, that their trip had been a success. Having completed that part of their homage they then, in turn, began to open the boxes of gifts. Their servants stepped forward and offered them to the family.

Mary gasped – gold, frankincense and myrrh! "Oh, but we can't accept these," she protested, pointing at the gifts, "for what is this honor?"

The men bowed again and then explained through their translator what they had already told Joseph outside. "What is more fitting for a king than gold?" asked one.

"Worship is accompanied by frankincense," another explained.

"But the myrrh?" Mary asked. That is so expensive."

"Nothing is beyond giving to a king," was the reply. Mary hardly knew what more there was to say. Joseph at her side listened again to their report and explanations of the gifts.

As the guests, apparently having completed their purposes, finally stood up to leave, one of them said in the best Aramaic he could muster, "Thank you for letting us see this child, this future king the star told us about. He will indeed someday be a great ruler. Our mission is accomplished. We can return home with great joy and in peace. Some day we will hear about this king and his rule."

Joseph & Mary followed them to the door. Suddenly remembering his culture's expectations of being hospitable, Joseph addressed the guests,

"Our place is small, as you can see. And I am afraid we have no accommodation for your animals. Where will you eat? Where will you stay for the night?"

The spokesman answered. "Thank you for your concern." He translated for the other men and Joseph heard them respond and gesture in a way that suggested they did not need anything. Indeed, their spokesperson turned back to Joseph, "We have been able to look after ourselves thus far on this journey and we can do so again. If nothing else," he pointed to some of the big bundles on the camels' backs, "We have tents and even some extra food for both ourselves and our animals. We stocked up before we left Jerusalem, knowing it would be some time before we came again to such a large center."

Indeed, the men were bowing once more and again blessing the family and child. Joseph and Mary bowed in return and blessed them in return, wishing them a safe journey back. They thanked them sincerely for the gifts. Joseph also followed them out to bid them further farewell.

Joseph watched as the caravan of camels and their riders reassembled and wheeled around to leave. By now, a few neighbors were milling about, wondering what was going on. "Joseph," they said, "What was all that about?"

"I really don't know what to say," Joseph replied carefully. He still could not trust letting too much be known by too many. "They seemed to say they had determined from some astrologers in their homeland in the east that something important was happening here. They stated they had been directed to come here as determined by the stars. You know the strange ways of the Gentile pagans." Becoming a little bolder Joseph added, "Imagine, here in little Bethlehem! I guess we'll just have to wait and see what happens."

Some of his fellow citizens looked somewhat askance at him, as if they didn't quite believe him. However, it was the middle of the night and, to Joseph's great relief, they slowly all turned and went back into their homes and silence once more descended on Bethlehem.

Chapter 20 – Refugees!

When Joseph turned back into his home, Mary looked up at him as he approached, "What do we make of all this? Isn't The Highest One amazing? He sends angels, shepherds, Simeon and Anna in the temple, and now these travelers. But what do these gifts mean? Gold makes sense for a king. We can always use it. Frankincense does fit in with worship and offering respect, as our guests said. But myrrh?"

Mary did not even want to voice it but all she could think of was that myrrh was something sometimes used to embalm the bodies of the dead. But these men knew they had come to worship a newborn. So why bring something that seemed to have to do with death? Mary shuddered at the implications. She did not want to imagine death happening around them. There was still so much she did not fully understand.

But then Mary brightened when she remembered something else the men had said, and added more animatedly, "Do you remember what else they said? It is written in the prophets that the Messiah is to be born in Bethlehem! I did not remember that prediction. So, our having to come to Bethlehem seems now also to be part of Jahweh's plan! Isn't The Highest One wonderful? Who knows what might have happened to us if we had been back in Galilee? Surely, Jahweh is reinforcing with us that he is directing everything according to his plans. What responsibilities we have been chosen for - including this little one," she added, looking fondly down at her son. "But then she looked up again with an expression of grave concern, "But now King Herod knows there is a special baby here. We keep being told this child is destined to be the Messiah, our Savior and ruler. Are we safe?"

Joseph sighed as he lowered himself down beside her, "I just don't know, Mary, our life certainly seems to be out of our control, doesn't it? We have been told who this child is, but we have no instructions as to how to raise him safely or what we are to look for to help him grow up to fulfil the purpose for which he is born."

"Well," Mary responded with quiet resolution, "we have been told much already. We must just wait on Jahweh and he will surely tell us what we need to know in his time. Now, we need to sleep."

They had drifted off to sleep when Joseph had a feeling he thought he had experienced before. Indeed, he seemed to be surrounded by brilliant light and there at his feet stood an angel again! "Joseph," the angel was speaking softly but urgently, "Get up, take the child and his mother and flee to Egypt. Stay there until I tell you, for Herod is going to look for the child to kill him. I warned the wise men from the east in a dream not to return to Herod so now he is going to be enraged and come after you!"

Joseph shot up from his cloak. He blinked, again – all was dark and still. Another dream. But what the angel said confirmed their worst fears. They were not safe before King Herod. Oh, were they never to live in peace, free from fear?

"Mary, Mary," he called, grabbing her arms and shaking her awake.

"What, what, what is it?" she asked, troubled by the alarm in his voice.

"An angel just came to me in a dream again. He told me we have to flee to Egypt – now – because King Herod is going to come and look for our son to kill him!"

"Oh, no," Mary cried, "what shall we do? What about our families?"

"We will just have to send word to them later," said Joseph. "We have to go now though. We have no choice. Do you think I would choose to do something like this?" He was gathering up the gifts and beginning to wrap them up in their blankets. Mary, realizing Joseph was serious, moved to let him finish and quickly began gathering what she thought they might need. She also collected what food she could to take along to eat.

"Mary," Joseph said, "You continue your preparations and feed Jesus and I will go and pay our landlord what we owe in rent and buy one of his donkeys. We will need it for the trip. I will explain as much as I need to but of course I will not say where we are going. We can't let Herod find that out." Before Mary had a chance to respond, Joseph vanished into the darkness.

It wasn't long before he was back. "The Highest One was with us," he said, "I got the donkey with no problem and not too many questions. And as for your parents, I asked him to send word to them that we had to leave but would communicate with them later, to tell them that we are doing what The Highest One is telling us to do. From what I have saved from my work, and thank the Lord the pay is better here than in Nazareth, I gave him some extra and asked him also to take care of what we have left, but to feel free to rent to others, as who knows when or if we will return."

By now, Mary had as much ready as she thought they could take. "Let's just get ready and go then," she said. "Jesus has been fed. I'm just glad he is quiet and I pray he stays quiet until we are well away from this town. Thanks for remembering all that and taking care of it. I don't know if I would have thought of that, so it's good you did."

Joseph helped Mary and Jesus on to the donkey and slung all their possessions over its back. Talking Mary's hand in his he raised his eyes to the dark sky and quickly sent up a plea to the Lord for wisdom, guidance and safety on this journey they believed he had sent them on. Then, grabbing his walking stick, he began to lead them down the road and out of the town. They were tired but fueled by fear, and with the growing conviction that Jahweh was with them, they made sure they were well out of the region of Bethlehem before they stopped by the side of the road to get some sleep.

The sun was already up when they woke next morning. The family hurriedly consumed a little of the food supply they had been able to bring. Then Joseph quickly helped Mary and Jesus back on to the donkey with their possessions and they began trudging on towards Egypt. Now, of course, this was somewhere they had never been before. However, Joseph knew that if they continued on this road to the sea they would find the famed highway that would take them on their way to Egypt.

"Joseph," Mary asked eventually, "Where in Egypt will we stay?"

"I really don't know," Joseph replied. "However, I do know there are many Jews in a city on the shore of the Mediterranean called Alexandria. Maybe we will find a welcome there. Since it is on the sea, it should be easy enough to get to. And," he added, looking back at their things, "we have those gifts that should come in handy to help us get established there until it is safe to return to Judea." Of course, Joseph had no idea how far it was, but he would find his way.

"Yes, Jahweh's hand has indeed been with us," Mary said with conviction. "We have not encountered any robbers or greedy tax collectors. And those gifts. They are so valuable. If those we met only knew… we must just continue to trust that Jahweh will lead us and take care of us, and his special child," she added, looking down at the toddler in her arms. "To be sure," Mary sighed, "I do sometimes wish we could settle down in one place in peace though. Don't you?" she asked Joseph. "Must we forever be on the move, basically homeless?"

Joseph sighed, "Yes, just when we were beginning to think life was becoming normal. I'm beginning to wonder if we will ever know peace."

The couple with their son traveled towards the sea and both were glad when they were heading south on the King's Highway, leaving Judea and Herod's grasp. Other than stopping to meet physical needs and to give Jesus a little time to stretch his legs and eat a little at the same time, they kept moving. Occasionally, they also had to stop to buy some food to keep going.

Eventually, some two weeks later, they knew from fellow travelers whom they shared the road with, that they were approaching Alexandria. Buildings appeared on the horizon. Far to the right they could see a large intriguing structure that they would later learn was a famous landmark of the city, indeed, one of the seven wonders of the world – its magnificent lighthouse!

They made their way into the city and after a number of inquiries found a place where they could stay. They were relieved. Finally, they could settle down again, at least for a while.

The young couple did not take long to establish connections with the Jewish community. Mary made some friends and Joseph was able to get some work. Of course, Mary was also busy looking after Jesus. Both parents were enjoying watching his development in spite of being away from home. They just wished they were nearer family to share some of their precious moments with their son.

Mary and Joseph were coming to realize that the Lord was always looking out for them. They could not help but conclude that it had something – everything? – to do with the precious child they bore. This certainly helped strengthen their faith and trust in he Highest One.

Joseph was invited by one of his associates to go with him to synagogue one Sabbath Day. It was a much larger and more grand structure than any synagogue he had ever seen before. They found a place to stand among their fellow-worshippers as the service began. His friend alerted him to the fact that some of the service and reading would be in Greek. At first this somewhat surprised Joseph – worshipping their Jahweh in a foreign, a Gentile tongue? But then he remembered having heard that in Alexandria the scriptures had already been translated to Greek because so many people used that language. From his work in Sepphoris he had picked up a few Greek words too, so occasionally he heard what sounded like a familiar word.

Joseph could not understand a lot of what was going, but his ears perked up when he heard the leader begin to read passages in Aramaic from the prophets, and particularly when - and he could hardly believe his ears - he heard the words, 'out of Egypt I have called my son.' He could hardly wait to get home to share this with Mary.

"Mary, Mary," Joseph blurted out when he got home, "Let me tell you what I heard at synagogue today! The prophet said Jahweh called his son out of Egypt."

"See," Mary said, "What did I say? If that is referring to our son, Jahweh is working his plans out, because here we are. And, even better, it reassures not only that we will not always be here, but seems to indicate that Jahweh will let us know when it is time to leave. Out of Egypt The Highest One calls his son," she repeated. "Now we just have to wait to see when that day will be."

III. Jesus Grows Up

Chapter 21. Nazareth at Last

The young family stayed in Egypt for some time. As the days passed, they prayed more and more earnestly for guidance. When could they return to their homeland? Besides getting homesick, they worried about what their families in Judea and Galilee would be thinking. Mary & Joseph could see their little son growing right before their eyes and so wished his grandparents could see him too. Then, they received their answer.

Joseph and Mary had heard that King Herod had died but they were still fearful and uncertain. They needed some assurances. Then, one night when the family had gone to sleep as usual, Joseph became aware that an angel was speaking to him in a dream again. This time he was less afraid than in the past. In fact, he was eager for the message, hoping it would be about going home. Sure enough, the angel gave him the direction the family had been waiting for: "Get up, take the child and his mother, and go to the land of Israel, for those who were seeking the child's life are dead."

This reassuring message gave Joseph some peace and after thinking over the message and what they would now need to do, he fell asleep again. He did not think he needed to waken Mary to tell her now. When Mary awoke in the morning though, he eagerly told her about his latest dream.

Mary was overjoyed at the news. They quickly ate breakfast. Mary began to pack their things and feed Jesus while Joseph went to settle what he owed the owner of their current home. He also went to his employer, thanked him for the work he had given him and told him about their leaving. Joseph was a good worker and the man was sad to see him go but gave him his blessing, generously adding a small gift to help them on their way.

The couple had sold their donkey sometime after their arrival too, as they did not need it in the city and the extra money came in handy. Joseph knew the family he had sold it to still had it so he went to explain the circumstances to see if he could buy the donkey back. Sure enough, things worked out there too. All of this seemed to confirm to Joseph that they were making the right move. Jahweh never failed in his guidance.

Later that morning, the family set out. They were not looking forward to the long trek across the barren lands to Bethlehem, but they did want to go home. When they reached Judea, they met some of the citizens of Palestine and talked over what had happened since they left. They heard the awful news of how Herod, intent on killing Jesus, had sent and massacred all the children in the Bethlehem area under age two. Mary was heartbroken when she heard this. It brought to mind those troubling words of the prophet Simeon in the temple, the meaning of which she had never fully understood. Now, she began to catch more of a glimpse of the meaning of his prediction, "This child is destined to be the cause of the falling and rising of many in Israel and to be a sign that will be rejected. Indeed, as a result of him the thoughts of many hearts will be revealed – and a sword will pierce your own soul as well." Her heart ached when she thought of all the families who would have lost their sons – she scarcely wanted to think of it – because of her son. She could not believe that was what Jahweh wanted, but that he, being The Highest One, would of course know what was going to happen. She certainly did not anticipate that someday this child in her arms would himself explain this troubling story to her.

As they moved through Palestine, Joseph asked people they met how things were going under the new king. When he and Mary heard that Herod's son Archelaus was reigning over Judea in place of his father Herod, they were not sure they should stay in Judea. The things they heard about Archelaus were no better than what they knew of his father.

The night after receiving this news, while they were still travelling north along the sea, Joseph had another dream. He received a warning suggesting they not return to Bethlehem. That confirmed their fears and told them they were right to question going back there. After sharing this with Mary and talking things over, they decided to go back to Galilee. They simply continued north along the coastal highway and eventually eastward to Nazareth. They were so glad to arrive back in Nazareth and settle down in familiar territory with Joseph's family. It had been over two years since they had left. Again, they did not know it at the time, but this too was later going to be shown to be a fulfilment of prophecy.

Needless to see, Jacob and Naomi were overjoyed to have Joseph and Mary back. And finally, they got to see the little grandson who had been so much on their minds. It had been a long time. And what stories the young couple had to share!

Joseph's parents were amazed at how The Highest One had been looking after their children and special grandson every step of the way. What they heard only reinforced their belief that their little Jesus was indeed going to grow up for a specific purpose as Jahweh's Anointed One. How that would come about and what it would look like, they still did not know. Just the same, hearing from Joseph and Mary about their harrowing flight to escape Herod's attempt to murder their grandson, also renewed their resolve to try to keep things quiet as long as possible. This would not always be easy. They would have loved to share more widely the stories of what The Highest One had done for them, knowing how much it helped deepen their own faith. However, they reasoned that it was best to wait.

Naomi loved learning to be a grandmother to Jesus. He was the most delightful child she had ever known, obedient to a fault. She had never known it could be such a pleasure to raise a grandchild. He was more loving and kind than any other child she had ever known, and so intelligent. Indeed, as the whole family enjoyed this child as he grew up, they had to believe that there was something unusual about him. They concluded this could only be explained with his being a miracle child, conceived through the Spirit of Jawheh, as the angels had told them.

As for Joseph and a return to employment in Galilee, it turned out that the new king of Galilee, Herod Antipas, was on something of a building spree. In fact, he was trying to rebuild Sepphoris into an even more important center. Joseph was very fortunate in being able to go to work there again, and at better pay than he had ever earned before. As in the past, he struggled with his role in completing some of the projects, as he knew the intent of the king and his supporters was to appease their foreign overlords by making the city even more Greek and Roman, less Jewish. Temples to foreign gods and even a theatre for drama and other spectacles were being constructed.

It was not long either before Mary's parents came from Jerusalem for a visit. What a reunion that was! They were relieved to have the family home. They were especially eager to meet their grandson, of whom they had already heard so much, even before he was born. Of course, they were also told the amazing stories Joseph and Mary had already shared with his parents. They were as pleased as Joseph's parents too, to see what a lovely child their grandson was turning out to be.

After a satisfying visit, Joachim and Anna returned to Jerusalem, confident that things were finally going well, strengthened in the belief that all was still in Jahweh's plans. He was no doubt working them out.

As life settled into more of a routine, Mary sometimes still longed to be able to join more fully in the exchanges she had with the neighbors. When the women would chat at the village well where they gathered to fetch water, Mary felt there were some things she could share, but a lot more she did not feel free to divulge. She also deemed it better to hold back in letting on what a perfect child her son was. She sensed that would simply raise questions and possibly eventually cause others not to believe her. They all knew no child could be that good. They would decide she had to be lying and wonder why. That could just create more gossip and Mary certainly did not want to feed into that. It did sometimes make her feel lonely though, not having anyone to share her deepest feelings and thoughts with except her in-laws, although she had no complaint there. The result was nevertheless that the citizens of Nazareth never really got to know who was growing up in their midst. Little did Mary know how this would indeed play out so hurtfully in their future.

Chapter 22. First Passover in Jerusalem

Life seemed to pass uneventfully for a number of years after the adventures of the first couple of years of Joseph and Mary's relationship and Jesus' birth. Joseph continued his work as a builder. Jesus actually gained some siblings, notably younger brothers James, Joseph, Jude, Simon and sisters Tirzah and Salome.

Mary and Joseph had given some thought to whether they should have more children or not. In the end, given the good health and fortune they were experiencing, they decided they would. On one hand, they looked forward and thought that if Jesus went on to fulfil whatever his mission in life was really going to be, he might not be around much once he got older. More to the point, in the present, they understood it would make their family look more normal to have more children, especially when their fellow citizens would look at them and wonder why not. No one voluntarily stopped having children. One could never guarantee an only child would be around to look after the parents in their old age. Was that not one of the reasons to have children?

When Jesus came of age, his father enrolled him in the local synagogue school, as was the custom. There, Jesus began to hear more of the scriptures than when he just went to synagogue with his father. He also learned to read and write Aramaic at an elementary level.

Jesus was a promising student who most definitely impressed his teachers. His parents were proud of him. However, Jesus' superior intelligence was a mixed blessing. Some people, sometimes jealously, questioned how Jesus could do so well, coming from what was considered a poor family. Sometimes his classmates accused him of currying the teacher's favor, although they could never really support their accusations with evidence. His classmates' parents sometimes wondered if the teacher was favoring Jesus for some reason, so it even added an extra burden on the teacher. Jesus' family felt sad that this all had to be endured. However, they were not prepared to share whom Jesus really was, as this could open up a whole can of worms.

Just the same, this also meant that when he approached his twelfth birthday, his teachers and other friends who knew the family well told Joseph and Mary they should enroll Jesus in school beyond age 12. Only the better students were known to be given such opportunities. Friends and neighbors might not have understood, but to Joseph and Mary, this did not come as a complete surprise. If Jesus was a special child of Jahweh, destined for the future role the angels had told them of years earlier, it was not surprising that he learned so well.

Unfortunately, there was no further teaching available in Nazareth. After much discussion, over a period of time, and with the advice of the teacher and the promise of financial support from Mary's parents, they made a decision. They would let Jesus go to a higher school in Sepphoris. If he was destined to become a light to the world, he would begin to make the acquaintance of that world in Sepphoris. He would learn better Hebrew and even some Greek. That Joseph could take Jesus with him when he went to work, was also a factor that influenced their deliberations.

Coming of age at his twelfth birthday meant Jesus was eligible to celebrate Passover with his parents in Jerusalem. Given Jesus' history as they knew it, Joseph and Mary both agreed this was something they should certainly arrange. Thus it was that Jesus travelled to Jerusalem with his parents in the spring of his twelfth year.

The family joined an ever-growing crowd of other pilgrims bound for the same destination as they wound their way southeast through Galilee and then alongside Samaria until they came to Jericho. Jesus listened to the stories he heard from his peers and his elders about the Samaritans they bypassed, but he did not join in the negative remarks that were made. Leaving Jericho, he heard stories about the dangers of that leg of the journey up to Jerusalem. Robbers loved to lurk around every hillside, so there was always a concern about being robbed, injured or even killed.

By this time though, the pilgrims were a steady throng of celebrants, providing safety in numbers. They sang together from their scriptures the Psalms of Ascent to Jerusalem customarily sung at this time when en route to the temple. Jesus had learned the songs in school and synagogue too and loved to join in as best he could. Excitement built as the pilgrims' singing of the well-known hymns became an ever more jubilant chorus as the wayfarers neared Jerusalem.

Passing through Bethany, the crowds crested the summit of Olivet and there lay the city and the temple, gleaming in the sun. Jesus wondered whether the emotions that ran through him as he surveyed the scene before them were shared by his fellow travelers. He was not filled with any sense of being superior to his peers and their parents but he felt a certain calm, a growing conviction that no one else, certainly not anyone his age, understood the significance of all of this as well as he did. He wondered if his peers felt the sadness he did, mingled with the joy they were all feeling. As they continued down and across the valley, Jesus thought over the rituals, the offerings and sacrifices they were soon to take part in.

Of course, the celebrations would all begin with a Passover meal. He looked forward to this, which would take place at his grandparents Joachim and Anna's home. That was their first destination. Jesus already knew from his studies of the Torah and the prophets, as well as the stories his family told of their people, that not everything done in Jerusalem, particularly at the temple, was as it should be. It was common knowledge that the priests had come to see the sacrificial system to which they were all bound by their Law as a business. Their wealth and power was all too evident. Jesus was troubled by this but knew that these practices were so entrenched there was little the people could do. Sometimes it seemed those who came to the temple with their offerings were even exploited, made to give up the offerings they had brought for ones the priests deemed satisfactory, at a higher price of course. To make matters worse, the whole priestly caste seemed to be in bed with the king and the occupying powers. They seemed to be more concerned about hanging on to their privileged position than teaching and practicing holiness and justice.

Jesus knew too, that the temple was the one place on earth Jahweh had chosen, among the people he had called, to be present on earth in a unique and yet mysterious way. Over the centuries good things had happened here. There had been times of reform and rededication, of real attempts to return to keeping the special covenant the Jews had with Jahweh. Many sincere and devoutly faithful Jews and even proselytes from among the pagans, the Gentiles, came here to worship. Focusing more on these thoughts allowed Jesus to enter more fully into the spirit of the occasion which those around him were exhibiting.

As they approached the gate into the city before them, the group began to disband. Jesus and his friends looked for their parents in order to join them in going to where they would stay. Jesus knew his family was going to his grandparents and he was eager to see them. Eventually he spotted his family and waited for them to catch up with him.

"We were wondering whether you were going to get lost," his father half-teased.

"Oh, I think our son knows where he belongs," Mary opined.

Jesus face was beaming as he joined his parents as they made their way to his grandparents. Joyous greetings and blessings were exchanged on arrival. They washed up from the dusty journey and relaxed together for a while. Then grandma got up and began preparing for their dinner.

"It's been a busy week," Anna declared. "Cleaning the house to make sure there is no leaven about. Making unleavened bread. Preparing the bitter herbs for tonight."

"Let me help, mother," Mary volunteered.

Grandfather, meanwhile, took pride in explaining to Jesus what the procedure was going to be for celebrating the Passover. Having made sure Jesus knew what it was about, he was invited to join in the preparations. Joachim had already purchased a lamb for the occasion. It was tied to an iron ring on the gate to their courtyard. Jesus looked at it with a deep sense of wonder, and also some sadness, this animal who was going to be sacrificed to take the place of the firstborn son, according to the ancient Exodus story.

When it came time to slaughter the lamb, Jesus was invited to join his father and grandfather as they took the lamb to the temple for the priest to bless and slaughter, provided he approved of it. Grandfather grabbed a pole leaning against the wall near the lamb. It had a piece of old cloth tied to the end with several coils of rope.

"This is to carry the lamb home with," grandfather explained.

Jesus was amazed at how willingly the lamb went with his father and grandfather, having no idea what was in store for it. The streets were crowded and as they neared the temple the cacophony of music, the cries of merchants and money changers, chants of priests, the sounds of animals and the mixed aroma of the burning flesh of the sacrifices and incense was overwhelming. The other worshippers jostled the three of them with their lamb as they edged forward, waiting their turn to appear before the priest.

Joachim was experienced with the whole affair and his lamb was quickly approved of. The priest then took the lamb towards the altar. The priest laid his hand on the lamb's head and, turning his eyes to heaven, offered a prayer of thanks for Jahweh's faithfulness in delivering Israel in the past with a plea for deliverance now. He also offered a blessing for Joachim and his family. The innocent lamb made no sound of protest. The priest was so efficient in ending its life, the blood was pouring from the wound on its neck into his basin a Levite held for him before Jesus really had time to follow the action.

Jesus' grandfather and father took the lamb, now slain and drained of its lifeblood, and wrapped the gaping neck wound with the cloth they had brought along. They then took their rope and tied the lamb's legs to the pole they had brought along to carry it with. They hurried back home along with many others taking their lambs home for the Passover meal.

Jesus, trailing the men with their burden, reflected on what had just transpired. He had learned the meaning of the lamb being sacrificed to take the place of firstborn sons back in Egypt nearly fifteen hundred years earlier. He thought about all the other offerings people brought in thanksgiving, fulfilment of a vow, or for atonement. These rituals did keep people mindful of their position in relation to Jahweh. They were thankful for what Jahweh provided. However, they also believed they were sinful in Jahweh's eyes and needed to pay a price for forgiveness.

At the same time, it seemed such a waste to offer all these sacrifices time and time again. The din in what was supposed to be a house for prayer and worship also bothered him. He wished it could be otherwise. He wondered if he could help make it different. The Jahweh he had come to know through his parents teaching and the humble synagogue in Nazareth was a God of love, faithfulness, mercy and forgiveness. He was not the demanding harsh master many believed him to be. He cared for his people and longed only for them to be free.

Once they reached home, Joseph helped grandfather skin the lamb and prepare it for roasting. Once it was ready they used the pole they had carried it with as a spit to roast the lamb over the home fire. As the family gathered for the meal, Joachim led them all through the ritual of the stories and the prayers, interspersed with the requisite bowls of wine before, during and after the meal. Jesus was filled with a deep sense of the gravity of the occasion. He realized how significant it was that his people were still faithfully carrying out these practices. They had been put in place by the prophet Moses at Jahweh's command centuries before. They served as an annual reminder of the miraculous delivery from Egypt that Jahweh had performed for his people at the time. As he looked around at the faces of his family, Jesus' heart filled with appreciation for the faith they displayed in their celebration of the Passover meal.

Jesus' heart was touched by it all. At the same time, he enjoyed what he was learning. In his growing understanding, he saw how it all fit together in fulfilment of long held understandings of the occasion.

As they sat back and conversed further after it was all over, Jesus remembered the reminder from his parents to thank his grandparents for their financial support for his schooling in Sepphoris. Joachim placed his arm around his beloved grandson's shoulder and said he was glad he could do that much, but that he missed them being so far away or they could have even more talks. Jesus' thirst for knowledge knew no bounds, which had always pleased his family and teachers, even though it often presented challenges for which they had no answer.

Chapter 23. Jesus - Lost!

When the Passover Festival came to a close, the family from Nazareth prepared to return. They all said their farewells to their Jerusalem family, Joachim and Anna and their relatives from Ein Kerem, Zechariah, Elizabeth and John, and set out. The streets were still full of people so it was hard for the travelers to keep together. Joseph and Mary had all they could do to keep their little ones together without being too concerned about the whereabouts of Jesus. They knew he could probably find his way back. They had already seen him joining some friends so knew he was in good company.

When they passed beyond Jerusalem and joined the throngs of pilgrims heading east, they still assumed Jesus was somewhere in the crowd. However, when they got to their first night stop and Jesus was nowhere in sight, they did begin to feel some concern. They searched the area where they were staying and asked many fellow travelers if they had seen Jesus. Of course, they had to provide a description but it was still all to no avail; there were dozens of young boys like Jesus on the road. They decided they had no option but to return to Jerusalem next morning to find him.

They went straight to Joachim and Anna's but he had not returned there. Now they were even more concerned, and so were Jesus' grandparents. This was not like Jesus, to do things without telling them. Mary's parents joined Joseph and Mary in the search as much as they could, while still keeping an eye on his younger siblings. It wasn't until the third day of searching that they found him. Some citizens had told them they had seen a boy in the temple for the last couple of days, surrounded by rabbis who all seemed to be taking a keen interest in him.

Hearing that, Joseph and Mary left their little ones with their grandparents and rushed to the temple. They could not help but feel a return of the anxiety they so often felt about Jesus. Would he, in his boyish enthusiasm, say more than he should about whom his family believed he was? Joseph and Mary prayed that would not be the case. The did not want to imagine what the results of that could be.

Sure enough, there was Jesus, surrounded by rabbis, scribes, and even some Pharisees and members of the Sanhedrin. Understandably, all those dignitaries were somewhat intimidating to the couple from Nazareth. Joseph and Mary were not sure what they should do in the face of this august gathering. They timidly indicated to some of the men in the outer circles that this was their son and they needed to take him home to Galilee from the Passover feast. Some said, "Well, then you must simply inform these men and claim your son."

The group was so intent on their discussion they hardly noticed Joseph trying, as respectfully as possible, to push his way through the circle until he was right behind Jesus. Mary was right behind him. Some in the circle looked somewhat disapprovingly at who this was intruding upon their meeting. However, before anyone could say anything to them, Mary had reached Jesus and, touching him on the shoulder, trying not to be heard beyond her son, in order not to draw too much attention, said softly, "Child, why have you treated us like this? Look, your father and I have been searching for you in great anxiety."

Jesus looked up at her, almost too innocently, and placed his hand over hers, "I'm sorry mother. The time just got away on me. I have been learning a lot. It is helping me understand myself better but also what our people are really thinking. But why were you searching all over for me? Didn't you know that I would be in my father's house?"

Jesus' parents were unsure of how to respond to that. "I'm not sure what you mean by that," Joseph replied, "But can you please come home with us now?"

The learned men around them murmured approvingly and some of them said to Jesus, "Yes, now you must obey your parents and return home with them."

Turning to his parents they expressed their awe at Jesus' ability, "This boy is unbelievably knowledgeable and mature. He can debate with the best of us. And the questions he asks. Even the wisdom he shows. Way beyond his years. He is going to have a bright future. He must have had an excellent teacher."

"But you are right, this young man should go home with you. After all, do our commandments not teach that children should honor their parents?"

Turning back to Jesus, they said, "We have enjoyed our time with you. It has been most stimulating. But now," they nodded sagely in agreement, "Passover is over, it is time for you to go home." Addressing both Jesus and is parents some added, "But we must thank you for this time we have had with your son."

As Jesus then stood up to join his parents, some of the religious leaders said to them in farewell, "Take care of him. See to it that he gets the best schooling you can afford. I am sure we will hear more of him."

The three from Nazareth bowed as they thanked the men for their interest and praise as they backed away from them, with Mary grasping Jesus' hand tightly in hers. Then, Joseph, Mary and Jesus turned to make their way out of the temple. They had not yet reached the exit when someone tugged at Joseph's arm. "Excuse me," the stranger said, "I was one of those with whom Jesus was discussing things these last few days. Forgive us for not inquiring about how he could stay here and whether he did not need to return to his family. More to the point," He rushed on, "Let me introduce myself. I am Joseph, from Arimathea. I am also in Jerusalem for Passover. But tell me," he spoke more slowly now, having gained their attention, "Where are you from?"

"Nazareth," they replied.

"Oh," Joseph frowned, "that's so far away. If you had said you lived nearer by, I was going to make a proposal. Your son really needs the best education that can be offered here, to help him fully develop his obvious potential. I could help you locate such teachers," he continued earnestly. "In fact, I would be prepared to help pay for that education, if that would help."

Joseph paused, searching their faces for an answer. Joseph, the one from Nazareth, looked at Mary and was about to turn back and venture his response when Mary beat him to it. "Sir," she bowed her head slightly in respect, then looked warmly at him. "You are most kind, and generous."

Then she added. "But we really can't take you up on that. It's hard to explain, but for now, I think our son is still better off with us in Nazareth. That is where we live, but we have already found a better school for him to continue on at Sepphoris, so he can still live at home with us."

Mary was concerned, and she knew her husband's mind was also thinking what she was, that they could not yet be sure of what would happen if Jesus were to leave home and his true identity come out. It was flattering to receive this attention and such a generous offer from one of their religious leaders. However, they had received so much guidance as to steps to be taken with Jesus to this point, they did not want to go out on their own if they did not believe Jahweh had decreed it. Sometimes they really felt that they were simply little more than blessed guardians of a most valuable gift from The Highest One, one they needed to watch closely.

Seeing the disappointment on Joseph of Arimathea's face, Mary leaned forward to place her hand on his arm, "I'm sorry," she said, "but we really believe it is best this way for now. Isn't that right," she looked at Jesus' father. Her husband nodded.

"I'm sorry too," the other Joseph responded, 'but if you are certain, I won't press my point. However, remember, if you ever come to the point where you are thinking about your son going on in his schooling, I will be glad to help. Just remember, Joseph from Arimathea."

"Young man," he continued as he turned to Jesus, "You have good parents. They do want what they believe is right for you. Right now, it is to go home with them and be obedient to them." Wagging his finger at Jesus with a smile, he said, "Don't cause them trouble like this again."

Jesus looked up at him, "Sir, I must add my thanks for your offer to what my mother has said. I will now return to Nazareth with my parents. We might well meet again," Jesus bowed as he finished.

"I am sure we will," the man said as he bowed to the trio and turned back with a swish of his opulent robes to join his fellows who had remained seated in the temple.

Jesus, meanwhile, having stood by meekly, not interrupting, knowing he had already upset his parents, now followed them as they made their way to her parents to collect the other children and explain what had happened. Joachim reprimanded Jesus gently for the worry he had caused and Jesus apologized. He seemed genuinely sorry for the anxiety he had caused but at the same time did not suggest he had really done anything wrong by staying behind. Mary noted this change with some concern.

Just the same, they said farewells once again and started over on their return trip to Nazareth. This time Jesus' parents made sure they kept Jesus near. He obliged and seemed quite happy to be travelling back with his parents, brothers and sisters. Eventually, they all reached home together.

Mary kept pondering the strange things that had happened in her life, not the least being this last action of Jesus himself. She still did not know what to make of it all. Nor did she know where this was really leading. However, as things settled down again, Mary was thankful for the return to routine.

Chapter 24. The Firstborn Son Grows Up

Jesus was now enrolled in the advanced synagogue school for promising boys in Sepphoris. He loved this and delighted in coming home and sharing with his parents what he was learning form the scriptures. They, in turn, were amazed at what he gained from them, how he seemed to speak of what he read with such authority. He also often seemed to see things in the law, the prophets especially, and wisdom literature that no one else did. At the same time, he started learning to help his father in his trade and Joseph noted that he was a quick learner and did very good work. He soon became a real asset to his father's business. This made him proud of this unusual son.

All told, Jesus continued to grow and seemed unusually wise for a boy his age. However, no unusual or unacceptable behavior, such as they had experienced in conjunction with that first Passover for Jesus, happened again, for which his parents were glad. Once again, life seemed as normal, as routine, as it had ever been for them.

Time passed and we resume the story many years later. Mary has been through a lot and Jesus is now a full-grown man. Life has not been kind to them. Some ten years after the last unusual event, the incident at Jesus' first Passover, Joseph was killed in a work-related accident. It had been a terrible blow to them all. Joseph had been such a good father. Mary was especially grieved. She did not know how she would manage without Joseph's companionship and support. They had come through so much together. Furthermore, he was the only one who knew as much as she did about their special eldest son.

However, Jesus now showed his maturity and ability. As the eldest, he took over as the man of the house. Having had years of experience working with his father, he was capable of working on his own and supporting the family. Mary told Jesus she did not want to tie him down with such a responsibility, knowing that at some point he was going to go out on his own to accomplish that for which he had been born. However, he insisted on taking on this role, "If I don't do this for you and my brothers and sisters," he had told Mary, "I dishonor my father and am not worthy of being your son. There will be time for my calling later."

Mary had to reflect on what a good son and brother Jesus was. She could see how much he really loved and cared for his younger siblings. He was such a good role model, playmate, and so gentle with them when young, yet firm as they got older. She knew he would never abandon them. Years later she would be reminded of all of this.

"But what about your mission?" Mary asked one day. Jesus had talked increasingly, as he grew older, of what he believed The Highest One had called him to do. He had also long ago told her that his understanding of his life's vocation meant he would never marry. "This is not something easy for me," he had said. "There are lovely young women around whom I would like to marry and have a family with. However, I know there are some things in life I am learning I must deny myself, and having a family of my own is one of them."

Mary could see how Jesus struggled with this. He felt more deeply about these things than anyone else she knew. She had been saddened by this too. She had sometimes dreamed about what wonderful grandchildren Jesus could give her. Being his mother though, she had replied, hoping to still encourage that, "I am sure you would make a wonderful husband and father."

"I don't think it's wise though, considering what I increasingly have a sense of what my life will be like," had been Jesus' answer. Mary had seen how good he was with his younger siblings and truly believed he would be a wonderful father. As it was, he made good use of those characteristics to help her raise her other children.

Sometimes Mary wondered what he was really beginning to understand what that would be. The insights he shared from the scriptures told her he was beginning to realize who the Messiah was to be, what his life would be like. Sometimes though, as he read far into the night, he would sigh and look up from the scrolls with a troubled expression. Mary saw the heaviness in his expression, and it did not sit well with her. When she would ask about it, her concern also evident in her voice, Jesus would put aside the scrolls, come and give her a hug and say hesitantly, "Mother, I wish I could tell you more, but I don't want to say things prematurely. Especially things that might be hard to understand and could even be upsetting. You have enough on your plate."

Such answers were not always reassuring. Indeed, even though these responses sometimes deepened her concern for her son's future, Mary knew her son well enough to realize there was no point in pressing further. Jesus would tell her what he could, what she needed to know, when he was ready. She was sure of that. The not-knowing still sometimes left a deep ache in her heart though. There was a foreboding feeling that something had come between them. Something was developing that was moving beyond her grasp. As a mother, she sometimes just had to bear these pains and let go. It was not easy, but nor did it mean she was really letting go of Jesus. These were the times when she poured out her heart most heavily to The Highest One, knowing things were secure in his hands and that was where she had to leave them.

Jesus meanwhile, gained experience as an elder brother-cum-father figure. As he worked he also gained more understanding of the dynamics that shaped the society in which he found himself. It had been some years since he had stopped attending synagogue school. His teachers had seen that he did not need their help anymore; they were not sure how much more they could teach him. They had encouraged Mary and Joseph to send him away to school. However, his father's death had put an end to any such ideas, with Jesus taking over the breadwinner role. Mary had not forgotten Joseph of Arimathea's offer though. She had asked Jesus about it but he had firmly but gently put an end to any ideas along those lines, reminding her he was here to help the family as long as he could. "I think I am coming to know the scriptures well enough," had been his answer. I don't need 'school learning' anymore." Mary, once again, had to let it go.

Sometimes, as Jesus talked with her, Mary grew concerned. Jesus would talk with her about what he saw wrong in their world. It intrigued her that it was not so much the situation with their being under the thumb of Herod and the heel of Rome. He had more to say about how he perceived their own religious leaders had failed them. However, he always had kind words for his teachers.

When Mary thought Jesus was old enough to grasp the significance of what she remembered of the message the angels, then the shepherds and finally the visitors from the east had said about him and what they had done at his birth, she had shared all this with him. She told him what Anna and Simeon had said when they had first taken him to the temple. He had sighed when he heard some of those words, especially the part about a sword piercing her own soul.

Taking her hands in his, she thought she had seen tears forming on his eyes when he had spoken so tenderly, "I wish for your sake in some ways the things you heard will not happen. However, what you have just told me does sound like some things we read in our scriptures, things I have learned in school and in synagogue, does it not? I believe it is all pointing to what I am meant to do with my life. Someday The Highest One will reveal to us when all this will take place. Until then, we have to wait. It will happen in the fullness of time."

Mary marveled at what Jesus understood from all of this, and tried to keep it all together in her head as the time passed.

By this time, they had heard that Mary's nephew John had begun his mission. Jesus and his parents had sometimes talked about the annunciation of John and the path his life might take. Word filtered back that he had left his parents' home in Judea and gone east into the wilderness, living an ascetic life. Then they earned that he was preaching repentance. A repeated theme seemed to be "Repent, for the kingdom of heaven is near." Later reports said people from Jerusalem, as well as all Judea and all the region around the Jordan, were going out to him, and he was baptizing them in the Jordan River as they confessed their sins. That was a new phenomenon and Mary wondered what it meant.

Then, one day, a neighbor who had traveled down to see this all for himself, came back to Nazareth with word that John was talking about baptizing with water, for repentance, but that someone was coming after him who was more powerful than he was. Indeed, John was saying that he was not worthy to carry his sandals. John had said this person would baptize with the Holy Spirit and fire. While this man was telling this to Jesus and his mother, their being curious about what was happening with Mary's cousin, Mary looked over at Jesus to see how he was taking this all in. Indeed, Jesus was leaning forward, listening most attentively. He wanted to know everything the man could tell them, even where John was generally to be found.

After the neighbor had left, Mary felt a sadness come over her. She had noticed how intently Jesus had listened to the guest's report. She knew that what Jesus heard was bringing into focus that for which he had been born. She had not forgotten that John's mission had been to prepare the way for the coming of the Messiah. Her son was the Messiah. Things were falling into place. She knew that meant he would be leaving them at some point to carry out this mission, and she really did not relish the thought. Jesus was such a positive presence in the family and neighborhood.

However, she knew she had to let him go at some point, or she would be standing in the way of the plans of The Highest One. When the man had gone, she leaned toward Jesus and asked softly, "What does this mean to you? What do you understand by all of this? Do you need to go and see what John is doing? We do know that what The Highest One called him to do had something to do with -."

"-what I am called to do," Jesus finished.

"Yes, I do want to go and see John," he continued, "I think he holds the key to when I am to begin my ministry. But when is the right time for me to go and see him?"

"Son," Mary began, "I know you feel responsible for us here. But you know James and Joseph are able to help us get along. We will be all right. You must fulfil the words given to us around the time of your birth." Mary tried to be strong as she mouthed what she felt were the right words for her son to hear. Deep inside though, her heart was heavy as she uttered these words. She knew she needed to release Jesus to that for which he had been born. But at the same time, she loved her son dearly and really wished she did not have to let him go.

Part IV. The Mission Begins

Chapter 25. Jesus is Baptized

The day that Mary was dreading came soon enough. One morning before Jesus went to work, he simply said to his mother, "I have been spending a lot of time in prayer and thinking about what we heard John was doing. The time has come for me to go and pay him a visit. I want to hear what he has to say to me, about me. I believe his words will make it clear to me what I should do and when."

"Jesus," Mary responded, sighing inwardly with a heartache only a mother can have, especially one having some foreboding sense of what lay before them, "I know you and John have a deep connection. You have shared with each other what you knew as far back as when we went to your first Passover in Jerusalem. To be honest, I have been afraid of this. I don't think I know much, but I have told you what I know. We have experienced and heard enough that we know your task will not be easy, for you nor us, your family. However, when the angel told me about your birth, I accepted that I was in the hands of The Highest One as his servant. That is still true. Therefore, I must let you go and, indeed, give you my full blessing, love and support. I will pray for wisdom for you, and that you find joy and fulfilment in your task. Of course, I will also pray for your life."

"Thank you mother," Jesus replied, taking her in his arms. "I know this is not easy – for any of us. Rest assured, for my part, I will do what I can over the next week or two to prepare James and Joseph to carry on in my absence. They know enough to be able to do much of the work and they can learn more over time, as I did. I must also let our customers know, that in future, James and Joseph will be their contacts for future jobs, not me."

True to his word, Jesus discussed and arranged this with his brothers and their employers. Then, some ten days later, Jesus bade his family farewell.

"I can't promise when I will see you again," he said truthfully. "You know I will keep you all in my prayers, as I have all these years when we have been together, especially since father died. However, I believe the time has come when I must fulfil my heavenly father's calling, and I know he will look after you too."

This reference to The Highest One as his heavenly father was an expression Jesus had begun using when he had stayed behind in the temple in Jerusalem years before. Mary still wondered what he had learned there that had brought this conviction to him. She knew too though that he only spoke like this in front of the family. No one else ever referred to Jahweh that way, and although the family had gotten used to Jesus doing so, it still seemed strange.

Jesus left Nazareth and trekked down to the Jordan Valley in pursuit of his increasingly renowned relative. As the days went by, Mary waited and yearned for her beloved son's return. Understandably, her mother's concern grew as the weeks passed to where she had really begun to wonder what had happened to him. She was not used to not hearing from or at least about him, but she heard nothing.

Finally, one day, some six weeks later, to her great joy, Jesus was at the door. Mary dropped everything and ran to greet him. She was adamant he stay with them. She quickly made him something to eat and insisted he tell them what had happened.

Jesus was pleased to do so. He loved to be with his family, especially as he knew these times were fast disappearing.

"I found John," Jesus began, "and I persuaded him that I too needed to be baptized by him. I just thought it was the right thing for him to do. And you know, mother," he continued, leaning towards her and looking at her, "You could never imagine what happened next. Mind you, given all that you and father experienced in your lives because of me, you won't really be surprised either.

"When I came out of the water, my heavenly father spoke to me in a clearer way than I have ever heard before. He said, audibly, 'This is my Son Jesus, I am very pleased with him.' John and others with us heard the voice too! Oh, I tell you, that was wonderful. You have no idea how reassuring this was. That was just the sign I was looking for, the identification I needed. But you won't believe what happened next," he said, pausing for effect, "It was as if something entered me. Those with me said they saw a shape like a white dove descend on me. Then, before I knew it, I was somewhere - I had no clue where – I just knew that it must be somewhere in the wilds of Judea. I realized after that it was somewhere west of Jericho. I can only believe it was The Spirit of Jahweh came upon me and took me there. In fact, I know it was. The Spirit was the gift of baptism, giving me the power I need to carry out this mission for which I have come.

"I did not know where I was but I had this strong conviction there was a purpose to be there – to fast and pray and prepare for my mission. It reminded me of how our people spent time in the wilderness after leaving the slavery of their world in Egypt by coming through the Red Sea so long ago. That was a time of purifying and preparation for them to enter this land to fulfill Jahweh's plans for them here. I too began to prepare for my mission, to help bring freedom to our people again, but not only ours. You know The Father is concerned for everyone in the world, not just the Jews.

"After enduring nearly forty days of fasting and praying about all this, I had the sense there was more coming. Indeed, then I had a most terrifying experience, one I hope never to repeat and one I would not wish on anyone. I had this foreboding feeling something evil was at hand. Sure enough, the evil one himself appeared.

"That was a trying time, let me tell you. He tried to tempt me to go in different directions than what I knew Jahweh was calling me towards. It was all earthly. He wanted me to succumb to the lure of economic power, political power and religion, all under his control, of course. It was only with my father's help and the use of passages from his word that I used in my defense that I could fend off the evil one. I was sure glad I had learned the scriptures as well as I had. The answers just came to me. Well, really, I have to say it was because of the Spirit of The Highest One. When it was all over, I was starved and – mother, you know about these things – angels came, and fed me! Just like the prophet Elijah, huh?" Jesus smiled. "The next thing I knew, I was on my way home."

Mary marveled at all of this. She couldn't help but shudder though when she heard about Jesus' encounter with Satan. She could not imagine what that must have been like, let alone grasp what it all meant. "Well," she said finally, "I'm just glad you're home safe and sound."

"But you realize, mother, I can't stay," Jesus responded gently, "I have to leave again to be about my father's business. However, as I have done before, I will do my best to make sure my brothers are able to carry on and support you."

Mary dearly wanted to know what 'my father's business' really meant. However, going on past experience, she knew Jesus might not even really know what it was all going to entail. It seemed he left it all up to The Highest One and obeyed whatever message he got when it came. Mary wished she had that degree of faith, that she could trust Jahweh as fully as that. As she reflected on this she realized that her miracle son was already beginning to teach her something about dependence on Jahweh that perhaps could be hers as well. However, she also knew, given what she understood about who her son was, that her relationship with Jahweh would never be what Jesus' was.

Chapter 26 – At a Wedding with Jesus and his Friends

In the following weeks, Jesus came and went from his Nazareth home. Mary was never quite sure what he was all up to, as he often left early and came home late. He didn't always take the time to tell her much. She, being a typical mother, would always have liked to know about what he had been doing or where he had been. However, she also knew that Jesus would always tell her what she needed to know. Sometimes he still stayed at home and helped his brothers with some of their work. They all appreciated this, for they had really come to love Jesus as a son and sibling.

Mary did know from some of the things that Jesus said and what occasionally drifted back to her through her neighbors that Jesus was making new friends around the Sea of Galilee. Some of them were apparently young fishermen. Was he recruiting them to be his supporters in his mission as the Messiah? Was he preparing to be the liberator of his people? Young fishermen seemed unusual candidates to help him carry out this role. Would he not start working with gaining the acquaintance and support of the religious leaders? Would he not need to get their support and cooperation with his mission? After all, who should be more knowledgeable about it and more desirous of seeing the prophecies they knew so well fulfilled?

It seemed that the followers Jesus was gathering saw him as a teacher. He was, according to some, even developing something of a reputation as a rabbi. Mary also learned that the people who heard Jesus' teaching were very impressed with his knowledge, his wisdom, conviction and originality. He was teaching with originality and authority, not just rehashing what previous rabbis had said. Many were already beginning to congregate wherever they found him and were calling him 'Teacher.'

It so happened, that about that time, Mary and her family were invited to a wedding in the nearby village of Cana. Mary let Jesus know that he was also welcome to attend. He was not home when Mary decided it was time to leave for the wedding, so she was not sure he had received her message. However, when she arrived, she was not surprised to find Jesus already there, along with some of his new friends. He seemed glad to have the opportunity to introduce them to his mother. She, in turn, seemed to find them good enough company for him. She took a special liking to one of them, whose name she learned was John. He seemed to be a very gentle soul who responded to her favor. He told her in all seriousness what a good companion Jesus was turning out to be and how she ought to be very proud of him.

At the same time, Mary noticed that Jesus in the company of these young men seemed happy in a way she had not seen before. They were enjoying each other's company, talking and joking convivially, as young men do.

After wedding ceremonies were completed, everyone settled in for what they all enjoyed most, the feast. Mary saw with some satisfaction that Jesus and his friends seemed completely at ease as they ate and drank heartily together. It was good to see him finally find a group of friends of his age, whose company he could really enjoy. Sometimes she had felt sorry for him. With the extra time he had spent going to school, and then having to take over as family breadwinner at a young age, his life had not allowed much time to develop such relationships.

Suddenly, Mary noticed a worried look on the face of the steward of the feast. To her horror, she heard him say the wine was running out. This was a major catastrophe for such a social event! Someone had certainly erred in making adequate preparations. This would not end well for the family or the steward of the feast.

Mary, stirred by the steward's plight and her knowledge of things that she had seen Jesus do around home and in their community, felt obliged to tell Jesus about the steward's distress. She knew of the compassion Jesus exhibited when people ran into troubles such as these, where they were not really totally to blame. Besides hearing about Jesus' ability as a teacher, Mary was also aware of some things suggesting Jesus was beginning to display miraculous powers like the prophets of the past. Perhaps Jesus could help.

Mary hesitated to intrude; Jesus was so enjoying the feast with his friends. She was still caught off guard with his rather curt reply when she did get his attention. "Woman, why are you saying this to me? My time has not yet come." His response sounded disrespectful, out of character.

Really though, he had done no more than simply address her as men were accustomed to do to women in public, even close kin such as their mother. However, the last sentence of his response told Mary she was on the right track. Jesus had not completely negated her request.

She quietly pulled back, but not before she discreetly said to some servants passing by, "If Jesus," gesturing towards her son, "tells you to do something, do it." Mary then retreated to her place but kept her eyes on Jesus. His presence with his friends was already quite evident. She had a strong premonition that something very much out of the ordinary was about to happen. She was not disappointed.

Mary had observed the usual large stone water jars there for Jewish ceremonial washing, each holding twenty to thirty gallons. It was not long until she observed, with no little pleasure, that Jesus, in spite of his remark, was following through with her request, even more quickly than she had anticipated. She heard him call the servants over and direct them to fill the water jars with water. Mary wondered how that was supposed to help with the wine supply. However, the servants, hearing the authority in Jesus' voice, filled them up, to the very top. The servants were well aware that Jesus' reputation made him a guest of honor. They had seen him and his retinue of young followers all welcomed, so they did not question Jesus' command. Then Jesus told them, "Now pour some into a cup and take it to the head steward."

When the head steward, at their request, tasted what they brought him, he was amazed. He thought the wine supply had been exhausted. "Where did this come from?" he asked. The servants could see that there was something different about what he was tasting, but he did not speak further with them. He turned quickly and called the bridegroom and exclaimed excitedly, "Everyone serves the good wine first, and then the cheaper wine when the guests are drunk. You have kept the good wine until now!"

"Master," the servants interrupted, "this came from the jars of water reserved for washing."

"What? How could that be?" the steward exclaimed, "Wasn't that water in there? How are the guests now to wash? No matter, I guess they have all washed by now. Leave that be and party on! We should have plenty of wine now!"

Mary was both relieved and pleased at the turn of events. She understood immediately what had happened. Jesus' friends also quickly realize what had occurred. Soon everyone was thanking Jesus for his amazing help. Some of the young men, not knowing Mary knew very well what had happened, came to tell her what they had seen. She smiled and told them that this was just a beginning of what they could expect from their new friend, Jesus.

"You already know from your own experience," she said to them, "that Jesus is no ordinary young man. Who knows this better than his mother? I tell you, I have been told about these things since before his birth. I am now beginning to see what has been prophesied by angels and people of wisdom alike. Jesus is a very special servant of The Most High, as you are beginning to see for yourselves."

As far as Mary knew, and Jesus friends corroborated this, this was the first time Jesus had ever done anything like this in public. They realized this was nothing short of a miracle. Jesus had revealed, in a new way, what Mary and the young men with him all came to understand as further evidence of who he was. These young men, Jesus' followers, now believed in him all the more.

Mary and some of Jesus' followers were still talking about this when Jesus joined them.

"I think I've had enough of weddings for today," he laughed as he sat down beside them, "I'm tired." Looking fondly into Mary's eyes, he went on, "Mother, why don't you and the family come down to Capernaum for a few days? You could see where I am staying and what I am doing."

There was nothing Mary would have liked more at that moment. As if reading her concern before she voiced it, Jesus added, nodding towards his friends and looking about at them as if to get agreement, "We'll come to your home with you to help get things in order so you can come with us."

The young men with Jesus all voiced their agreement. So, it was arranged and off they went, but not before they wished the newlyweds appropriate blessings. Not without Mary noticing Jesus' use of the phrase 'your house' though. She couldn't help but reflect with some sadness, 'My son is really growing up and moving on. He doesn't even call our home his anymore.'

Chapter 27 – Rejection!

After spending a few days with Jesus in Capernaum, Mary decided she needed to go home. She had enjoyed being able to spend time with Jesus' new friends, and even their families. The family of the one called Simon, in particular, had been such good hosts.

She was continually filled with wonder at the teachings she heard Jesus sharing with the young men, and not only them, but the crowds that seemed to gather around nonstop. Jesus was getting known. More amazingly, she saw Jesus healing people of diseases and even casting out evil spirits. Sometimes she wondered if Jesus was overdoing it. He hardly seemed to take a rest. Mary found it hard to believe her son was doing all this. She realized anew what all those voices from the past had said about her child. Now, she was seeing it come true. But where would it lead? She knew she was just beginning to find out.

Mary pulled Jesus aside one morning a couple of days later and said, "I think I need to go home. The children are getting restless. The boys need to go back to work. Why don't you come back with us? Our people in Nazareth could also benefit from your teaching and healing."

"Thank you, mother, for your invitation," Jesus replied. "I must ask the Father about it. Why don't you go on home with the family and I will follow if it is his will." Suddenly pulling her close, Jesus kissed both of her cheeks and added, "You know I love you mother, and always will. Our Father will take care of you. Go in peace."

Mary turned to gather her children and her things, warmed by the love shown in Jesus' affection, but marveling again at Jesus' manner of speaking. Suddenly he was a mature man, speaking with authority. Where had this come from?

One Sabbath day, not long after, Jesus, having made his way back to Nazareth after all, went to the synagogue to teach. His disciples were with him too. People had heard about the things Jesus was doing and were glad to see him. Those who had known him better growing up and knew what a brilliant student he had been, were eager to hear what he had to tell them. Some had seen and heard for themselves and most had at least heard of the teaching and miracles he was doing in the villages and towns around the Sea of Galilee. They hoped they could see some miracles here too.

When Mary was told Jesus was at the local synagogue, she hurried to see what was happening. She had not seen Jesus since the parting in Capernaum and missed him dearly. She was beginning to realize how much she had come to depend on him after Joseph's death. She knew he had made his home in Capernaum, staying at the home of Simon, where Mary and her children had stayed too. Of course, they had met already at the wedding in Cana.

Jesus' brothers and sisters followed along with Mary to the synagogue, arriving just as Jesus was making his way to the front. Doing so indicated he was ready to take a turn at reading. The leader of the synagogue gave him the scroll of the prophet Isaiah to read. Jesus took the scroll, turned and looked over those assembled there and unrolled it to find this passage: "The Spirit of the Lord is upon me, because he has anointed me to proclaim good news to the poor. He has sent me to proclaim freedom for the captives and the recovery of sight for the blind, to set free those who are oppressed, to proclaim the year of the Lord's favor."

Then he rolled up the scroll, gave it back to the attendant, and sat down. The eyes of everyone in the synagogue were fixed on him. He faced the congregation and told them, "Today this scripture is being fulfilled in your hearing, just as it was read."

As he went on to explain what he meant, his fellow Nazarenes nodded in approval and amazement at the wondrous words coming out of his mouth. They turned to one another, all speaking well of him. They believed they knew what it meant to be poor. Many also had experienced being captives. They certainly felt oppressed, both under their own King Herod, and also under the Romans. Hearing that it was time to proclaim "the year of the Lord's favor" lifted their spirits. That meant Jubilee, when slaves were supposed to be freed, land given back and debts canceled. Was Jesus going to help them shake off the yokes of all this oppression! It all sounded too good to be true.

As they listened to Jesus, some began to question what he said amongst themselves. "Where did he get these ideas? Who does he think he is? What is this supposed wisdom that has been given to him? Isn't this the carpenter, Joseph's son? Isn't he the son of Mary and brother of James, Joseph, Judas, and Simon? Aren't his sisters here with us?" Mary could not help feel some dis-ease when she heard these sarcastic remarks, especially when she saw some of her townsfolk look around to see if she was present. It almost made her wish she had not come.

Why did there always have to be naysayers and doubters? Did there have to be those who could not accept that one of their own could rise above them? She longed to tell them, as she had so often wished she was free to do, "You don't know Jesus, he's not like that. He's not putting on airs. He has been sent by Jahweh to do a mission and he's fulfilling his calling." On one hand, she did not want to get into that, as she was not sure whether she could answer the questions that might lead to. But she also had concern for herself and her children. What did they think hearing this about their beloved brother? Would these people also turn on them?

Whereas just a short time ago, some of these same people had been buoyed by his words, now they took offense at him. They questioned how a local boy like Jesus could make these claims for himself. They soon had everyone discounting what Jesus was saying. They had expected him to do some miracles for them but he was doing nothing of the kind. Without such deeds, how could they believe he had any power?

As if reading their minds, Jesus seemed to outrightly challenge them when he heard him say, "No doubt you will quote the old proverb, 'Doctor, heal yourself' I know you just want me to do here what you know I did in Capernaum." What he said next really did make some present become upset. He seemed to choose stories, from their own scriptures mind you, about help Gentiles received in times past. It was as if he was saying, I'm not here just to please you.

"Let me remind you of the old truth: no prophet is acceptable in his hometown, among his relatives, or even in his own house," Jesus proclaimed. "Let me remind you of the stories from The Prophets: "There were many widows in Israel in Elijah's days, when it did not rain for three and a half years, and there was a great famine over the whole land. Yet Elijah was not sent to help any of them. He was sent only to a woman who was a widow at Zarephath in Sidon. And there were many lepers in Israel in the time of the prophet Elisha, yet none of them were healed except Naaman the Syrian."

When they heard this, all the people in the synagogue were filled with rage. How could Jesus talk of occasions where Jahweh had seemed to pour his favor on Gentiles. Given the Jews animosity to the Gentiles, going back especially to the time of Babylon, then Greece and now Rome, this was not something they could accept. They did not want to hear about Jahweh helping pagan Gentiles. How could Jahweh help the Gentiles? Had Jesus forgotten all they had suffered under the Gentiles? The Gentiles had not done them any favors. Jahweh was here for them, was he not? He was their god. If Jesus was serving Jahweh, he should be helping them.

How could Jesus speak only of good things done to Gentiles? It sounded as if he was twisting the words of the prophets to make them say something different. They really did not know what Jesus was trying to tell them. They only knew they did not like the sound of it. This was new! To misuse the words of the prophets and attribute grace to the Gentiles to Jahweh! This was nothing short of blasphemy!

Suddenly they were all on their feet, rushing to the front of the synagogue. Jesus' followers were caught off guard by this sudden onset of hostility. Before they could intervene, the crowd pushed forward, grabbed Jesus and practically carried him from the front of the synagogue out to the street on their shoulders. The penalty for blasphemy was death and from the shouts that Mary heard, it was clear this mob was intent on that.

Mary had been standing with Jesus' siblings just outside the door of the synagogue. She was shocked as she saw her beloved son treated this way. As the angry mob pushed past them, she wanted to cry out and tell them they were mistaken, to beg them to let Jesus go. Jesus would never say anything to favor evildoers like the Gentiles. But seeing the murderous looks on her neighbors' faces and hearing their angry cries, she suddenly felt afraid for herself and for her other children. How could her fellow Nazarenes turn on one of their own like this? What if they turned on them, as Jesus' family? And where were Jesus' young friends? Could they not have helped stop this?

Where were they going? Mary followed from a distance, keeping well back of the crowd. She saw Jesus' friends trying vainly to break through to help their teacher, but to no avail. She had to see what was happening to Jesus. She gripped the hands of her younger ones and ordered the older ones to stay with her. She saw the crowd carry him to the brow of the steep hill at the edge of the town. They wanted to throw him over! They really were intent on killing him! Then, suddenly, she saw Jesus simply walk back through the crowd and into the circle of his friends and disappear with them. No one touched him!

Mary had seen it all unfold. She was too terror stricken to really appreciate what she had just seen, that Jesus had been spared. She had felt powerless in the face of these angry citizens. She wished she had not come; she felt especially sorry that Jesus' siblings had seen and heard this. What questions they would have, never mind the confusion in her mind. What would they think of their neighbours? What would be their opinion of their brother when they saw how their fellow Nazarenes treated him. That Jesus deserved to die for what he had said? What would Jesus have had to do to get the crowd to at least listen and consider his words? How could people be so closed-minded and so quickly turn violent? Was Jesus partly responsible because of what he had said? It made Mary wonder if Jesus was going too far, getting carried away with his deeply ingrained sense of mission and Jahweh's calling. As he had grown, he had become increasingly confident and sometimes it even irked Mary that he always seemed to be right.

Mary's heart ached as she hurried her children home. She was glad to hear that some people had cried out in his defense. Later she did hear that others, still begging for his help, had been healed by Jesus simply laying his hands on them. Mary assumed this had happened before the teaching in the synagogue. Some of the towns people moved towards Mary as she passed on her way home, placed their hands on her arms and murmured their sympathy. She expressed her thanks to them for that. She was just glad the angry folk did not bother them.

Mary prepared the evening meal and fed her children, but she really had no appetite herself. They were all quiet. In a way, she was glad for this, as she did not have to answer any questions, at least not yet. She needed to think on this and be prepared to give some answers to her children. As she wearily lay down for the night, she just felt exhausted, and was glad for sleep. All she had energy for was to a quick silent prayer to Yahweh for

Jesus, first of thanks for the deliverance she had witnessed, but also for his safety and his future, as well as that of her family and herself, and even his followers.

Chapter 28. A Mother's Concern

After the incident in Nazareth, Jesus returned to Capernaum. After all, this was near where many of his new friends were from. He got more of a welcome in this area than in his hometown. Capernaum was the centre for a number of villages around the Sea of Galilee. Jesus loved the hillsides around the large inland lake with the natural theatres that made for natural teaching venues.

Mary had difficulty getting used to Jesus not being around though. He had been such a pillar of support over the years since his father's death. All she could do was keep her ears open for reports that filtered back from the area around the Sea of Galilee, and these were becoming more astonishing all the time.

Mary received reports of Jesus performing miraculous healings and driving demons out of possessed individuals. He had gone to Jerusalem to the Passover and run into some challenges there. Apparently, he had gotten angry at what he saw going on at the temple. Some of the leaders had gotten very upset when he tried to stop the buying and selling that went on, along with the exchanging of money in the temple courts.

Mary appreciated Jesus' zeal for his heavenly father, but she grew concerned when she heard that what he was doing was raising the ire of some of the leaders. She knew as well as anyone that the religious leaders were not innocent; too many were complicit in exploiting temple-goers. Others were more interested in retaining the favor of the king and emperor than Jahweh. However, she wondered whether Jesus was going about things the wrong way by arousing their opposition so early on.

Conversely, Mary believed Jesus had the right idea with all the good he was doing for people. She even heard about some of his wonderful messages. But Mary knew enough about the Sanhedrin, the council that basically ran things in Jerusalem, and the High Priest's family which ran the Sanhedrin, to be concerned. Then, as always, there was the spectre of Herod and his supporters, and behind them all, the Romans. They tolerated no unrest.

Mary was unsure how to handle her growing unease. She really was not sure where to turn. Ever since the incident with Jesus in the local synagogue, she had been wary of her neighbors. Finally, she disclosed her fears to her sons James and Joseph. They did not have the wisdom and maturity Jesus had displayed at their age, but they were growing up. Jesus had been a good influence on them.

James, as the eldest male at home now, thought he should have a voice in these matters too. His response to all this was that they should simply go and see Jesus and talk to him about what he was doing. They did talk about how to approach Jesus, but were at a loss for constructive ideas on which they could all agree. Mary knew the boys would probably be more rash about things than she might want. Having no better ideas than a face-to-face encounter though, Mary accepted James' proposal. The family made the necessary preparations and began the trek to Capernaum. Meanwhile, Mary implored The Highest One for wisdom in this venture. The last thing she wanted Jesus to think was that they did not appreciate what he was doing or that they were opposed to him.

When Mary and her sons arrived at Capernaum, they went to Simon's home. He was the one they knew best and Mary also knew Jesus spent time here. When they arrived, Simon's family filled them in on the latest. To her dismay, Mary heard that Jesus was getting so besieged by crowds looking for help he wasn't taking time to eat properly. He was not always getting his sleep either.

James, being the bolder and often more abrupt of her children, simply responded to this news by saying they had to confront Jesus and help him rein things in. "He's out of his mind," was James' opinion. Mary had some misgivings about that. After all, she knew Jesus firmly believed he was doing what he ought to do. He might be overdoing it, but it might not be that bad.

Nevertheless, they went to the home where they were told Jesus was staying. Sure enough, the crowds thronged the doorway, making it practically impossible for them to push their way through. People were pushing to get in for help and hear what Jesus was saying. Finally, Mary's family had to resort to asking those in front to pass on the message to Jesus that they were outside and wanted to see him.

The message was delivered. Those sitting next to Jesus told him, "Look, your mother and your brothers are outside looking for you."

Jesus' response seemed unusual. "Who are my mother and my brothers?" he asked. Looking at those sitting around him in a circle, he said, "Here are my mother and my brothers! Whoever does the will of Jahweh is my brother and sister and mother. Those of us who have confessed and repented of our sins and wish to follow the Lord with their body, heart, mind and soul are Jahweh's family."

When this response was transmitted back to Jesus' waiting family, James was of the opinion they should force their way in and talk sense into Jesus and get him to come home with them. However, Mary knew her son best. She recognized in the response that they were best not to interfere further or they might indeed be guilty of keeping Jesus from doing Jahweh's will. She really could not disagree with what Jesus had said. She knew Jesus wanted to look beyond the groupings of society, the traditions, to create something new and free from all such limitations. She pulled James by the arm and said, "Come, let's go home."

"But mother," James replied, "What Jesus is doing is -" he stopped short, "He does not know what he is doing!"

Mary looked her son squarely in the eye and stated firmly, "James, I think he knows exactly what he is doing. He might not understand fully yet what purpose he is carrying out, but I don't think we can or should try any harder to stop him. Your brother believes strongly that he has a unique mission to complete, given by Jahweh. You know that message was given to both your father and I from before Jesus' birth. I think the best we can do is go home and pray for him, that he will receive the wisdom he needs to do the will of The Highest and that Yahweh will look after him."

Grudgingly, James and the rest of Mary's children fell in line as she turned and led the way out of the village to the road back home. Mary felt a sadness and heaviness in her heart. She tried to help Jesus' siblings understand him, but sometimes she felt she was perhaps trying to convince herself as well as them. Deep inside though, she trusted Jesus was doing what he felt called to do. Was he not the son of The Most High? As such, he would not take a wrong path.

Chapter 29. Lives Are at Risk

Not long after the above incident something occurred that really heightened Mary's anxiety for the wellbeing of her firstborn. Besides trying to keep track of what her eldest son was doing, she had also been keeping an ear open to what was happening to a special relative of Jesus, her Aunt Elizabeth's son John. Mary always remembered the special bond between Elizabeth and her going back to their pregnancies. Then, there was the key role John had played in the beginning of Jesus' ministry, not that long ago.

John had become very popular among many of the inhabitants of Judea and Galilee. People flocked to hear his message and be baptized, symbolizing their repentance and receiving forgiveness. They listened to his teaching on how they were to live. Some enjoyed hearing their religious leaders challenged by John's preaching. Mary heard of all of this. She knew that John, although he continued his work, was telling his hearers that someone he had baptized was more important than he and was also teaching in their land, namely Jesus.

Then news came to her that really shook her. Mary had known that John didn't flinch when it came to critiquing those in authority. His words could be as sharp as a sword to some hearers, and cut just as deeply. She knew John's message was meant to convict, to bring confession of sin and repentance. This penchant of his to preach so boldly concerned her, just as Jesus' words and actions could heighten her anxiety for him. However, as with Jesus, she knew John also believed he was doing what the Spirit of Jahweh wanted him to, that he was speaking messages from The Highest One. Slowly, in spite of her fears, reinforced by the recent events at Nazareth, she was coming to accept these things. If they were doing the will of Yahweh, surely the Highest One would look after Jesus and John. At the same time, she knew how her own people had treated prophets in the past. It was all there in the scriptures. As difficult as it was, she knew there was not much she could do but accept that John and Jesus' lives would always be at risk doing what they were doing.

A Sword Shall Pierce Your Soul

The terrible news that had reached Mary was that John had been put in prison by King Herod. Apparently, John had spoken out against Herod marrying his brother's wife. These doings of the kings were common knowledge, but most would not dare to say anything against the king. But John had, and now he had paid the price. Not only had Herod imprisoned John, it had not taken long before he had killed him!

Mary had heard some details of what had transpired but you never knew what was gossip, and what was truth. That was immaterial now anyway. What did matter was that John was gone. What a horrible shock. Then, she remembered Simeon's words: "A sword will pierce your heart also." That's how she felt in her grief over her beloved cousin's murder. Now, it began to bring into focus what might be in store for her son if he continued on his path. But no, if he was the Messiah, he should become king, not be killed. She tried to reassure herself with such thoughts, but they weren't always enough.

Of course, Mary also thought immediately of her aunt and uncle. Here was their only son, promised of Jahweh, born for a special mission – and now he was killed? She wished she could go and see them and comfort them. That was not so easy with a family and she was not as young as when she had made those earlier trips. Fortunately, John's disciples had been allowed to retrieve the body and give it a proper burial. His parents would no doubt have been part of that, which would have provided them some comfort.

Mary's thoughts turned just as quickly to how this news must have affected her own son. Jesus' and John's lives were linked from before their births. They knew what they meant to each other. To be sure, she had learned that John had wondered after his imprisonment whether Jesus was really the one for whom he had come to prepare the way. Perhaps, having been silenced himself, he just needed reassurance that Jesus was not stopping with their mission.

John was already in prison when he had sent some of his followers to ask Jesus if he was the Messiah. Perhaps he was still unsure whether what Jesus was doing matched John's vision of the role of the Messiah. Perhaps he knew he could be facing death and really wanted to know whether the most important part of what he had done in his own lifetime, announcing the arrival of Jahweh's chosen, had been misguided or not. In any case, Jesus had sent John's inquirers back to tell him all of what he was doing: "The blind were receiving their sight, the lame were being made to walk, lepers were cleansed, deaf made to hear, the poor were hearing good news and even the dead were being raised to life."

This was what Jesus was doing. This was why he was becoming so becoming popular with the people. They were receiving attention, compassion and care in ways they had never experienced. Jesus had indicated that these actions of his were proof of who he was. Mary had to wonder though, and no doubt John had entertained similar questions. The Jews had always thought of the Messiah as someone who would come on the scene in power, someone who would restore Israel to what it was meant to be, at least in the eyes of all faithful Jews: a kingdom of peace, prosperity and happiness for all. Above all, this would be accomplished by shaking off the shackles of all the foreign influences that oppressed Israel. But Jesus did not seem to be showing any signs of moving in that direction. Mary could hardly doubt all that she had been told by angels and others. But still…

After answering John's disciples, Jesus told the crowds that John was the greatest prophet of all because of his role in making ready peoples' hearts for the Messiah's coming. He had actually said that John was the Elijah who was to come. That was part of the Jewish narrative, that the Messiah's coming would be preceded by the return of the prophet Elijah. And now, John had met the same fate as so many prophets before him.

Mary's heart ached. How she wished she could go to Jesus! She needed to see how he was taking this, but hesitated after her reception when she had so recently gone to see him in Capernaum. She was not sure how she would be received. He was so busy. All she could do was pour out her breaking heart to Jahweh. He never failed those who trusted in him. She needed to hear the still small voice of Jahweh's Spirit telling her things were going to be all right. But what mother would not be afraid for her son when you had a king like Herod, with the work Jesus was engaged in? Mary could not help but wonder when Jesus' mission would attract the paranoid and jealous Herod's attention in a similarly negative way as had happened with John. If Jesus was to be a king in David's line, well, Herod would never stand for that – but Mary just had to put those thoughts out of her mind. With the help of The Highest One, she would.

Chapter 30. The Women in Jesus' Life

Months passed and Mary saw little of her son. Neighbors, friends and sometimes visiting relatives would share snippets of information. One of Jesus' followers, the young fisherman John, whom Mary remembered from the wedding at Cana, had family in Jerusalem. Jesus and his friends would apparently stay there when he went to Jerusalem. At least he has somewhere to go when he's in Jerusalem, thought Mary. Of course, Jesus would have known that he would always be welcome at his grandparents or his great uncle and aunt's too.

Then Mary heard some news that made her take notice. Apparently, Jesus now also had some women who followed along with him. This was something new. Traveling teachers usually only had male students. Indeed, many were now referring to Jesus as 'rabbi,' 'Teacher.' Mary tried to learn who these women followers were and what had brought that about.

Mary learned that there were actually quite a few of these female devotees. Some, Mary discovered, were women who had been healed of evil spirits and disabilities. One name in particular figured prominently in this group: another Mary. However, this Mary had quite a different background. She was from Magdala on the west shore of the Sea of Galilee, south of Capernaum. Evidently Jesus had cast out seven demons from her. There were also rumors she had been a prostitute. No wonder she has become a follower of my son, Mary thought – the gratitude of being freed from all that.

Perhaps just as surprising was that another woman named Joanna, the wife of Cuza, King Herod's household manager, was in this group. Some of these women, such as Joanna and another named Susanna were women of means. It seems they provided for Jesus and his followers out of their own resources. Mary wondered what would make them do that, and how they could do so without getting in trouble. Especially if you were linked to Herod's household! All this was rather amazing. Mary was pleased though, that in yet another way, her son was being looked after and his material needs were being met.

The months passed by. Mary continued to hear of Jesus' teaching and his miracle working. Jesus had, on a couple of occasions, actually miraculously fed the crowds that gathered around him. I guess I need not worry about his getting enough to eat, thought Mary wryly.

She also heard that, on several occasions it was believed, Jesus had raised people from the dead. Mary found that hard to believe. Yet, that had been one of the 'proofs' Jesus had passed on to John when his followers had come to determine Jesus' true identity. That was something to ponder. Who but Jahweh had such power? Some of these had just died when Jesus intervened.

Then, Mary heard an even more amazing story. She had heard of Jesus friends in Bethany, the village where pilgrims often stayed when they went to the feasts in Jerusalem. The man of the household, Lazarus, had died. Jesus had not arrived until four days later, by which time Lazarus' body had already been laid to rest in a tomb. Lazarus' family had taken Jesus to the tomb at his request and he had called the man to come out! And he had; he had walked right out of the tomb! Mary could not help but wonder what this signified. Where was this all headed. What was Jesus' ultimate goal?

Mary also continued to hear increasingly of Jesus' confrontations with the religious leaders. She was beginning to pick up that some were so disturbed by Jesus' claims that they wanted to kill him. When she heard that Mary was shaken indeed. Were her greatest fears going to be realized? Again, she reasoned, trying to reassure herself, that was impossible. She was convinced her son was sent by Jahweh, although she too was still looking for him to fully reveal himself as she and her fellow Jews imagined the Messiah would.

Mary knew all too well what had already happened to their relative and Jesus' 'cousin', John. Would she never be free of fear and worry about her son? What had Jahweh really asked of her when she had promised so long that she was his servant and his will should be done? She had tried to leave things in the hands of The Highest One before and still believed she was doing that. However, these stories seemed to give her no choice. She was determined to find Jesus and see for herself that he was all right. She needed to get some answers! How far was Jesus taking this? Did he know what was ahead, what lay in store for him, for them?

Mary knew Jesus and his followers had gone to Passover so she decided to go to Jerusalem and find them. She arranged things with her family and informed her neighbors, just in case. She knew though that her children were old enough to take care of themselves. Wearily, she made her way down from Galilee to Judea and Jerusalem and went to her parents' place, glad now that they lived there so she had somewhere to go. She had often wished they were still back in Sepphoris so she could have talked more with them, sharing her concerns about what Jesus' life was turning out to be. Of course, she knew she would also have been welcome at her Uncle Benjamin's.

Mary was warmly received. It seemed a long time since her parents had seen her. After welcoming her in and letting her get refreshed form her travel, they settled down to talk over a meal. Mary was naturally curious about what her parents knew of Jesus' activities from their vantage point in Jerusalem. Her parents were just as obviously interested in what had brought her their way.

Mary told them of her increasing level of unease with what she had heard of Jesus' doings. Her parents understood her worries, her doubts. As they shared their reservations, they agreed there was little they could do, that simply allowing a negative frame of mind did not help. They would continue to bring their troubles to Jahweh and trust that Jesus was still in his hands.

Her father did tell her that when Jesus was in Jerusalem he spent time at the temple preaching and sometimes doing miracles. Here, he often also got caught up in debates with the religious leaders - the lawyers of the Torah, the scribes and even the Pharisees. Just like when he was twelve, Mary thought.

Things were different now though. Was Jesus simply becoming over-confident? Apparently, he had been quite hard on the Pharisees in one of his speeches. Why would he alienate the religious leaders? It didn't make sense. Mary wondered if he was being fair. People generally looked up to the Pharisees as models of law-abiding behavior, the Law of Moses, that is. Mary told her parents she was determined to go to the temple to find Jesus.

Next morning, Mary left her parents and went in search of her son. Her parents had told her to bring Jesus with her for a visit if she could. That way they could all talk with him about what he was doing and perhaps be enlightened instead of being left in the dark. "And do come back in time for *seder* with us," Joachim said. "It will be nice to have some company to commemorate Passover together."

It was not hard to find Jesus. Mary just had to go where the crowds were thickest. There he was, sitting on the steps, teaching. She wanted more than ever to run forward and feel Jesus' reassuring embrace, to talk to her son but she held back. She saw his young followers with him, hanging on every word. She gathered that the women with them were the ones she had heard about who helped provide his support for the group.

Jesus was busy teaching and Mary felt she could not disturb him. However, she did edge closer until she was next to some of the women. They were clustered more around the fringe of the crowd that was thronging Jesus. She greeted some of them, hoping to make their acquaintance. They seemed to be welcoming, sincere and caring persons.

Eventually, Mary mustered up enough courage to tell the women who she really was. She added how long it was since she had seen him, but immediately wished she had not said that. "Oh," they said, "We must tell our friends who you are. We have to tell Jesus you're here too, so you can talk with him."

"That would be wonderful," Mary replied, "but, really, I will be happy just to join you for a while. Let Jesus do what he needs to do."

The woman Mary had first spoken to quietly signaled to her friends and they all moved together behind Jesus. Mary was quickly introduced to the others. When she met Mary of Magdala, the woman rushed forward and grabbed Mary's hands and began kissing them. "We are so blessed to meet the mother of our rabbi. You are so honored and privileged to be his mother. May who you are and what you have done be forever remembered by our Jahweh, and by our people. You are a wonderful mother," she continued, "to be able to free Jesus to do his work like you have done. No wonder Jesus is such a loving person. He had you for a model mother."

"Oh, thank you," Mary returned, "you are too kind. I only did what any good mother would do."

"We really do think He is our long-awaited Messiah too," one of them added. At that Mary's ears perked up. Maybe all her fears were premature. What did these women know, what had they heard that convinced them of that? Did that not sound like what the angel and the prophets had told her years ago. Now others were coming to that conclusion. This was truly astonishing!

"Yes, one of the women chimed in, 'Last first day of the week we really saw what it would be like if he were our king, as the Messiah will be."

"What do you mean?" asked Mary.

"Oh, have you not heard?" they asked, seeing the puzzled look on Mary's face.

"Yes, it was incredible," the women all chimed in. "Jesus got hold of a donkey colt. Some of us put blankets on it and Jesus mounted it to go back into Jerusalem. Seeing Jesus like that really drove the crowds wild. They began to tear palm and other branches from the roadside and wave them before him as he rode. They even threw their cloaks down in front of him. Just like people do for a king! All the while, they were shouting, 'Hosanna! Blessed is he who comes in the name of the Lord. Blessed is the King of Israel.' Some of the religious leaders were not impressed. They tried to tell Jesus to use his influence to stop the crowds but it was to no avail. We know that some of them really want to catch him and put him on trial for blasphemy and treason."

"Blasphemy?" Mary said incredulously. She had never heard Jesus say a bad word in his life.

"Yes, Jesus talks about The Highest One as if Yahweh is his father and sometimes also makes it sound as if he is equal with him. Not surprisingly, that does not go over well with the religious leaders who are so zealous for protecting our faith. No human being should make that claim, but then, we have never seen or heard of anyone like Jesus either."

Mary's heart had skipped a beat and begun to pound to the point where she could hardly think clearly when she heard about the intention of the authorities. Was she still not going to be relieved of her fears? Where was Jahweh? The Almighty who had spoken to her and Jesus' father, telling them of what was to come. If only Jesus had listened to her a long time ago. But he always seemed to know what he was doing, what he believed he needed to do. She had learned long ago that there was no stopping him.

At the same time, Mary was glad she had made the acquaintance of these women. She could feel their support for Jesus, even for her. The women asked if she had a place to stay. She thanked them for their concern, their hospitality, and reassured them she was looked after. She told them where she was staying; at relatives.

Mary turned her attention away from the women to where Jesus was. So as not to disturb Jesus, the women had moved back as they chatted with Mary. Now they saw that Jesus had also moved off. Mary saw him in the distance, speaking and reaching out to people, no doubt healing them, reassuring them of forgiveness, reaffirming their faith, which she knew he did so often. As much as she wanted to talk with him, she felt reassured by her new friends' support.

Once again, she felt she needed to hold back and let Jesus do his work. Who knew how long he would have to complete his mission? With that she reassured her new friends that she was all right. She had seen her son. She had seen and met these supporters of his and was heartened by all this.

Mary had one request to make of her new friends though, "Please tell Jesus, she said, "that I have come to Jerusalem. I would like to see him. I am staying my parents'. I am fortunate in that. Jesus knows where that is. Perhaps he will have time to come and visit us there."

"Of course, we will tell him," the women chorused. "We'll tell him he should come and visit you. You are his mother." Mary was comforted by that, so with that promise, she bade her new friends good evening, Happy Passover, and went back to join her family.

Then came the day to celebrate the Passover feast. Would Jesus come and join his family as was the custom? The day came and the celebrations were completed but still no sign of him. Mary cold not help feeling let down, but she did not give up hope. She could not believe Jesus, knowing she was here, would not come and see her at some point.

Later Mary was to hear that Jesus had commemorated Passover with his disciples. He had instructed his young men to prepare a place for them. Everything had fallen into place just as he had predicted. Yes, Mary had thought on hearing that, 'He always seems to know what's going to happen.' Moreover, she remembered the time when she and his siblings had tried unsuccessfully to speak to him. He had declared that his followers were his family. So, he was celebrating with his new family.

V – Mission Accomplished

Chapter 31. An Unexpected Awakening

Mary awoke with a start. Someone was pounding on the door of her parents' home and calling for her! Mary listened to see if her father would respond, for she, as a woman should not go to the door of her host first, especially at night. Then she heard him moving towards the door. Understandably, she could hear a little annoyance in his voice as he asked what all the fuss was about in the middle of the night. She could not hear everything that was said but then she heard the hurried approach of his footsteps towards where she was sleeping and call out tersely, "Mary, this man at the door says he knows you. He brings awful news! He apologized for it, but he said to tell you that Jesus has been captured by the temple police and taken for trial before the Sanhedrin! At this hour of the night! They have already taken him to Governor Pilate who has sent him to King Herod! He says his name is John. He thinks you will want to join him and his friends, that you will want to be there."

Mary felt as if she was going to faint. Her head spun and she clutched at her clothes. First John, her cousin, and now her son! All the fears and dread that had been plaguing her these last few weeks were now being realized. "Oh, Jahweh," she cried in agony, "Help your maidservant! Protect your son! Oh, what can I do?"

It seemed as if her prayers were heard, at least enough to be able to pull herself together and try to get up. Joachim saw her unsteadiness and helped her to her feet, then supported her as she walked out to meet John. Yes, he was the kind young man she had taken a liking to ever since meeting him those years ago in Cana.

John bowed slightly as Mary approached, "Mother, he began," addressing her politely. "We had to let you know what has happened to your beloved son. I volunteered to come and tell you. Do you want to come with us?"

What else would she do? "Of course," Mary said.

"But Mary," Joachim interjected, "Will it be safe? If they find out you are his mother? Let me come with you."

"No, father," she said, looking lovingly at him, touching his arm affectionately, "It will be too much for you." She knew how much he had cared for his grandson and thought of how this too must be affecting him. "Stay here with mother. I will let you know what happens. I will be all right with John. John knows his way around Jerusalem." Mary had learned earlier that he actually was somehow related to some of these religious leaders.

Mary turned to go with John and then impulsively turned back and embraced her father tightly. She noticed that his body had become thinner and bonier with his aging. She was glad she had persuaded him not to come along. She pressed her lips against his cheeks and kissed him, "You can pray for us, please?"

"Of course," her father said, as Mary, reluctantly let him go, and then Mary was gone with the young man.

John took Mary's hand to make sure she was all right. Mary clutched her cloak tightly around her as she hurried through the chill of the dark night with John, praying earnestly in her heart for her beloved son's welfare. Then John began to fill her in on what had happened.

"We had gone with Jesus to the Garden of Gethsemane on the Mount of Olives after we finished *seder*, thinking we would continue on to Bethany for the night. Jesus seemed unusually troubled and went off by himself to pray, which you know is not that unusual for him. He did ask us to pray with him – more than once. We were so tired we kept falling asleep. I feel so bad now that we did stay awake and pray as Jesus asked. Then, what happened next might have been avoided. We had fallen asleep again when suddenly this crowd of noisy men with torches and clubs came storming across the valley and into the garden. And Judas was leading them! He took them right to Jesus."

'Judas,' Mary thought, 'I never really had liked that one–'

John was continuing, "Jesus said something to Judas about betraying him and the next thing we knew Jesus was in the hands of these men and being led away, back towards the city.

"Then what had happened at *seder* made more sense. Jesus was talking about one of us betraying him but the idea seemed so preposterous. We all asked him if he meant one of us. He said it was the one to whom he would give a piece of bread after he had dipped it, and he gave it to Judas. When Judas asked him whether he meant him, Jesus had said, 'You said so.' Then he told Judas to do quickly what he was going to do. Judas promptly got up and left. We thought Jesus had sent Judas to take care of some bill or something. We still could not believe that Jesus was really telling us who the traitor was."

"Where are we going?" Mary interrupted John.

"To King Herod's palace. That is where they took Jesus after taking him to the council and then the governor."

Mary shuddered. She did not want to imagine what would happen in front of Herod. She had never forgotten what this king's father had done all those years ago to all those innocent babies in the Bethlehem area when he could not find her own son. And then there had been the beheading of John. Poor John. And now? Now? Would it be Jesus' turn? Mary's heart felt a sharp pang as she remembered another happening from the past, the words of Simeon in the temple when they had dedicated Jesus: "as a result of him the thoughts of many hearts will be revealed – and a sword will pierce your own soul as well!" How often those words had troubled her. What did they mean? Now, she realized, she might be finding out. She shuddered at the thoughts flooding her mind.

Then another thought came to Mary. "John," she said, "Where are all the others? Are they all right?"

"No one else got arrested," John answered, "If that's what you mean. Most of us, once we came to our senses back there in the garden, tried to hurry after Jesus and the police, to see where they were going. Some ran off to tell those who were not with us."

Mary accepted that answer. She was almost too breathless to speak any more.

All seemed quiet as they neared the palace. Suddenly though, they could hear a growing roar of voices from the governor's quarters beyond that. They continued towards where the sound was coming from. It seemed things were happening awfully fast. When they got nearer, all Mary could hear was "Crucify him! Crucify him!"

Mary glanced over at John and noted the grim set of his jaw. "John," she said, hardly able to give voice to such thoughts, "Is it what I am thinking?" She almost did not want to hear an answer. "I don't know," John replied between breaths, "I hope not."

'Oh no,' Mary felt a tightening across her forehead, 'If it is - What is wrong with these people? What has happened? How can this happen? Crucify Jesus for what? What has Jesus done wrong?'

When they arrived at the edge of the crowd, Mary instinctively covered her face. She did not want to be recognized and get into trouble. But John saw some of his friends, Jesus' followers, and steered Mary in their direction. Mary saw the familiar faces of the young men who had been so close to Jesus. But someone was missing. Peter!

Mary tugged at John's sleeve, "John, where is Peter?"

John stopped and took both her arms as he looked into her eyes, "Peter left us. But he will be back. It's not easy to tell you this. You see, Peter – you know how he loved Jesus – he had followed the mob right into the High Priest's courtyard. However, when people began to accuse him of being Jesus' follower he got scared for his life. He said he did not know him."

"Oh no," Mary said.

John went on, "Some of us, who were a little farther out, all of a sudden saw him bolt from the courtyard, sobbing. We ran after him and when we caught up with him, we calmed him down to see what the matter was. Peter is anything if not honest. He told us what had happened. After the third questioner had spoken to him a rooster had crowed. It was morning after all. But the rooster crowing had made Peter remember that Jesus had told him at *seder* the exact details of how this would happen. He would deny Peter three times before the first rooster of the morning would crow. Peter had denied at the time he would ever do this, but he had. We tried to reassure Peter Jesus would forgive him, but he just could not bear to stick around. He wanted to go back to John Mark's so some went with him to make sure he would be all right."

Poor Peter, thought Mary. Yes, I know Jesus will forgive him. She could only imagine how terrible he must feel and quickly offered a prayer for peace and forgiveness for him.

At that point, the continued din of the crowd making it hardly possible to speak, John and Mary turned to join the others. Mary saw that some of the women she had come to know were there too. Joanna, Clopas' wife, Susanna, Salome and Mary from Magdala were all there. There was another woman, Mary was to learn later, named Veronica. Jesus had healed her of a bleeding problem that had plagued her for twelve years.

They were all weeping but they all hugged Mary when they recognized her with John. Through their tears, they shared their distress at what they were seeing. Then they all turned back to see what was unfolding before them. They gasped when they saw their beloved Jesus at the entrance to the governor's quarters.

There was something that looked like branches wrapped around his head and blood dripping down his face. Looking more closely they could see all too well; it was a wreath of thorns! Standing near him beside a throne-like chair was a man with gaunt appearing features, a sternly chiseled face, wearing a white toga. They all knew instinctively he must be the hated governor, Pilate. A number of Roman soldiers flanked the two men. Mary knew this was not good. Part of her wished she had not come to this place to see this. As if sensing her state if mind, John pulled her more closely beside him and wrapped his arm around her shoulder.

Chapter 32. A Rigged Trial

The Roman Governor, Pilate, raised his hands to quiet the mob that surged in front of him. As if to banish any thoughts of releasing Jesus, Mary heard the Jewish leaders shout out, "If you release this man, you are no friend of Caesar! Everyone who claims to be a king opposes Caesar!"

When Pilate heard these words, he slowly moved over and gravely took his place on what was obviously the governor's seat. He leaned towards the crowd, then waved his arm in the direction of Jesus, standing downcast behind him. He seemed to be mocking as he said theatrically, "Look, here is your king!"

Mary was awed. Where did Pilate get that idea? What had he been told? Or was he indeed just taunting the crowd? She knew Pilate had no respect for the Jews. To be sure, the angels' messages to her and Joseph when Jesus was conceived and then born had indicated that was Jesus' destiny, to be a king. She had not forgotten that and there had been a number of occasions since when she had been made to remember that. Her thoughts were quickly overwhelmed though by a roar from the crowd:

"Away with him! Away with him! Crucify him!"

Pilate called out, "Shall I crucify your king?"

The high priests and those with them roared, "We have no king except Caesar!"

Pilate then seemed to gesture to a servant nearby and someone then appeared beside Pilate with a basin. As they watched, Pilate methodically washed his hands in it and then turned to the crowd as the aide took it away.

Pilate then raised his hand, trying to achieve some silence, but with little success, as the crowd kept shouting, "Crucify him! We have no king but Caesar!"

A Sword Shall Pierce Your Soul

Mary was close enough to hear Pilate say in response, "I am innocent of this man's blood. You take care of it yourselves!"

The people in the crowd, who had moments before been chanting 'Crucify him,' now began to follow their religious leaders again in yelling, "Let his blood be on us and on our children!"

Mary could not believe what was happening. The fury of the mob! What the religious leaders were saying. None of it made sense. Had they all lost their minds? What possessed these people? Had they not seen the wonderful things Jesus had done? Had they not heard the teachings that had amazed so many? Mary just could not comprehend how things had come to this turn, and so rapidly! Not even a week earlier crowds had been hailing Jesus as king!

Still the crowd bellowed the over and over, "Crucify him! Crucify him!"

The governor, as if in resignation, covered his face in his hands momentarily before he rose from his seat. Normally, that would have been a signal to the crowd to quiet. However, nothing seemed to be stopping this mob. Pilate seemed to shrug and wave his hands in disgusted dismissal. Then he turned and appeared to say something to the soldiers.

'Oh no,' Mary thought, as her hands flew to her mouth, 'Is the trial over? Where are the witnesses?' She learned later that part of the proceedings had already been completed before she and John had arrived. The only charge that had been brought against Jesus was that he had claimed to be a king. There had been no witnesses to the contrary and Jesus had apparently not said a single word in his defense. Mary had found that hard to understand. Jesus? Who was so good with words? Later, Mary was also later told that initially, Pilate seemed dissatisfied with the evidence and had wanted to release Jesus. There was a custom of releasing a prisoner at Passover. However, the crowd had yelled for some other criminal and not Jesus. All of this was beyond Mary.

Suddenly, Mary's attention was caught by action on the floor of the hall. Several burly soldiers closed in on Jesus, grabbed him roughly by both arms and dragged him back out of sight of the crowd.

'Now what?' Mary wanted to ask, but there was no way anyone could have heard her above the din of the crowd. She felt utterly helpless.

The crowd continued to cry for Jesus' crucifixion, saying also that they would bear the responsibility. It seemed they would never stop. It was unbelievable. Mary looked at the distorted angry faces nearest her. 'They don't know what they are doing,' she breathed to herself. 'They don't really know who Jesus is.'

Suddenly, the crowd's angry chorus swelled and there was a rush towards the side of the palace. Mary knew the reason why as soon as she saw Jesus appear, barely able to stand, let alone walk, blood dripping through his clothes and from his face. Then she realized that part of the reason for this was the thorn branches twisted about his head, pressing into his skin. She knew immediately too, from the blood oozing through his garments and dripping onto the street, that he had been thoroughly whipped. She had not thought about that, but yes, that was what always happened to prisoners before they were crucified: the dreaded thirty-nine lashes! And there was Jesus, as if he had not already endured enough, struggling under the weight of a huge wooden cross they had just dropped on his shoulders, almost knocking him down. Two other men also came out behind him, bearing crosses as well.

Mary could hardly breathe, 'Oh, no,' she thought, 'Are those some of Jesus' friends, his followers? Were they tried with Jesus?' In spite of herself, she craned her neck forward and was relieved to see that she did not recognize either of the faces. At the same time, she felt a twinge of guilt. They might not have been Jesus' followers, but these men did not deserve such a cruel death either.

Jesus, going to be crucified? Mary began to weep uncontrollably. But yes, that is what the crowd had been yelling. She leaned into John, feeling as if she were going to collapse on the spot.

"What have they done?" cried Mary. One of the other women, tears streaming from her eyes, leaned in towards her, putting her arm around her and said, "He has just had a flogging. They always do that before they crucify someone."

"He is going to crucified like a common criminal?" Mary cried "How can this be? For what purpose is this happening?" She had to believe something positive was about to happen. Jesus could so easily shake all that off and disappear like he had in Nazareth when they had wanted to kill him there. He had the power. Mary knew that. Why would he just let this happen to him? Had he not come to be a king? To save, to free his people? As far as she could tell, that had not yet happened? Things were just not adding up.

Mary wanted to rush forward, to cry out, "Jesus, save yourself! You can do it!" She wanted to run to Jesus and get answers to these questions. She wanted to let everyone know what they were doing was wrong. Jesus was not guilty of what he was being accused. She knew that. What kind of trial would have ended up with a death verdict being passed on her beloved son?

However, on one hand she knew now was not the time for her to expose herself like that. She could be the next one arrested. She also knew, on the other hand, that in the state Jesus was in, it was impossible for more reasons than one, for him to engage in such an exchange. If he had not defended himself before this, he was not likely to do so now. Humanly, there was no further recourse. Once again, Mary had to keep her thoughts and fears to herself, heavy as they were. Once more, the only other place she could turn to in her heart, her spirit, was Jahweh, who was somehow behind all this.

Chapter 33. Enemies Get Their Way

Jesus was not doing what Mary wished, what she believed he was capable of. Instead of performing some miracle and freeing himself, he silently and bravely bore his cross and struggled out to the street. The soldiers were pushing the three men towards the nearest city gate. One concession Rome had made to Judea was not to crucify criminals within the walls of the holy city.

The crowd surged after the procession. Mary, John and the others were swept along with them. Suddenly, Jesus stumbled and fell. The woman Mary would come to know as Veronica rushed forward, pushed her way through the crowd and began to wipe the blood from Jesus' face. The soldiers pushed her aside so roughly she stumbled and almost fell. Some of the other women rushed, weeping, to her side.

Jesus looked back at them and, pausing, found the strength to speak, "Daughters of Jerusalem, do not weep for me, but weep for yourselves and for your children. There is one thing you can be sure of. The days are coming when they will say, 'Blessed are the childless, the wombs that never bore children, and the breasts that never nursed!' Then they will begin to say to the mountains, 'Fall on us!'" The soldiers pushed rudely at Jesus, as if to stop his warning. They tried to prod him forward, but he held his ground, stooped beneath the cross, to finish, "And to the hills, 'Cover us!' For if such things are done when the wood is green, what will happen when it is dry?"

Mary did not entirely understand what Jesus was saying. Some of it sounded foreboding. What was he predicting? At the same time, she got some comfort from hearing that he still had compassion on others, that he was still able to speak, in spite of the predicament he was in. 'Jesus,' she thought, 'You never stop caring about others before yourself.'

Jesus, now stumbling forward, staggering from side to side, looked as if he was going to collapse at any moment. The soldiers noticing this, looked about for help. Spying a tall, swarthy, well-built man on the side of the street, they grabbed him and dragged him out onto the pavement. Wresting the cross brutally from Jesus' shoulders, almost knocking him over in the process, they forced this man to carry it onwards. One of the soldiers grabbed Jesus, righting him, as he lurched on. The newly conscripted helper bravely carried the cross on to their destination. Mary could hardly believe that the soldiers would have had that much mercy on Jesus. Then she realized, no, they were probably more concerned with wanting to get to their destination and get their job done. They were certainly not about to help carry the cross. She was thankful for small mercies just the same.

The sorry procession continued on to the city gate and out to the small hill called Golgotha. They stopped at its peak where the soldiers grabbed the three convicted men and held them to the ground as they proceeded to nail them to the crosses. Mary, seeing what was coming, turned away and covered her ears at the sound of the screams. She couldn't keep from sneaking a look at her son, and was amazed that his mouth remained shut; not a sound came from him. She saw the soldiers try to give the men something to drink but Jesus refused it. Then they hoisted the men up on their crosses up and dropped them, screaming in pain, (again, not including Jesus!) into the holes already there from many previous crucifixions.

Mary noticed a sign at the top of the cross and wondered what it meant. As if to answer her question, John turned to her and said, "They have called him 'King of the Jews'." Mary still could not understand how that had come about. All she could keep in her mind was that there had been words to that effect in the messages she and Joseph had received years before, but there had never been any acceptance or acknowledgment of that so far as she knew. Nor had Jesus really shown anything to demonstrate that he saw himself as a king.

Then Mary remembered what had happened on the first day of the week. She had been told by Jesus' female friends about Jesus riding into Jerusalem on a donkey accompanied by throngs of pilgrims shouting 'Hosanna to the son of David, blessed is the one who comes in the name of the Lord!"

When had people realized he was a descendant of David? What had Jesus been trying to say by entering the city on a donkey? That was indeed the way kings sometimes did enter the city when they came in peace. Had he finally gone too far? She could see how all of that would have upset the leaders and especially Herod. So many seemingly unanswerable questions flooded

Mary's mind as she gazed at the spectacle unfolding before her. Would she ever get answers? Then again, she realized, as her mind cleared somewhat, would any of it matter once Jesus was crucified? What was left?

Meanwhile, oblivious to the suffering going on above them, the soldiers had taken the victims' clothing and were clustered at the foot of the crosses, seeming to be playing some kind of game. One of the women turned to the rest and explained disgustedly, "They're gambling on who gets Jesus and the others' clothes. They do that all the time with the crucified."

'How low can you get?' Mary thought. 'How utterly inhumane. Human beings are dying above your heads and all you can think about is what you will get out of it.'

As time passed, the crowd began to thin somewhat. As some of the throng left though, Mary's heart was pained again as she heard them make a point of passing below Jesus and mocking him, shaking their heads and saying, "Aha! You who said the temple would be destroyed but you could rebuild it in three days, save yourself and come down from the cross!"

In the same way, even the chief priests – together with the experts in the law – Mary could tell by their dress and demeanour – who were also still there, as if to make sure their victim got what they wanted, could be heard mocking him among themselves just as loudly as everyone else seemed to be doing: "He saved others, but he cannot save himself! Let the Christ, the king of Israel, come down from the cross now, that we may see and believe!"

Mary was aghast! How could their religious leaders, the people they were expected to respect and look up to, do and say such things! She was having a hard time believing what she was seeing. What would make these normally sedate and perhaps pompous individuals stoop to such abusiveness? What had happened to make them so angry?

Indeed, what was happening to her world? Everything seemed to be falling apart. Had they been deceived? Was Jesus not the Messiah after all? If he was, she could not fathom these things happening. This could not be the end. Where was the glory, the blessing, the 'ruling forever'? Part of her wished she had never come. But her mother instinct was strong and she could not bear the thought of leaving her son alone at a time like this.

As the crowd thinned, the women and Jesus' young followers - those who were there – inched cautiously closer to the cross upon which Jesus hung. The two men beside Jesus had also spoken out against him 'Who are they and what right do they have to say anything,' Mary thought. Sometime later one of them seemed to have second thoughts. One of the criminals hanging there had just called out in desperation, "Aren't you the Christ? Save yourself and us!"

But the other had rebuked him, saying, "Don't you fear Jahweh? You are under the same sentence of condemnation. We were sentenced rightly. We are getting what we deserve for what we did, but this man has done nothing wrong." Then, turning to Jesus, who was hanging between them, he gasped between his labored breaths, "Jesus, remember me, when you come in your kingdom."

Jesus was able to answer him! "I'll tell you the truth, today you will be with me in paradise."

Mary almost gasped. Jesus could still hear what people were saying and respond! Could still think, and talk, after all that he had suffered. Mary marveled at his strength. His answer told her too that he still had not forgotten who he was, what message he bore. Even in the midst of his suffering he was continuing to show compassion and offering forgiveness. Just hearing that gave her heart a little lift. As if sensing what was going on in her heart, Jesus suddenly gave a loud cry, "Father, forgive them, for they don't know what they are doing." Indeed, thought Mary. Does anyone here today know what they are doing?

But others continued to hurl insults at Jesus from where they stood at a distance, "He saved others. Let him save himself if he is the Christ of Jahweh, his chosen one!"

The soldiers also mocked him, coming up and offering him sour wine, and saying, "If you are the king of the Jews, save yourself!"

It had been around the time of the end of the first morning watch when the crowd had arrived on the hill. Suddenly, when it was about noon, an ominous darkness came over the scene. It was more than just dark clouds; it seemed the sun's light itself had failed. A chill settled over Mary and the others. They pulled their cloaks tighter around them but remained rooted to the ground. They were unable to tear themselves away from the awful picture playing out before them, from their beloved Jesus. They just wanted it to be over. But then what?

Suddenly, Jesus opened his eyes. He seemed to be aware of who was around him, for Mary saw the pained look on his face. He looked particularly in the direction of herself and John, trying to focus his eyes on whom he was seeing. Then, as if mustering his last breath of will, his gaze fixed on Mary and she could tell he was trying to speak to her. Impulsively she edged closer to and heard him say - yes, he was talking to her! "Woman, look," lifting his chin in the direction of John just behind her, "here is your son!" He then looked over her head towards John and said to his disciple, "Look, here is your mother!"

As if in obedience to his master's dying wish, John moved alongside Mary and put his arm back around her as they faced Jesus together. Mary burst into tears again and just buried her head in John's arms and wept. 'Oh, my Jesus,' she thought, 'What has it come to? Is this how it all ends? What about all those prophecies?' Somehow, she could not believe this was the end. There had to be more.

Then Mary remembered her family: her uncles and aunts in Jerusalem and Ein Kerem. What could she, what should she tell them? It would be a severe blow for Uncle Zechariah and Aunt Elizabeth. First John, now Jesus. And then there were her children in Nazareth. She could well imagine James' reaction. He had never been happy with what he saw Jesus doing. 'Lord, she pleaded silently, standing there with John on that cursed hill, 'I want to cry out to you, why? But now I also need your wisdom, your words, on how to deal with my family.' She shivered there in the gloom. She felt so alone. She just covered her face and sobbed. John, noticing her distress, pulled her closer, rubbing her back and trying to comfort her.

Three hours of this dreadful darkness had passed, when Jesus suddenly cried out with a loud voice, "My Lord, my Lord, why have you forsaken me?"

When some of the bystanders heard it they said, "Listen, he is calling for Elijah! Leave him alone! Let's see if Elijah will come to take him down!"

Before they could do anything, Jesus cried out again "I'm thirsty!" After one of the soldiers put a sponge soaked in something from a jar standing near, he put it on a coarse branch of hyssop and lifted it to Jesus' mouth. Jesus appeared to at least wet his lips with what he had received, after which he cried out with a loud voice, "It is finished! Father, into your hands I commit my spirit!" With that his head fell forward and he breathed his last.

Chapter 34. After the Crucifixion

The Roman soldier who stood in front of Jesus heard all that Jesus spoke from the cross. He had seen how Jesus had endured the trial, the beating, the thirty-nine lashes, and now he saw how he died. Mary heard him look up at Jesus, shake his head and say, "Truly, this man was the Son of The Highest One!" In fact, to the amazement of the women and Jesus' other followers standing there, he praised The Highest one and declared, "Certainly this man was innocent." Then Mary saw some of the soldiers approach the crosses holding large sturdy beams of wood. What now thought Mary?

She learned later that, because it was the day of preparation, the day before Sabbath, the bodies should not stay on the crosses. That was against their religious rules. This was particularly so because this Sabbath, coming after Passover, was an especially sacred one. What the soldiers were doing was coming to break the legs of the men hanging there. This way they could no longer try to push themselves up to get their breath. It would hasten their death so their bodies could be more quickly taken down. They took their beams and went first to the two men who had been crucified with Jesus, first the one and then the other. They just wanted to get the job done and get on with their other duties.

When Mary saw what was coming, she quickly averted her gaze, but she couldn't avoid hearing the terrible 'crack, crack' and the ensuing screams of pain as the soldiers swung the beams against the criminals' legs. She buried her face in John's cloak to keep away from what was going on behind her, fearing the same for Jesus. She could not bear to see her son bear any more punishment. Then she heard one of the soldiers call out, "Cornelius," which she took to be their superior's name, "This one is already dead."

Mary turned back to see whom they were referring to and immediately she wished she had not. "Oh, no," she cried, for just at that moment, one of the soldiers pierced Jesus' side with a spear, and blood and water ran out. That mixture proved Jesus was already dead.

'Oh,' Mary gasped, 'Did they have to pierce his body when they had already decided he was dead? I can't bear to see anymore.' She felt as though her own soul had been pierced. For a moment, she thought she was going to faint. She wanted to cry out to the heavens, 'Is Jesus really dead? Jahweh, you let your son die?' The questions that had been with her all of Jesus' life now just would not leave her. 'Is this the end of all his dreams? The mission he saw himself completing? What about all those things the angels told me, what Simeon and Anna said?'

Still, Mary and her new friends remained at the cross. They felt compelled to stay and see what would become of their beloved. With all the frenzied activity of the last hours lessening, Mary became more aware of her surroundings. She noticed that John had left her side and was embracing another woman. She realized that it was his own mother. He brought her to meet Mary and she tried to console Mary through her own tears. As they stood there together, it was as if the heavens themselves had seen enough, and no longer needed to try to hide the evil done in darkness. The clouds began to dissipate and the sky became bright once again.

Suddenly, a pair of well-dressed men with a retinue of servants arrived on the scene. They were carrying some large packages. They approached the soldiers and unrolled a scroll to show to their leader, the centurion whose name seemed to be Cornelius. The men gestured towards Jesus as they spoke. Mary wondered what was going on. To her wonder, those same soldiers who had moments before been beating the criminals, took down the cross on which Jesus hung and removed his body. Then the newcomers lifted it and placed it in the linen they had brought so it could be wrapped.

Mary and her friends hurried forward. "Where are you taking him," they asked.

The men looked at Mary and one of them said, "You are Jesus' mother, are you not? You don't remember me, I'm sure. We met when your son was in the temple at the time of his first Passover. I always kept my eyes and ears open to see what was happening in that remarkable boy's life." He said he too had become a follower of Jesus, and had asked Pilate for the body, in order to give it a decent burial.

He added, "I knew you might not know me for I never joined your group. I am ashamed to admit it, but I was keeping my belief secret for fear of my fellow council members. I want you to know though, that I never approved of this," he said angrily, gesturing towards Jesus' body. Then he turned to introduce the man with him. "This is Nicodemus, another member of the council who was also a follower of your son." Then he turned back towards his servants to make sure they were finishing what they had come to do. Mary was surprised to see that Jesus teachings had made at least some inroads into the Jewish leadership. At the same time, she breathed a sigh of relief and then a silent prayer of thanks. Something was going right. There were people who cared.

"Come with me," Joseph said when his men had Jesus' body wrapped, "I have a tomb that was made for me but we can put Jesus there for now. No one has ever used the tomb."

Mary wanted to step forward and embrace Joseph but knew such a display of emotion was not acceptable. Instead she approached both men, bowed, and simply said, "Thank you so much sirs. May Jahweh bless you richly for your kindness. We will be glad to follow you."

Joseph responded, "I am so sorry for you. May Jahweh give you strength." Nicodemus nodded in agreement. Then Joseph turned to lead his servants as they carried Jesus' body to the tomb.

The women who were still there, along with John, followed Joseph together to a nearby hillside. They watched as Joseph and his attendants undid their packages. There was a large amount of spices to wrap Jesus' body in clean linen. When the servants were done they gently laid it to rest inside a tomb newly hewn out of the rock. Then his servants began to roll a large stone over the entrance to seal it.

Mary Magdalene rushed forward, "Sir," she pleaded, "Do you have to do that? How can we embalm the body to show our love and respect for this our leader and Lord?"

Mary could not help but think of how, just days before, Jesus had called his friend Lazarus from just such a grave in Bethany. Now, who was there to call Jesus forth? How could he remain dead when he had raised others?

"I too am his disciple," Joseph reminded them, 'but I know that the leaders have been listening to Jesus and heard him talk about rising again.

If Jesus will do that, He won't need embalming. Nor do I think a stone will stop the Son of The Highest One from showing his power if he is to rise again. The Jewish leaders have actually stipulated this because they worry some of Jesus' followers will steal his body to say he has come back to life."

Mary Magdalene and the others could find no argument against that. But they could not get their minds off that huge stone in front of the tomb. They still would have liked to embalm Jesus' body. They had already been thinking about coming back with the requisite spices and ointments with which to do that.

The women also felt they had been chided a little for lack of faith. Those who had put Jesus to death put them to shame. They had heard Jesus talk about rising from the dead and thought by sealing the tomb they were going to prevent that. The women remembered Jesus' talking about rising; yes, he had said that more than once - on the third day. But with all that had happened they had completely forgotten that. They had nothing to do now but wait and see. There was little they could do now, because the Sabbath was already beginning.

Suddenly, Mary realized she was exhausted. When John and his mother suggested they would walk with her to her parents', she was too tired to say otherwise. Then she began to feel hungry and thirsty too. They tried to get their other friends to come along, but Mary Magdalene and a couple of the others insisted they were all right and would stay at the tomb a while longer. Mary thanked them all for their support. They embraced and kissed one another and then Mary, John and his mother left.

The women who stayed had not been there long when they noticed torches approaching. As the torchbearers drew nearer, the women realized they were being carried by a cohort of soldiers, temple police actually, heading in their direction. The women looked at one another. Now what? Were they also going to get in trouble?

They backed off, crouching low to the ground. They stayed motionless, hoping the soldiers would not see them in the growing darkness. However, as the troop neared, the leading soldier did spot them. He raised his arm and the whole company came to a halt, "Stop! Who are you?

Mary Magdalene, hesitated, pulled her shawl tightly around her face, then said, "We just came to see where they laid the teacher," she offered.

"Humph," snorted the burly guard, "you waiting for him to rise again? You believe him when he said he would rise again in three days?"

Without waiting for an answer, the guard signaled the rest of the troop to continue and they pushed their way roughly past the women and tromped on. The women noticed the guards were carrying some heavy-looking containers and wondered what they were.

The women's curiosity was piqued by the soldier's remark. They paused and watched as the guards reached the tomb. Then it became clear what was in the containers. The soldiers set down the containers, opened them and quickly began scooping out the contents, sealing the circumference of the stone with masonry.

"Oh, no," the women murmured to each other, "The stone was bad enough, now it's sealed. What can we do?"

"I'm not sure," Mary Magdalene finally declared, "but I am coming back in the morning to see what we can do. I think we had better leave now."

Chapter 35. The Darkest Sabbath

John took his mother home first, as it was nearer to the troubling scene they were leaving behind them. Then he walked on with Mary to her parents' home as dusk deepened. They hurried through the streets, quieter now with families in their homes for the Sabbath. As the cool of the night enveloped them, they pulled their cloaks closer around them. Little was said. They were all too distressed and dismayed by what they had just witnessed. Words could not do justice to their shared experience – yet.

When they reached Joachim and Anna's home, Mary was surprised to see some strangers just leaving the gate. She wondered what was going on, so quickly thanked John for everything. She wanting to rush inside to find out but felt compelled to step forward and embrace John. She looked up into his surprised eyes through her own tear-filled eyes and said, "Don't forget, you now have two mothers!" Then she kissed John's mother and said good night to them both. As they turned and walked away, Mary could not help but note the droop in his shoulders. They were all grieving, and so unexpectedly; it was nothing short of a shock. With that she turned quickly towards the door of her parents' home.

Mary was surprised to see some other people with her parents when she entered. She quickly realized, of course, that the news of what had happened to Jesus had probably spread, and neighbors were already coming to mourn with the family.

When Joachim and Anna saw Mary, they immediately rushed towards her. Their tear-stained and drawn faces told her they had indeed heard the news. They both wrapped her in their arms and all burst into tears together. Once the floodgates were open, Mary could hardly stop sobbing. She clung to them, burying her head in her father's shoulder. Finally, she pulled herself up and said softly, "I don't know what to say. I never imagined this happening to your beloved grandson. What shall we do?"

"I just don't know her father replied. "I have no words either. But Mary, do you know what happened to Jesus' body?"

"Oh," and Mary's tears came again.

"I don't want to think about it," Mary's father continued, "But we need to think of a place to lay Jesus' body and have a burial. Our friends here," He gestured towards the people sitting with them, "tell us someone came and took the body. Someone from the Sanhedrin? What does that mean?"

"Oh, don't worry, father," Mary explained. "You probably don't remember any more than I, but the council member who showed special interest in Jesus way back when we found him in the temple – remember that?" Mary did not wait for an answer, "He came while Jesus' followers and I we were still wondering what we should do. He said he had asked Governor Pilate for the body. He wanted to give Jesus a proper burial." Seeing her father lift his eyebrows in question, Mary went on, "Yes, he said he wanted to do this to honor Jesus because he too was a follower."

"But, but, do we know where the body was taken?"

"Yes, yes, we do," Mary continued excitedly. "Some of us went with him. His name is Joseph, from Arimathea. We needed to see where he was taking him. He placed Jesus' body in the tomb he had prepared for when he passes on. We can go there if you wish."

Mary's father turned wearily and slowly made his way back to join her mother who had already settled herself down again among their guests. "Well, it seems there is not much we can do today anyway. We will have to think about what our next steps should be. This is all so unusual, so sudden, so unexpected."

Joachim buried his face in his hands. Then Anna spoke up. "Mary, you must be exhausted. You probably have not had anything to eat or drink either. Let me get something for you." Looking meaningfully towards their guests, she bowed and said, "Thank you for joining us. As you see, things are not unfolding the way one expects. May we please be excused for now. We will let you know what we decide to do tomorrow. I think we all just want to sleep now. You are probably tired too."

The guests looked at one another, then all silently rose to their feet. They bowed towards the family and murmured words of condolence and respect as they filed out the door.

Mary agreed that she needed sleep, realizing at the same time she really had no appetite. However, at her parents' insistence, she had a little to eat. Then she once again hugged her parents as they all retired for the night. They all knew Mary was too upset to ply her with questions about what she had seen, or what had really happened. They reasoned they could talk about this further when Mary was ready.

Initially, Mary had trouble falling asleep. The awful images of what she had seen kept rolling before her weary eyes. The tears still came, but not as heavily as when she had first witnessed the awful scenes of the day unfold before her. However, eventually her brain succumbed to her fatigue and she did sleep.

The next day seemed to drag on forever. Little was still spoken in the troubled household. They had no heart for going to synagogue or the temple. Was there any point to it?

Friends and neighbors, who knew what had happened, came by, seeking to comfort the family. Some brought food. Mary and her parents were grateful for their concern and thanked them. However, things had developed so rapidly and unexpectedly, the family was still at a loss. They had no answers for the usual questions about rites after death, such as a funeral.

It was thus with some relief for the family when, not surprisingly, Uncle Benjamin and Aunt Tirzah also appeared. They all embraced each other and tried to comfort one another through their tears. They were all still so numbed that they really could not speak of what might need to be done or how to go forward from here. Benjamin and Tirzah had thoughtfully brought some food and they did eat together, mostly in heavy silence. They uttered the requisite prayers, some ritually and audibly, as they had shared their Sabbath meals. They ate little, as there was really no pleasure in it.

Benjamin and Tirzah stayed and kept Mary and her parents company. This helped them face some of the well-wishers that continued to drop in, so their company was appreciated. When evening came however, Joachim and Anna assured their caring kinsfolk they would be all right and encouraged them to go home and get some rest.

When night fell, they all retired to their beds again. Just as on the previous eve, Mary did not immediately fall asleep. This time it was not so much the images of yesterday, although they were still present. It was more the questions and thoughts that swirled around in her mind. What were they all to make of all that Jesus had done in his short life? What had been the purpose? What did it mean? Surely, all those messages had not been in vain. And what had Joseph, the man who let Jesus be buried in his tomb reminded them of – that Jesus had suggested he would rise again if he were killed? Mary was not sure she could even put any energy into believing that and building up some hope. She felt somewhat guilty for not having observed the Sabbath better, but she was sure she could be forgiven for that. This had indeed been the darkest Sabbath she had ever known. Eventually, she slept again.

Chapter 36. The Tomb Is Empty!

At dawn on the first day of the week, having rested on the Sabbath as commanded in the Law of Moses, Mary Magdalene, Joanna and Mary the mother of Joses went to look at the tomb. They had prepared the requisite myrrh and other spices to anoint and embalm Jesus' body, giving it the last care Jesus deserved. They remembered the big stone in front of the tomb and wondered what they could do about it. However, they felt compelled to go anyway. They just could not stay away from where their beloved teacher's body was. Now there was the added complication of the guards who had further sealed the tomb. Something – hope? – drew them to the site, as if things would change when they got there.

Suddenly, as they were making their way through the last darkness of the night, the women felt the ground shake as a sound like distant thunder rolled over the land. The women knew at once it was an earthquake. They trembled, hesitated, but kept doggedly moving forward, as the sound stopped almost as soon as it had begun. Then, out of the darkness, loomed the figures of the guards they had been worrying about, hurrying in their direction. At first, they paused in fear, afraid of what could happen to them. However, the guards ran right by the women with looks of sheer terror on their faces. The women looked at one another but turned forward and kept walking determinedly towards the tomb in silent agreement of completing what they had come to do.

When the women rounded the hill to where they could see the tomb, they saw that the stone was gone from the opening. But what else they saw caused them to pull up short in alarm! The tomb was open, and its doorway was flooded with the most intense light they had ever seen! What was more, a being that could be nothing other than an angel of the Lord was sitting on the stone that had been against the tomb entrance, but was now lying on the ground beside it. His appearance was almost as blinding as the sun, and his clothes were white as snow. Suddenly a second angel was standing next to them. They fell back in fear, startled by the bright light that surrounded them.

Then, still so blinded they could scarcely see, they heard the angel nearer them say, "Why are you looking for the living among the dead? He is not here, he has been raised to life! Remember how he told you, while he was still in Galilee, that the Son of Man must be handed over to sinful men, and be crucified, but on the third day he would rise again? Do not be afraid; I know you are looking for Jesus, who was crucified."

As if he needed to emphasize what he was saying, the angel repeated firmly, "He is not here, he has been raised, just as he told you." Then he added, more gently, "Come, see the place where he was lying. Then go quickly and tell his disciples, he has been raised from the dead. Tell them also, that he will go on to Galilee, where you are to go. You will see him there." Again, perhaps to be sure the poor speechless women would hear and remember the importance of the message, the angel added, "Listen to what I am telling you!"

Still overwhelmed by a combination of fear and disbelief, really not comprehending the incredulity of what they were hearing, the women forgot all about the angel's offer to show them where Jesus' body had lain. Instead, they turned and fled from the tomb to tell the other disciples. But who should be in their path but Jesus himself!

Then, that familiar voice greeting them! The women could hardly believe their eyes! Overcome with emotion they ran and threw themselves at Jesus' feet. They held fast to his feet, as though afraid he would disappear again, weeping and kissing his feet through their tears.

Jesus gently backed away from them, and as they then looked up questioningly into his face, he said comfortingly, "Do not be afraid. But do not cling to me either. I must still ascend to Father. Go and tell my brothers I must go to my Father and your Father, my Lord and your Lord. Then tell them to go to Galilee. I will meet them there."

The women were in such shock they said nothing to anyone as they raced back to where the disciples and other followers of Jesus were meeting. They tried to tell them everything they had seen and heard. However, in their excitement, their words tumbled out too incoherently. Those gathered there heard their words, but were really not sure if they were getting the story right. Did they hear correctly, that Jesus was alive? Could this be true? They could scarcely bring themselves to believe what they had heard.

Chapter 37. Unbelievable News

Meanwhile, while all this was happening, Mary woke to see sunlight streaming in through the windows. Such a bright morning would usually give her energy and hope for a new day. If she were at home she would get up and cheerfully begin her daily tasks. However, any such thoughts were quickly banished as the memories of the last two days came flooding back.

But life had to go on. She had her parents and aunts and uncles here in Judea. However, her family was up in Nazareth. Slowly, she rose and wearily began to get ready for the day. She really had no choice; she would have to think about returning to Nazareth.

At breakfast, Mary and her parents slowly began to sift through what had happened. Now that there was more distance between them and those terrible events, it was not so draining to discuss them. Of course, the big question, especially on Mary's mind, was 'What now?' She still could not accept that it was all over. So much hope had been awakened, had been promised. Jesus had done so much in the last few years. He had become so popular, well-loved even. Many owed so much to him with the healing he had brought them, the freedom from their demons. Others had been inspired by his teaching to change their lives and were the better for it. No one had ever heard a teacher like him and no one had ever performed so many miracles.

The three of them finished their breakfast, mainly in silence. They then began to clean up and slowly drag themselves to do what they thought they needed to.

They kept about their activities as if hoping that being busy would help them keep their minds off the terrible events and emotions of the last couple of days. It was already well on in the day when, still considering all these thoughts, they heard a knock. Who should appear again at the door but Jesus' disciple John. Now what did he have to say?

Mary could see by the glow on John's that face there was something of great import on his mind. Sure enough, John could hardly wait to go through the niceties of normal greetings before he reached forward. Taking Mary by the arms, he looked lovingly into her face, "Mother, Mary, the tomb is empty! Peter and I saw it for ourselves." He rushed on, "You remember how Mary Magdalene and some of the other women had prepared spices and oils and wanted to go to the tomb and embalm Jesus? Well, they of course had been wondering how they would roll the stone away from the entrance that they had seen Joseph and his servants roll in front of it. We understood the authorities thought they needed to do that to make sure we didn't rob the grave and say Jesus had risen. Can you believe that?"

"John, John," Joachim broke in, "Sounds like you have a lot to tell us. Please, make yourself comfortable," he said, gesturing to the mats the rest were sitting on. "Can we get you something to eat, to drink?"

"Thank you, you are very kind," John bowed as he settled on the mat beside Mary. "I don't need anything to eat or drink."

John began again, "Indeed, the Jewish leaders had been so afraid something would happen, the women who had stayed at the tomb in mourning had seen temple police come and seal the entrance. Not only that, they had posted guards at the tomb yesterday evening. But they were no longer there when the women arrived, and the stone was rolled aside!

"They did not know what to make of that but when they came nearer, a bright light had shone from the tomb and Mary from Magdala said two angels appeared. They had been terrified, of course, but the messengers had told them not to be afraid. They had told the women Jesus had risen, as he had said he would. They even reminded the women with words we remembered afterwards that Jesus had indeed said. We were just too skeptical at the time to pay heed to that. Actually, we just did not want to think about our Lord dying, so why would we pay attention to talk of rising from the dead? The angels had said, 'Remember how he told you, while he was still in Galilee, that the Son of Man must be handed over to sinful men, and be crucified, and rise again on the third day."

John had so much he wanted to say no one could interrupt him, "The angel had invited them to look inside and see that the tomb was indeed empty. Some of them had been too terrified to go nearer. But the angel had been firm with them. He told them to go quickly and tell us, his disciples, that Jesus was going to Galilee and we would see him there!"

Mary's mind was spinning. Was it really true? Was Jesus alive again? Mary could not believe her ears. Had Jesus really come back from the grave as he had in fact said he would? It was one thing to see him raise others from the dead, but himself? He raised others, yes, but who was there to raise him? But to raise himself? It had seemed too impossible when he had first begun such talk. No one had really believed him. But John was still not finished.

Mary could hardly contain her growing excitement as John continued, "We really could not make sense of what the women were pouring forth in their excitement. It just seemed so impossible! It sounded like pure nonsense, so we did not believe the women."

The glimmer of hope springing up in her heart wanted to make Mary shout, "No, they were wrong! He is alive!" But could she be sure? If these men, following Jesus more closely over the last three years than she had been, were not listening to the women who had returned from the tomb with such an amazing report, why would they listen to her? Was she hoping for too much? She held her silence while John carried on.

"As I said, we really could not believe the women at first. But then Mary from Magdala came running with an even more startling report. She had stayed behind when the other women had come running. Her heart had been too heavy for her to even have the strength to leave the place where her beloved teacher had been buried. But then she said she saw Jesus in the garden. At first, she had thought he must have been the gardener. She had even asked him what had happened to Jesus' body. Then, he had called her by name! She needed no more proof. Jesus himself had then given her the same messages the angels had given to the women. He also reminded her to tell us to go and meet him in Galilee!

"But that was not enough for Peter. Although he wanted to believe what the women were saying, he had to go and see for himself," John went on. "Mary Magdalene's story seemed so unbelievable that Peter and I ran to the tomb and saw for ourselves that it was just as they had said. We bent down and saw only the strips of linen cloth used to wrap the body. We still wondered what had all happened. But it does seem true. Jesus' body is not in the tomb. We decided to head back to Jerusalem, still wondering what had happened."

John stopped as if to catch his breath. Then bowed his head and was silent for a moment. Mary was just speechless.

Finally, she found her tongue and responded, "John, this is amazing. It has to be a miracle." She finished wistfully, "Oh, I hope it is all true. I just want to see Jesus."

Mary looked at her parents to see their response. She could see they were just as dumfounded as she was.

"Mother, father," Mary implored, "What do you think?"

Before they could answer, John straightened up as if re-energized and looked Mary in the eye as he answered, "According to Jesus, we now need to make plans to return to Galilee. After all, that is our home. In fact, before all this happened, Peter and some of us had already talked about going back to work. We have to fish to earn our living."

Moving closer to Mary, John spread his arms out to her, "You must have thought about returning too. What else would you have done? Why don't you come with us? It will be better for you than travelling alone. Galilee is where Jesus said he would meet us."

Mary hardly knew how to respond to all of this. She wanted so much for Jesus to be alive, but his death was still so real. Still, as John said, she also knew she had to face reality. But now, could it really be that Jesus was once again going to be part of their future? What was in store for them? Mary could not begin to imagine!

As John had continued to explain this and try to make sense of it all, Mary began to grow somewhat weary. It was so much to absorb. It was getting late. She told him she thought she would stay at her parents for the night. Still, she could not quell the feeling that something momentous had happened with her beloved son. Something that was going to have a profound effect on their lives.

"You are very kind, John," Mary murmured, "Let me think of your offer. We will let you know what I decide. I will have to do some shopping here before I return. I would like to say goodbye to my Aunt Elizabeth and Uncle Zechariah too. They will want to know what you have told me too."

"I understand," John replied. Turning to Mary's parents he bowed respectfully, "I know I have told you all a lot. Time will tell what is really happening. Now, we do seem to have some hope though." With that, John bade them all farewell and left.

Mary's heart ached. What did this mean for her dear parents, as well as for her uncle and aunt? Elizabeth and Zechariah had been so happy when the long-awaited John had been born to fulfil Yahweh's promised. But he too had been killed by that wicked King Herod. All the hopes for him had also seemed to be unfulfilled. What had he really accomplished with his life, cut off so prematurely? Just as she and her Aunt Elizabeth had shared so many questions and feelings at the beginning of their sons' lives, they now both faced the same thoughts about the ends of their sons' lives. It almost did not seem fair that there was no sign that John would return, but there seemed to be hope for Jesus.

Sleep still did not come easily to Mary that night. Now it was not the heavy sadness but the stimulation of all that John had told them; the exhilaration of hope kept her awake.

Chapter 38. Through a Locked Door

The following morning Mary rose and talked further with her parents about what had happened. Then she began preparations to return to Nazareth. Neither she nor her parents could see any reason for her to stay in Jerusalem. She felt a strong pull though, to first go back to the place where Jesus' followers were all meeting. She was anxious to see if there was more news.

Mary had not even started out on her quest when John and some of the other disciples appeared at the door. May could tell again by their haste and the expressions on their faces there must be something momentous they were eager to share. She was getting used to John appearing with unusual news! She knew they were not simply coming to accompany her back to Galilee as John had promised yesterday.

"Mother Mary," John could hardly contain himself, "You won't believe what happened yesterday. We were all gathered at John Mark's home making preparations for our trip today when two of our group, who had been on their way home to Emmaus rushed in. We knew something must have happened that made them hurry back like that. Sure enough, they had an unbelievable story! As they had been returning home from Jerusalem, a man had suddenly appeared and fallen in with them. They had begun to talk and it seemed this stranger had no knowledge of what had gone on in Jerusalem these last few days.

"Our friends had filled him in abut Jesus having been killed, crushing their hopes that he was the Messiah. They had also related to him the unlikely report from the women that said they had seen him alive that morning.

"This stranger had chided the two travelers on their failure to understand the scriptures and begun to teach them how the Messiah had to be crucified and then rise again in fulfillment of what the law and the prophets had written."

These disciples had then recounted how he had gone through the scriptures with them as they walked on towards Emmaus, still oblivious to whom they were listening. When they had gotten home, they had invited him in, as it was late and they wanted to hear more. He accepted the invitation to eat with them and took the initiative of asking the blessing on the meal. There was a familiarity in the manner, tone and words he used. Then it had dawned on them; this was Jesus! No sooner had they realized this, then he had vanished from their midst. However, they had been convinced enough of what they had seen and heard to cause them to rush back to share the news with the others in Jerusalem.

Then, even more excitingly – news that made Mary's heart leap to her throat with joy! John had continued, "But what happened next yesterday evening was even more incredulous! The two followers had barely finished telling us this story when whom should appear among us but Jesus himself!"

Seeing the astonishment on Mary's face, John insisted, "Yes, yes, it was really him! It was absolutely amazing! We were at first somewhat afraid because suddenly there was this figure in our midst. He had appeared so suddenly, without us even knowing anyone wanted in. We thought we were seeing a ghost."

Mary knew they had been keeping the door locked because of their fear that the police would come after them, as followers of Jesus. "He had not even knocked on the door," John continued, "It seemed he had not come through it at all. He was just – there! But when he spoke, telling us not to be afraid, there was no denying it. It was the same familiar voice."

Jesus had definitely calmed their panic when he had said to them in that beloved voice, 'Peace be with you.' Then he had asked them why they were afraid, and why they still doubted. He had told them to examine his hands and feet. He had insisted it was him, chiding them that a ghost did not have flesh and bones like they could see he had.

"When he said this," John said, "he showed us his wrists and the tops of his feet, which still bore the scars from his crucifixion, but they were all healed! He persisted in asking us to touch him and see that he was real, but we were all too ashamed because we had doubted."

Hearing this about Jesus' wounds, thrilling and positive as the larger story was, brought back some of those awful memories Mary had been trying so hard to erase. If Jesus had scars on his hands and feet, was there a scar in his side where the spear had pierced him? It was not a sword, but the thought of it brought back another memory. That memory had raised questions and fears in her ever since Simeon had been spoken to them so many years ago. Neither she nor Jesus had suffered from the sword... so far. Perhaps it had only referred to emotions, not a real sword. She had certainly experienced that. She hoped that was all it was. Mary quickly tried again to push those concerns down and focus her attention on the present, as John was still speaking.

"We had still been eating supper when the friends from Emmaus had arrived, so Jesus asked us for something to eat to help prove he was not a ghost. We gave him a piece of broiled fish, and he took it and ate it in front of us and it was gone.

"Yes, I tell you, Jesus made us all feel rather guilty. How many people, starting with our sisters Mary from Magdala, Joanna, Susanna and others, had told us in the morning Jesus was resurrected, but we had not believed! He really rebuked us for our unbelief and how dense we were not to believe those who had seen him resurrected, particularly the women.

"'My sisters,' Jesus said, 'saw me and believed.' He had thanked them especially for their devotion and care, for what they had wanted to do for his body.

"I tell you, on one hand he seemed so different somehow, that we were still rather taken aback and apprehensive about how we should relate to him. On the other, we were all so excited we just could not keep from quickly crowding round him to see if he was real. Of course, we also wanted to hear whether there was anything he had to tell us."

As if the most important news had now been shared and he could not think of what more he could say at this moment, John admitted, "Well, now we do believe that he is alive because we have seen him with our own eyes and touched him with our own hands. That is what is most important."

For a moment, John seemed lost in thought, remembering the momentous scene. But then he went on. "Jesus said to us again, 'Peace be with you.

Just as the Father has sent me, I also send you.' After he had said this, he had breathed on us and said, 'Receive the Holy Spirit. If you forgive anyone's sins, they are forgiven; if you retain anyone's sins, they are retained.'

"These words had seemed somewhat strange to us. Send us for what? Receive the Holy Spirit? What did that mean? But before we had a chance to ask Jesus what this all meant he disappeared, just as quickly as he had come. As we discussed this amongst ourselves though, we realized what our Teacher was expecting of us now. We began to remember what he had said after the Passover meal. He had talked then about the Holy Spirit and what was to come. Obviously, Jesus wants us to carry on what he began. Now, he was continuing to lay it out for us. But we still had so many questions."

Mary could not believe her ears. Was this possible? Was Jesus alive after all? Had he in fact risen from the dead? The conviction with which John and the others told her of what had happened slowly erased her doubts. Now all she wanted was to see her beloved son for herself. What did it mean for them all that he was alive again? What would he do now? What were they supposed to do?

"So, Mary," John interrupted her thoughts, "We were going to take you with us to Galilee, remember? Now we have all the more reason to hurry back. We will meet Jesus again!"

The simple conviction with which John said this was enough to galvanize Mary into action. She nodded and quickly gathered her things together. Then she bid her parents an emotional farewell. They were so happy too. In her excitement, she almost forgot about her desire to see her Uncle Zechariah and Aunt Elizabeth. Remembering, just as she approached the doorway, she turned to her parents, "Oh, Uncle Zechariah and Aunt Elizabeth. I had wanted to see them. Please, pass on my condolences for their loss of John. I am so sorry for them. Their only son..." tears came to her eyes as she finished, "Pass on my apologies for not coming to see them. Tell them what has happened and what we must do. They will understand. They will forgive me."

Then, turning to join the young men already making their way out the door, she was gone. This was indeed going to be another exciting chapter in the book of her life. She could hardly wait.

Chapter 39. Mary Sees Jesus at Last

Mary and the young men hurried through the city, back to the home of John Mark and his mother. Their friends were continuing to gather here and talk about all that had happened. They also began to formulate what course of action they should take in the coming days. There was so much everyone wanted to discuss, they could hardly settle to make their preparations for returning to Galilee.

Mary found herself getting caught up in the conversations that carried on through the day. The disciples were recalling things Jesus had said. They slowly put it all together, especially with what the two from Emmaus remembered of what Jesus had told them. Mary listened with rapt attention. She was hearing things she had never heard from Jesus. However, it was all beginning to make sense to her too.

She remembered what the angels had told her and Joseph. Then there were the startling pronouncements Simeon and Anna had made when they had brought Jesus to the temple in Jerusalem for his dedication. She realized she also needed to share what she knew. The others needed to hear these stories, because they had probably never been told to them. Indeed, when she began to talk, the disciples were eager to hear her. They were impressed with how much they were learning, and how it all fit together. It was very powerful.

The day had passed quickly as they all shared story after story. They grew increasingly amazed at what unfolded. Before they knew it, it was time for the evening meal again.

Thomas, who had not been with them the previous evening when Jesus had appeared, rejoined the group. He found it hard to accept all he was hearing. He said firmly, "Unless I see the wounds from the nails in his hands, and put my finger into the wounds from the nails, and put my hand into his side, I will never believe it!"

Mary could understand Thomas' need for proof. Some thought he doubted but he just wanted to know. Mary believed though. She felt a growing contentment.

Although the doors were locked, suddenly there was once again a figure standing in their midst! Everyone started and fell back. Mary gasped when she saw the figure and then heard that familiar voice, as Jesus addressed them all, "Peace be with you!"

It was really him! Jesus eyes scanned the room, and when his gaze fixed on Mary, a quick smile flitted across Jesus' serene face. But he turned to Thomas who had pulled back in fear, stretching out his arms towards him, palms up, and there, indeed, were his scars, "Thomas, my friend, put your fingers here, and examine my hands." Beginning to pull aside the clothes he wore, Jesus added, "Reach out and put your hand into my side too. Don't continue to doubt; believe!"

Thomas dropped to his knee before Jesus and exclaimed, "My Lord, Jahweh!" Jesus reached down to grasp his hand and pull him to his feet, saying, "You believe now because you see me? Blessed are those who do not see but still believe."

Leaving Thomas stunned and wondering whether he was still supposed to touch Jesus' wounds, Jesus abruptly turned. Suddenly, he was at her side and Mary felt again those strong familiar arms around her. She buried her head in his side and just sobbed. The rest of the group quickly gathered around them and embraced them both, at the same time spontaneously lifting their eyes heavenward, calling out in joyous thanksgiving to Jahweh, whom they were beginning to know as Father. Jesus, still holding on to his mother, had barely lifted his eyes to heaven to join in their chorus of prayer and praise when he once again disappeared, vanishing as quickly and mysteriously as he had come.

For a moment, everyone was silent. What had just happened? Was what they had just all seen and heard real? Once again, Jesus had disappeared as suddenly as he had appeared. They were at a loss to explain this. Suddenly they were all talking at once! Their excited chatter led to one conclusion, of which they were now all certain. They were not imagining things. Mary and Thomas especially, had no doubts.

As the renewed excitement diminished, they returned to their original discussions of their plans for both the present and the future. Realizing that night was drawing on, some of their number, who lived nearby, gradually dispersed. Those who were going to Galilee knew it was too late today to start their journey. Some wanted to talk more of what had happened but they all recognized they had a few days of travel ahead, so their thoughts turned to getting some rest.

Their hosts helped them all find a place for their weary heads, but sleep was slow in coming. They were all too excited. How could they sleep with all that was on their minds? Some did nod off sooner, while others continued to talk softly into the wee hours of the morning. Eventually, these quietly turned together to prayer before they too felt settled enough to sleep.

Chapter 40. Reunion in Galilee; The Sword

Mary was glad to be home, away from those terrible scenes in Jerusalem. The journey had been tiring but the excitement of seeing Jesus and the excited discussions with his friends made it all worthwhile. How amazing it had been to hear the stories and put together the passages of scripture fulfilled in Jesus. He had to be the Messiah! However, the picture that was emerging was certainly different from much of what they had all been taught by the Jewish leaders.

After the bustle of Jerusalem, Nazareth was so peaceful in comparison. Now, she just hoped her son would join her again. He had told his disciples he would meet them in Galilee, but had not said where. All she could really do was wait and hope. Well, she did pray that her son would come home to visit. She had also made John promise that when they met Jesus – if they saw him first – they would tell him his mother really wanted to see him at home. Mary found life rather lonely here now, with her other children grown and gone, although they were all nearby.

As she tidied up, she looked at what she needed in terms of food and supplies besides what she had brought home from Jerusalem. She had just decided to take a break for lunch when, suddenly, there he was! Sanding across the table from her like in old times. She started and a cry of surprise escaped her. For a brief moment fear gripped her. But then she remembered how Jesus had made his appearances in Jerusalem, just like a ghost out of thin air.

"Oh, Jesus," she cried, jumping to her feet. Jesus, at her side in an instant, caught her in his arms and stroked her hair as she sobbed in his strong embrace, "I didn't know when or where I would see you again, or even if. But you are here! At home. At last."

"Mother," Jesus said comfortingly, "Where would I go first in Galilee if not home? What kind of a son would I be if I put others before you? I know

I did not come home as often as you would have liked, but you know I had a task to do. Now, my work on earth is almost done, and I must return to our heavenly Father."

"Oh, Jesus, I'm just so glad to see you," was all Mary could say. She clung to him a bit longer but then pushed herself back, gripping his arms as she looked up into his face. "Oh, is it really you? It's so hard to believe. I saw you die. They said your body was in a sealed tomb. And then, it was empty. It's just beyond anything I ever imagined for you. I can't tell you how wonderful it was to see you in Jerusalem too, although it was far too short a time," Mary smiled to soften the mild rebuke. "Will you stay longer now?"

Before Jesus had a chance to respond, Mary began to voice the questions that she had held so long. "You just talked again about the task you had to do. You know, Jesus," Mary said, "I am still not sure what 'your work,' as you say, really was. I just don't understand how what you have done fulfils the prophecies about the Messiah. Forgive me, but you know what we, our people, have believed for centuries. That the Messiah would come and free us from all oppression and finally lead us into the golden age of our nation, our people."

"Mother," said Jesus gently, "Let me explain it to you now, and I know you will see how everything that happened was planned by my heavenly Father. But you were going to have lunch. Let's do that first."

After Jesus had blessed what Mary set before them, they quickly finished eating. Both were eager to pick up where they had left off. Jesus then began to give his mother his story.

Starting with Genesis and The Law, working through the Psalms and The Prophets, Jesus showed how his coming had been predicted so exactly. As the wonderful story unfolded, Mary began to see how Jahweh planned things versus what the Jews had erroneously come to expect of their long-awaited Messiah. Mary's eyes were indeed opened as she realized how contrary much of what she had come to expect was to what Jahweh had actually accomplished through her son.

Jesus was describing how he had fulfilled his mission. But his mother still had other burning questions. She took advantage of a momentary lull to interrupt Jesus with what was on her mind.

"Jesus, what about the prophecies that say an eternal king will come from the line of David, that the Messiah will come to free us, his people, from all the oppression we have endured?"

"Ah, mother," Jesus smiled. "You do remember that the angel told you I was the son of The Highest One, Jahweh. I am indeed the Son of Jahweh, in all Jahweh's fullness. I am Yahweh. Does Jahweh need an army to accomplish his purpose of bringing liberation? The freedom the Messiah brings is deliverance from spiritual and psychological, even social and physical, oppression. It is freedom of the heart, the soul and the mind. It isn't about freeing Judea and Galilee from Rome."

"Jesus," Mary broke in again, "May I ask you one more question?" She leaned toward him across the table and placed her hands on his. "I think I told you, when you were old enough to hear these things, what the prophetess Anna told us in the temple when we brought you for dedication to Jahweh. She said a sword would piece my soul. You can imagine the dread of that I have suffered ever since. Now, I know I felt that when you went through those awful things and were crucified..." Tears came to her eyes and she couldn't go on. She covered her face and all the pent-up emotions of the last weeks just poured forth.

Jesus immediately came to her side to comfort her in his arms. He too was unable to stop his own tears.

Eventually, their weeping together subsided and Jesus lifted his mother's face to his, "Mother, I can't tell you how sorry I am you had to go through that. I felt a sword in my heart seeing you there too. But that was how it had to be."

"But Jesus," Mary said, "Is there more to the sword than that? I have always felt there was a different, a more profound meaning."

"Oh, Mother," Jesus smiled, "Jahweh chose well when He appointed you to be my mother. For all you have suffered, you will be richly rewarded by my Father. For all that you are and have done, you will be remembered and honored forever." Mary noted the conviction with which he continued in deliberate measure, "You are most blessed among women."

Both sat silently for a moment. Then Jesus acquiesced, "You are right, there is more."

This time Jesus did not overlook what he knew to be Mary's concerns. He launched into a full explanation of what he was about. He spoke of how he had come to accomplish Yahweh's liberation on earth through his word and his hands. Just as Jahweh had created the universe through his word, Jesus was introducing a new world through his word. However, his kingdom, his being enthroned as king, did not depend on a literal sword. At the same time, and Mary could understand this, Jesus clarified, sometimes my word does act like a sword. That's when it creates divides between people, even between family members who don't agree about me. Finally, Mary was getting the answers to questions that had troubled her for so long.

"My sword," Jesus declared firmly, "is not cold, hard metal. My sword is my word. My father," Jesus continued, "shaped mankind from the dust of the earth to enjoy the world he had created for them, and to rule it together with him. You know how sin spoiled all that. I came to use my hands to heal, to comfort, to reshape lives so those who believe in me can rule with me in the Kingdom of Heaven. This is the kingdom our Father had in mind from the beginning. Now, it is being re-established.

"I used my sword, my word, to proclaim what the new kingdom is about and what one needs to do to really be part of it. Sometimes, my word cuts deeply, not unlike a sword. But it is not meant to harm or kill. Instead, it is to pierce the depths of one's being, one's soul, and to awaken in each person the realization of what is missing. My word helps people see what needs to be forsaken, what one needs to turn one's back on. In turning to me, one can have a fulfilled life, abundantly beyond can be imagined.

"This kingdom of repentant, forgiven and healed souls is what I was always speaking about. People once again reconciled with their Maker. My kingdom is not national or political."

Being at home in Nazareth for most of Jesus' three short years of ministry, Mary had not heard nearly all that Jesus had taught. Finally, now that Jesus was explaining his mission, she knew she had heard some of it, but had largely misunderstood even that. Jesus put it all together for her.

Suddenly it all hit Mary. "Jesus," she exclaimed, "Is this why our leaders, our most religious people killed you? You were not acting according to their expectations of a Messiah, just like I had a wrong idea of who the Messiah would be? They thought you were another of the many would-be Messiahs we have had who have just brought grief upon us, and they wanted to get rid of you before that happened again?"

"Mother," Jesus exclaimed as took her hands in his and gazed lovingly into her eyes, "This has been revealed to you by Jahweh's Spirit. You are most blessed to understand this. But you are absolutely right."

"Jesus," Mary hesitated. "How does this relate to John being killed. He did not get to live again." She sighed wistfully, "I feel so bad for your aunt and uncle, and for you," she looked into his face and saw the tears well up in his eyes.

Jesus blinked back his tears. "Ah, yes, my 'cousin'. He was so special to me. You have no idea. I was so upset at the injustice of it all, knowing I would never see John again here on earth. But you do know we will meet after the future resurrection."

"Yes, I know that," Mary replied. "But why did he have to die?"

"Unfortunately, humans make evil choices, mother. Herod had the earthly power. Remember what you told me about what Herod did when I was still a baby? We had to flee to Egypt to avoid my being killed. Don't you think the Father's heart was also pierced by those swords? It pierced my heart when I heard it, to think those innocent babies had to die and their parents had to suffer their loss because of the wicked choice of one evil man. It was definitely not the will of The Father for that to happen.

It was the same for John. King Herod simply wanted John gone for speaking the truth. You know it has been that way for so many of our prophets. But John had accomplished his mission. For that he will always be remembered and revered."

Jesus paused, leaned back and continued, "You remember, as I told you, the prophets predicted the Messiah would not be recognized by his people, that he would be rejected and suffer, as I did. But it was all part of The Father's wonderful plan, foretold in so many ways so long ago. By my death and resurrection, I defeated all the evil forces that have been, are and will be. These forces brought so much suffering and death into the world Jahweh created good." Jesus then went on to tell her some of what his plans were for the immediate future and how she could now be part of that.

When Jesus had completed his discourse, Mary took a deep breath and responded, "This is still so new. However, it makes so much sense. It is beautiful, what The Father has done. Nevertheless, it is still hard to accept, to understand, especially for me as your mother," Mary smiled at her son as she laid her hand on his, "what you had to go through to accomplish this. I will never fully fathom your love and commitment, your obedience. You have certainly shown us the face and the mind of The Father in a new way, which we will never forget."

"Thank you so much, mother, for everything. This time together has been so precious," Jesus responded. With that, he stood and moved toward her, opening his arms to her once again. "You will be an important part of what happens from now on. But I still have work to do here. I must go and tell my brothers, my disciples, what I have told you. I have to trust them – and you – to carry on with my mission.

"Mother, thank you for everything you have been and done for me. I could not have wished for a better mother. Jahweh knew what he was doing when he chose you. I know we will miss each other dearly. I must soon return to The Father. However, as I said, I will send my Spirit to be with you all and comfort and strengthen you as you carry on what I have only begun." Jesus leaned in close, nuzzling his mother's hair as he held her even more tightly, "And, mother, I will come again and this time you will be with me – forever."

Then he pulled back, kissing her on both cheeks. Mary looked up again into Jesus' face, her eyes filling with tears. Before she could say anything more, she noticed his eyes glistening as well, and then he was gone.

Chapter 41. Epilogue - To the Ends of the Earth

Mary never did see Jesus again. His disappearance left an ache in her heart that she knew would never completely fill. However, she wasn't entirely sad about it. He had told her where he was going and that someday they would re-unite again, forever. She had been so happy to hear that! She began to dream about what that might be like. How she looked forward to that day. She wanted nothing more than to be with her beloved son.

Mary could not help wondering though, where Jesus was. What was he doing? Who was he with? For a while, she continued to hear stories about Jesus being around and meeting with people. She felt a surge of excitement every time she heard such news. He spent most of his time with his disciples, which was understandable. Mary knew there was a lot he wanted to make sure they knew and understood about what he had all been about. She knew he had to make sure they were ready to carry on his work, his mission. However, he had not limited himself completely to his disciples. At least once he had met with a large crowd, which again heard him teach and experienced his healing.

Then she heard the last story of Jesus' life on earth. Jesus had gone back to Judea with his disciples, leading them again to one of their favorite spots, the Mount of Olives, looking over Jerusalem. This was where he had been so violently torn away from them just weeks before. Mary wondered what it must have been like for Jesus and his disciples to visit that place again.

It was not the same this time. Jesus was now their resurrected leader. After assuring them of his love and continued presence through his Spirit, he had unexpectedly left them again. This time though, he had been in control of his leaving. Before doing so, he had given the disciples a departing message, reassuring them of his return, but that they had an important mission to fulfil in the meantime. Then they had observed him simply, slowly, ascend out of their view. What's more, an angel had appeared, reinforcing Jesus' message that he would return, just as he had left.

When Mary heard all this, something inside told her she needed to go back to Jerusalem. She felt drawn to rejoin Jesus' friends. She spoke to her children about it. They too had heard the stories Mary had heard. She had told them what she could remember of what Jesus had told her. They confessed they had been skeptical, even oppositional. However, Jesus' awful death had brought them together in a way they had not experienced before. During the years of Jesus' ministry, they had all gone on with their own families' lives, trying to ignore the stories. However, what they had heard about Jesus' death and resurrection and what he had explained after, had changed all that. They too were beginning to understand what Jesus had really been doing during his short time on earth with them.

Mary's younger children had also come to know how special her relationship was with Jesus. Whereas they might sometimes have been jealous of that in the past, now they understood more of what was really behind it. They had become more open to really hearing the whole story of how Jesus had so marvelously come to be Mary and Joseph's first child, with all that had happened even before they were born.

Jesus' siblings knew they could not deny their mother's wish to join Jesus' followers in Jerusalem. Actually, some of them were contemplating being part of carrying on what Jesus had started. As they reviewed these things together, her children reassured their mother that her home would be looked after when she was in Jerusalem. James, now her eldest, had insisted he go with her, that it was unthinkable that she should make the trip alone. They gathered some things together, including some food, and began the long trek to Jerusalem.

Uncertain as to how things would go, Mary and James went straight to the house where Mary had gone with John and the others. This was the home where Jesus had so recently appeared to them all, Peter, John, Andrew and the rest of the remaining eleven – they had told her already the sad story of what had happened to Judas after his betrayal of Jesus - including the women.

They were all really glad to see Mary return. They were also happy that James could be with them. He soon also felt that he was being accepted as one of them.

Mary hoped to hear more of the stories of what had happened after she had returned to Galilee. She was particularly interested in hearing what had really happened on the Mount of Olives. What was the real story about Jesus' disappearing again. One might have expected Jesus' friends to be sad, but that did not seem to be the case. Jesus had told them they were to wait in Jerusalem and he would send them his Spirit, and they were eagerly awaiting that event.

To be sure, they still feared what the authorities might yet do to them because they were Jesus' friends. They knew that their leaders, especially King Herod and the Romans, did not take kindly to any group that formed and grew in numbers and strength. They had good reason for this, as there always seemed to be some Jewish leader appearing who claimed to be the one Israel expected and that he would free them. Too often this had fomented bloody rebellion. These zealots always met the same fate though, just as Jesus had - a cruel death which was supposed to drive enough fear into their followers to cause them to disband and give up whatever plans they had been making. As a result, the disciples kept their doors locked and were always somewhat cautious when they went out. They tended to go after dark and never alone.

Mary, along with James, did get to hear the fascinating account of Jesus' last moments on earth. She could just imagine the scene as Jesus' friends shared with her what had happened.

The way they described it, it had been a beautiful sunlit spring day, with just the type of breeze that warms your body as it whispers around you. The blue sky had been as clear as could be. The new grass on the hill and the leaves on the trees had never seemed so green. The flowers on the hillside were blooming in all their colorful glory. Even the singing of the birds around them had never sounded so sweet.

No one had disturbed this intimate group this time. They had sat down in the warm spring sun and enjoyed one another's company in a way they had never really done before. The disciples were literally basking in the light of The Son.

Jesus had taken the opportunity, as it turned out, to give them what were some final instructions. He had said to them, "These are my words that I spoke to you while I was still with you, that everything written about me in the law of Moses and the prophets and the psalms must be fulfilled."

Then he had summarized everything again in such a way that it really did open their minds so they could understand the scriptures. He had added, "Remember, it is all there in your scriptures, that the Christ would suffer and die. I kept telling you I would rise from the dead on the third day. Now you have seen the proof of all of this.

"Furthermore, your task now is to continue to proclaim my message. In short, the good news that repentance is freely available for the forgiveness of sins. This message of freedom from the bondages that enslave one is to be proclaimed in my name to all nations, beginning from Jerusalem. You are witnesses of what I taught and did, and you will do the same, including the miracles. I am sending you to do what my Father promised. All authority in heaven and on earth has been given to me. That power is there for you as it was for me!

"But stay in the city until you have received this power from on high. It will be yours once the Holy Spirit has come upon you. You will be my witnesses in Jerusalem, and in all Judea and Samaria, and to the farthest parts of the earth. I am charging you to go and make disciples of all nations, baptizing them in the name of The Father and The Son and The Holy Spirit, teaching them to obey everything I have commanded you."

Then, before they had quite realized where this was leading, he had comforted them with these words "And remember, I am with you always, to the end of the age."

After delivering this powerfully encouraging message, Jesus had stood up and lifting up his hands, he had blessed them. During the blessing, he was lifted up from the earth, seemingly floating weightlessly upward until a cloud appeared and hid him from their sight.

As they were still staring into the sky, suddenly two men in dazzling white clothing had stood near them and said, "Men of Galilee, why do you stand here looking up into the sky? This Jesus who has been taken up from you into heaven will come back in the same way you saw him go into heaven."

The disciples had realized immediately these were angels. Given their knowledge of the role of angels in Jesus' story now, including their own experiences, the presence of the angels had not invoked the fear it had before. They knew this was a message from Jahweh that could be trusted. As soon as the angels had gone, they had knelt right down on the spot to worship Jahweh with praise that sprang from deep within.

"Too bad you were not there, Mother Mary," John had whispered to her as she listened to these amazing stories.

Jesus was gone, but the fact that he had fulfilled the prophecies of the ages, as they had now come to understand, and his own promises, had so energized them, there was no sadness among them. He had spoken so often of the Kingdom of Heaven being near. Indeed, in their eager anticipation of Jesus' last promise, they believed it had already come. They worshipped and praised Jahweh with fervently thankful hearts for all that had been given them.

All the followers of Jesus, Mary, the disciples, the women and many others, looked forward excitedly. What thrilling adventures lay ahead? With utmost anticipation, they contemplated their futures.

Mary, who had pondered so many things in her heart, was content. Her son, Jesus, had accomplished what Jahweh had prophesied. The messages she had received from the angels, those many years ago, were all true. Not to mention the scriptures and those special prophets in the temple when Jesus had been presented on his eighth day. Praise and wonder overwhelmed her!

In spite of their fears, they all remained in Jerusalem, filled with a great joy and peace. They continued to meet in John Mark's home, the same place where they had celebrated the last Passover Jesus had with them. They decided that everyone who had been close to Jesus should join them in Jerusalem to wait for this special event. They wanted all of them to receive the same blessing of the Holy Spirit they had been promised.

An invitation was extended to Jesus' mother Mary and her family to be part of this. This made Mary's heart overflow with joy! She was so very glad she would now be part of her beloved son's ministry. She smiled to herself as she thought, 'Now we will all bear witness to The Word, the sword Jesus spoke of. It has pierced my soul. It is not a weapon of death, but of truth and freedom. This sword is not for evil but for good.'

End Notes

I hope you enjoyed reading this story as much as I enjoyed writing it. If you are like me, the reading, or the writing as in my case, might even have brought out some emotions in your reading it that the original text hardly does.

If this story has made you more interested in exploring the biblical texts – and I hope it has - in brief, they are largely in the first portion of The New Testament of the Bible, in the Gospels According to St. Matthew, Mark, Luke and John. You can read the entire gospels to get the full story. Mind you, even that does not suffice. There is so much in The Old Testament that points forward to Jesus and so much written after the Gospels that relates how the impact of His life and words has formed and still informs life in The Way.

To aid you in searching the biblical texts that form the basis of The Story of Mary, the key references on which the story is based can be found below. Some are from the Old Testament: these would include texts Jesus would have expounded on when he taught his followers, particularly after his resurrection. In my story, I imagine him also referring to them when he explained himself to his mother. These references are followed by parentheses containing the related New Testament passage. Most citations are from the New Testament itself.

This compilation is by no means exhaustive. If you are interested in delving further into this, a good study Bible, commentary or even concordance will help make links from these references to others.

Biblical References Behind the Story

Old Testament

Psalms

- 2:6-8, 110:1 The Son of Jahweh, Jesus and King David (Matthew 22:41-46, Mark 12:35-37, Luke 20:41-44)
- 22:1, 31:5 Jesus' last words on the cross (Matthew 27:46, Mark 15:34, Luke 23:46)
- 22:6-8 Jesus' treatment when arrested and tried (Matthew 27:39-44, Mark 15:29-32, Luke 22:47-23:25, John 18:1-19:16)
- 22:12-18 Jesus' experience on the cross (Matthew 27:32-56, Mark 15:21-41, Luke 23:26-49, John 19:16-37)
- 22:20 The Messiah will not experience the sword (John 19:33-34)
- 34:20 The Messiah will have no broken bones (John 19:36)
- 69:9 The Messiah's zeal (John 2:17)
- 118:26 Blessed is he who comes in the name of the Lord (Matthew 21:9, Mark; 11:9, Luke 19:38)

Isaiah

- 7:14 A child named Immanuel to be born (Matthew 1:22-23)
- 9:1-7 Those in darkness will see the Light (Matthew 4:13-16)
- 40:3-5 A voice crying in the wilderness to prepare the way of the Lord (Matthew 3:1-3, Mark 1:2-3, Luke 3:1-6, John 1:19-23)
- 42:1-9 Jahweh's servant, a light to the nations (Matthew 3:17, 12:15-21, 17:5, Mark1:11, Luke 3:22, 9:35)
- 53:4 Jesus took away our disabilities and healed our diseases (Matthew 8:17)

- 53 Jesus suffering and death foretold (Matthew 8:17, 26:47-27; 61, Mark 8:31, 9:30, 10:32-34, 14:43-15:47, Luke 22:47-23:56, John 12:38, 18:1-19:42)
- 56:7 The temple to be a house of prayer (Matthew 21:13, Mark 11:17, Luke 19:46, John 2:13-16)
- 61:1-2 The tasks of the Anointed One (Matthew 11:2-6, Luke 4:16-21, 7:18-23)

Hosea

- 11:1 Jahweh calls his son out of Egypt (Matthew 2:15)

Micah

- 5:2-5 Bethlehem to be the birth-place of the Messiah (Matthew 2:6)

Zechariah

- 9:9-10 The Messiah to ride into Jerusalem on the foal of a donkey (Matthew 21:2-7, John 12:14-15)

Malachi

- 4:5-6a The prophet Elijah to come before The Day of the Lord (Matthew 17:10-13)

New Testament

Matthew

- 1:1- 4:11 Jesus' genealogy through Mary, the stories of angelic visits leading to the births of John the Baptist and Jesus, Mary's visit to Elizabeth & Zechariah, the visit of the wisemen, the trip to Egypt, John the Baptist's ministry, his baptism of Jesus and Jesus' temptation (see also Mark 1:1-13, Luke 1:5 – 24, 57-80, 1:26-56, 2:1-40, John 1:19-34)
- 9:20-22 Unnamed woman's healing (Veronica, according to legend/tradition; see also Mark 5:25-34)
- 10:34-39 Jesus did come to bring a sword (see also Mark 8:34-5, Luke 12:51-3)
- 11:2-19 John the Baptist questions Jesus (see also Mark 6:14-29, Luke 7:18-35, 3:22-30)

- 14:1-13 The death of John the Baptist (see also Mark 6:14-29, Luke 9:7-9)
- 21:1-17 Jesus' triumphal entry into Jerusalem; 'cleansing' the temple (see also Mark 11:1-11, 15-18, Luke 19:28-40, 45-48, John 2:13-22)
- 23:1- 36 Jesus denounces religious leaders (see also Luke 11:37-54)
- 26:14-27:66 Jesus' betrayal, arrest, trial, crucifixion and burial (see also Mark 14:10-25, Luke 22:39-53, 22:63-23:56, John 13:21-30, 18:1-19:42, I Corinthians 15:3-4)
- 28:1:20 Jesus' resurrection (see also Mark 16:1-20, Luke 24:1-49, John 20:1-18, I Corinthians 15:4)
- 28:16-20 Jesus commissions his disciples, his ascension (see also Mark 16:14-20, Luke 24:50-53, Acts 1:1-11)

Mark

- 1:1-13 John the Baptist's coming, Jesus' baptism and temptation
- 3:31-5 Jesus' family comes for him (see also Luke 8:19-21)
- 5:25-34 Unnamed woman's healing (Veronica according to legend/tradition)
- 6:1-6 Jesus' rejection in Nazareth
- 6:14-29 The death of John the Baptist
- 11:1-11, 15-18 Jesus' triumphal entry into Jerusalem, 'cleansing' the temple
- 14:10-25, 32-65, 15:1-47 Jesus' betrayal, last Passover meal, arrest, trial and crucifixion
- 16:1-8 Jesus' resurrection
- 16:9-13 Jesus appears to his disciples
- 16:14-20 Jesus commissions his disciples, his ascension

Luke

- 1:5 – 24, 57-80 John the Baptist's birth
- 1:26-56, 2:1-40 Jesus' birth
- 2:41-52 The boy Jesus stays in the temple
- 3:1-22 John the Baptist, Jesus' baptism
- 3:23-38 Jesus' genealogy through Joseph
- 7:18-35 Jesus and John the Baptist
- 8:1-3 The women in Jesus' life
- 8:19-21 Jesus' family comes for him
- 11:37-54 Jesus denounces religious leaders

- 19:28-40, 45-48 Jesus' triumphal entry into Jerusalem, 'cleansing' the temple
- 22:1-23 Jesus' last Passover meal
- 22:39-53 Jesus' betrayal and arrest
- 22:63-23:56 Jesus' trial, crucifixion, burial
- 24:1-49 Jesus' resurrection
- 24:50-53 Jesus' ascension

John

- 1:19-34 John the Baptist and Jesus' baptism
- 2:1-22 The wedding at Cana, 'cleansing the temple'
- 3:22-30 Jesus and John the Baptist
- 7:3-9 Jesus and his brothers
- 12:12-19 Jesus' triumphal entry into Jerusalem
- 13:1-20 Jesus' last Passover meal
- 13:21-30 Jesus' betrayal
- 18:1-19:42 Jesus' betrayal, arrest, trial, crucifixion and burial
- 20:1-18 Jesus' resurrection
- 20:19-29, 21:1-14 Jesus appears to his disciples

Acts

- 1:1-11 Jesus' commission to his disciples; his Ascension

I Corinthians

- 15:5-8 Jesus appears to his disciples

Printed in Canada